Every Witch Way but Vamped

Magical Misfits Mysteries - book 2

K.E. O'Connor

K.E. O'Connor Books

EVERY WITCH WAY BUT VAMPED

ISBN: 978-1-915378-43-9

Written by: K.E. O'Connor

Chapter 1

A heated encounter

"You haven't eaten your fancy fish treats." Zandra Crypt gently nudged me with her elbow. "Are you feeling okay? You usually inhale them in five seconds and then demand more."

I stood and circled in my bed in the passenger seat of the work's van. "I'm not hungry."

"Hmmm, should I take you to the vet?" Concern filled Zandra's dark eyes. "You've been off your food for days."

I narrowed my gaze and extended my claws. "Don't even think about it. Those monsters don't know what they're doing."

"Juno, I need to make sure you're not ill." She placed a hand on my head as if checking my temperature.

"I'm an all-powerful, all-magical cat. Of course I'm not ill." I licked one white fluffy paw. There was nothing physically wrong with me, but my mind was muddled, and when my thoughts were occupied, my appetite took a hit.

It had been three weeks since Angel Force discovered Zandra's mother's purse at the ghoul factory. Since then, I'd been doing discrete digging, as had my friendly half-angel sidekick, Finn, but neither of us had found new information as to why Adrienne's purse would be there.

I wanted to remain hopeful, but my instincts told me something was wrong. Until I had definitive proof about what happened, I wouldn't worry Zandra.

She reached over and scratched between my ears. "You're not bored with this job, are you? I know you didn't sign up to search for misbehaving animals and lots of paperwork. And boy, I didn't expect all the paperwork that comes with this job. There must be a spell to speed that up."

"Barney insists on good record keeping, so I can't fault him for that. And I have no problem working in animal control. So long as you're enjoying it, it's good enough for me."

Zandra's mouth twisted to the side. "Weirdly enough, I am. Even though I nearly got my arm chewed off by that brown, bug-eyed sloth three days ago, it's nice we're restoring order in Crimson Cove. This place has so many weird animals, though. A crazy high percentage of fluffy troublemakers find their way here."

"There's no such thing as a fluffy troublemaker, just a badly trained magic user not taking proper care of their charge." Although, when we'd taken this job, I hadn't expected the diversity of miscreants who'd landed in our cages to appear so frequently.

Zandra's mobile snow globe, which was propped on the dashboard in the van, flashed to life. Glenda Ridgeback's red, sweating face appeared. "One of the baby dragons from Finn's sanctuary has escaped and is making his way to town. I tried to cut him off, but he almost took my head off with his tail. That thing is madder than a snake who just realized he married a garden hose."

Zandra was already starting the van, and I was on my paws, listening intently. There was nothing babyish about a dragon, new born or not. They came out roaring and didn't stop.

"We're in the center of town," Zandra said.

"Perfect. He's crashing his way through the woods. I reckon, so long as he sticks to the path he's taking, he'll come out by our office." Glenda panted as her image jiggled.

"We're five minutes from there."

"You head him off from the front. I'll follow up from behind. If he doubles back, I'll make sure he doesn't get past me again. Darned thing nearly blasted my face off. I can still see him, but he's moving fast."

"We need to neutralize his fire," I said. "A dowsing potion will do it, but we'll have to be close enough for a direct hit, or we'll only make him angrier."

Glenda nodded. "Good plan. See you on the other side. Hopefully, not chargrilled and toasted."

Zandra was nodding as she rocketed the van along the road, heading to Crimson Cove woods. "When we get to the trees, you go one side of the path, and I'll go the other. You throw out a containment spell and slow the dragon, then I'll cast a dowsing potion.

Be careful of his claws and tail. Even the little ones can shatter bone."

I wiggled my booping snooter. My magic hadn't been on its best behavior, and I wasn't certain I could hold a powerful containment spell for more than a few seconds.

"You good, Juno?" she said. "Happy with the plan?"

"Bring restraining nets, too. It never hurts to have extra supplies. And call Barney. He'll be closest to the scene."

"Nope. Barney is in High Woods. He's dealing with that report about the flesh eating bugs. The mayor's been on his back again."

"What about Oleander?" Zandra's colleague, Oleander Yockley, was a jerk of the highest order, but he could handle difficult animals, being part golden jackal.

Zandra grimaced. "We've got this. And Glenda is a pro. I expect she's already contacted Finn and told him what's going on. We can tackle this dragon between us."

I still wasn't certain, but I had to trust my witch and my magic. It would be there when I needed it the most.

A moment later, Zandra pulled the van to a halt, unclipped my harness, which was attached to the seatbelt, and we leaped out. She raced around the back of the van, opened the double doors, and hunted through the potions.

"Get two dowsing potions, just in case your first one misses the target," I said.

She pocketed two vials of red liquid and grabbed the magically doused nets. "Any sign of our scaly little friend?"

I scanned the trees, looking for smoke and feeling for vibrations under my paws. "Nothing yet."

"Maybe he's changed course and is heading back to Glenda."

With my magic so unstable, I'd be happy for Glenda to handle this dragon. She was a tiny slip of a woman, but her size meant animals and magic users underestimated her. They always lived to regret it.

"Keep watching for him. He'll be here any second," Zandra said.

I scouted for a suitable hiding place for Zandra and selected a large oak with plenty of cover. Even if the dragon hit the tree with fire, she'd be protected.

"Still nothing?" She hurried over, the netting draped across her arms.

"Not yet. Use this tree for cover. I'll be on the other side of the path."

Zandra crouched. I hopped my front paws onto her thigh, and we briefly touched foreheads. My bonded witch meant everything to me, and the feeling was mutual. We'd faced plenty of danger in the decade we'd been together and always survived. This time would be no different.

"Let's teach this dragon it's rude to cause chaos in our hometown." Zandra booped the end of my nose and then dashed behind the tree.

I scurried away and hid behind a similar sized oak tree close by. I shut out all distractions and dug deep into the well of ancient magic inside me.

Before I'd been turned into a cat, accessing this power was as easy as clicking my fingers. And yes, I used to have fingers. I hadn't always been a cat. But three decades had passed since I'd been transformed into this magnificent, beautiful creature, so I was fully adjusted to this way of life. Well, almost.

One increasingly urgent problem was that my magic no longer wanted to perform.

I closed my eyes, relaxed, and hunted for a thread of ancient power that used to course through me like water tumbling down a waterfall. There it was! The power that slumbered inside me and no longer wanted to help. I prodded it until it lazily awakened.

Small, scurrying feet caught my attention, and I cocked my head, swiveling one ear. Something was on the move. It wasn't a dragon, but it piqued my curiosity.

My eyes opened, and I came face-to-face with a malevolent tree rat. The scourge that is squirrel. I'd had enough acorns and pinecones hurled at my head by these beasts to know they couldn't be trusted. They looked like cute, fluffy gray angels, but they were devils in disguise.

I growled, and the tree rat chittered and ran up the trunk.

My hunt instinct took over, and I charged after it, digging my claws into the soft bark as I sprinted up the tree.

The squirrel chittered another battle cry and kicked chunks of bark in my face.

It was the ultimate insult, and I hissed and leaped, almost catching its tail, but at the last second, the fluffy beast got away, and I clutched nothing but air. I dug in my back claws and clung on while I steadied myself.

Flames blasted around me, sizzling my fur and dazzling me with an intense, eyeball frying brightness. The dragon! I'd been so distracted by the evil tree rat, I'd lost focus on the mission.

The foul stench of burning fur flooded my nose, and I was horrified to see my beautiful, fluffy white tail on fire. I howled and dropped to the ground, rolling repeatedly in the dry leaves to extinguish the flames.

My rolling stopped with a bone jarring shudder as I hit a rock. I flipped over. Ah, not a rock. I'd arrived under the belly of the baby dragon.

The dragon's huge green scaled nose dipped down to sniff me. The rank smell of trapped meat between unbrushed teeth and sulfur wafted over me.

I wrinkled my booping snooter. "Greetings. I'm Juno. You may know me as Juno the Magnificent. May I suggest you visit the dentist? That stink won't attract the lady dragons when you're old enough to date."

The dragon pulled back his head and roared.

The stench was so gross I almost passed out. Never a good move when looking up at a mad as a coot dragon. I rolled away just before his huge, clawed foot tried to stamp me into oblivion.

"Juno! Where are you?" Zandra's voice was tinged with panic.

Her cry alerted the dragon to her location, and his head whipped up, a menacing rumble shuddering through him.

I flipped onto my paws, dug into my sluggish, lazy magic, and fired it to life, but the dragon was already on the move and racing toward Zandra. "Hide! He's coming your way."

"Have you slowed him down?"

"Working on it." Come on, magic. Don't fail me now. I had to keep my witch safe.

I concentrated so hard my head felt like it would splinter. The magic finally flared to life, and I shot out a restraining spell. It caught the dragon by the end of his tail and yanked him off his feet.

The dragon roared as he lost his balance and hit the ground with an almighty thud.

"You got him!" Zandra said. "Hold him still. I'll be right there."

The dragon thrashed his tail twice, shattering my spell's weak bond. He staggered to his feet, shook his head, and belted out a blast of brilliant flame, setting fire to several trees and skimming the top of my head.

Then the dragon was running again, straight at Zandra, and there was nothing I could do to stop him. My power was gone, and it felt like I had no magic left to use.

But I wasn't giving up.

I raced after the dragon as fast as my paws would carry me. I had my excellent murder mittens and a fine set of fangs. This dragon would still feel my rage. It would just take longer to destroy him, and it could get messy.

"Out of the way, fluffy knickers. I've got this." Glenda appeared alongside me, magic blazing on her palms. She thrust out the spell, and it covered the dragon from the tip of his tail, swiping along his body and up to his head.

The dragon slowed, shuddered, and fell face-first into the dirt.

A second later, both vials of dowsing potion shattered over him, and Zandra came into view, looking worried as her gaze darted around.

Zandra and Glenda circled the dragon as he rioted and roared under the powerful magic, but he was going nowhere.

"Pipe down. No one's impressed by your toddler tantrum," Glenda said. "Nice shooting, Zandra."

"You weren't so bad yourself."

I launched onto Zandra's shoulder, eager to be close to my witch.

She was focused on the dragon but gently touched my side to acknowledge my presence.

"You both good?" Glenda was panting, her eyes blazing a tawny yellow, giving away her werewolf heritage alongside her witch magic. It was quite a combination.

I nodded, too embarrassed to say anything. I'd messed up. My magic had failed.

"We're good, thanks. That was a close call, though." Zandra checked over the dragon, who was already snoring. "What did you use on him?"

"A sleep spell. And those dowsing potions you used were double strength concentrate, so he won't be breathing anything other than air for weeks. No flames for him. Serves him right, naughty baby." She petted the dragon's rump.

While Glenda inspected the dragon, Zandra stood back. She pressed her head against my side. "What happened? I thought you had the dragon pinned."

I hid my face in her hair. "Sorry. Maybe I'm not feeling quite myself."

"You should have said you weren't up to tackling the dragon. And look at your beautiful fur and tail. You're not hurt, are you?" Zandra gently touched the blackened ends of my once magnificent tail.

"It's a surface injury. I'll be back to normal in no time." My magic would take away the injury, so long as I could get it to work.

"I knew there was something wrong with you. First thing tomorrow, you're going to the vet."

"There's no need. I... I just got distracted."

"By what?"

I hung my head in shame. "A tree rat. It was being rude. It issued a challenge."

Zandra sighed. "You and squirrels. You're almost as bad with them as you are mice."

"We all have natural enemies. One of mine just happened into view at the wrong moment. It won't happen again."

"You're sure that's all it is? You'd tell me if something was wrong, right?"

"It's nothing a good night's rest and a decent meal of sea bass won't cure. Let's help Glenda with the dragon." I didn't want to dwell on my humiliating performance. I'd let Zandra down, I'd let myself down, and I'd let Glenda down.

Zandra spent a few seconds fussing over me, but I brushed away her concerns with a gentle paw swipe.

Between the three of us, we wrangled the dragon into the back of Zandra's van. He only just fit. He was a big baby.

Glenda stepped back, her hands on her hips. "I've had enough fun for one day. I'm taking a long overdue break and grabbing food. You good with getting the dragon back to Finn's place?"

"Sure. And thanks for the save. We couldn't have done it without you," Zandra said.

"My pleasure." She held her hand up for a high-five. "But you owe me."

"The office cakes are on me tomorrow."

"I'm buying," I said. "I should have stopped that dragon on my own."

"We'll go halves." Zandra winked at me, and it seemed all was forgiven.

Glenda strolled away through the woods, whistling, and we headed to the front of the van. Zandra kept glancing at me, but I pretended not to notice she was still concerned.

That had been too close of a call. I had to try harder. No more tree rat distractions, no more troublesome magic, and all my focus needed to be on my wonderful witch.

Otherwise, what kind of terrible familiar was I?

Chapter 2

Doubly dead with a side order of badger

Zandra pulled the van into a spot outside a plain brown barn with a handwritten sign out the front: *Creature Comforts Animal Rescue*.

"You'd never know Finn was so into his animals, given how pristine his apartment was the last time we visited." I waited as Zandra unclipped my harness, and then we climbed out of the van.

"Yeah, he lives in a typical minimalist bachelor pad. Come on, let's see how Archie's doing before we unload our scaled sleeping beauty."

I walked along beside her. I still felt sorry for myself after my failure with the baby dragon capture, but I'd perked up when Zandra suggested we see Archie, my favorite drooling hellhound. We'd rescued him after his owner, Osorin Greenbow, had been killed. It was a gruesome death, involving an exploding magical collar, shady gang members, and an expensive diamond hidden somewhere very intimate to Archie.

We walked around the side of the barn and the view opened, revealing vast green fenced off paddocks and several smaller barns.

The various sounds of different animals bleating, growling, and grunting reached my ears. This place was full. Finn must be busy looking after all these rescues.

There was a thud. Something crashed to the ground, and a second later, Archie bounded into view, racing toward us at full pelt.

Finn was right behind him. "Slow down! They're not going anywhere." He lifted a hand. "Archie's been bouncing off the walls with excitement when he heard you were visiting."

Archie was going so fast, he raced past us, had to hit the brakes, spin around, and trot back, his huge dark hellhound tail wagging.

"Greetings, Archie," I said. "You're looking good."

"I don't have a diamond wedged in my colon. That's why." He aimed his huge tongue at my head, but I avoided being drenched in hellhound drool by nimbly leaping to the side.

"And it looks like you've settled in," I said.

"This place is great. Better than Torrin's shed."

"Hey, now, Torrin did his best when he took you in." Finn had a grin on his handsome face as he stopped in front of us. "He's just less experienced than me."

"But much more modest." Zandra rolled her eyes as Finn laughed.

"I love it here. But did you hear the amazing news? Finn found me a foster family. They've got experience with hellhounds, and they're used to drool, since they have four St. Bernards. That's a kind of dog. A really drooly one." Archie bounded around. "I'm so excited."

"Calm down." Finn wasn't dressed in his usual white Angel Force uniform but had on jeans and a red and black checked shirt. The rugged, outdoorsy look suited him.

I glanced at Zandra to see if she agreed, but she was paying more attention to Archie, scratching behind his ears and telling him what a good boy he was.

"It'll do Archie good to be in a regular family, surrounded by other dogs. Although he's not house-trained, so he needs time to learn those skills. Best paw forward, buddy, so they want to keep you," Finn said.

"I do my best, but Osorin always had other things on his mind, so he'd forget I needed regular bathroom breaks." Archie's tail lowered, and I joined him in a moment of silence. It was the most heartbreaking thing to have your bonded magic user ripped from you.

Archie had lost Osorin in horrible circumstances, and there'd been a time when I'd thought he wouldn't survive. Thanks to my excellent magic and my witch's amazing skills, Archie now thrived.

"I'm moving in four days," Archie said. "I'll have my own bed and a water bowl. And, apparently, the family walks their dogs three times a day! I was lucky if I got out in the yard once a day." He huffed out a smoky breath. "Osorin made mistakes, but he did his best with me. And I know he loved me in his own way."

"He did," I said. "Sometimes, our magic users just get things wrong. Have I told you about the time Zandra tried to get me to eat only dried cat food?"

We poked out our tongues and snickered at that ridiculous prospect.

"Hey, I did it for your health. There's too much mercury in fish, and you eat way too much."

My expression soured. "Fish is the perfect balanced food for any fine feline. You only have to look at my fabulous fur to realize that."

"Usually, I'd agree. But you both look a little charred," Finn said.

"Your baby put up a fight." I tucked my tail underneath me. "It's only surface char."

"You're still the prettiest cat I've ever seen," Archie said. He tried to lick me again. "Even if you smell like ash and rotten eggs."

Finn chuckled. "How about me and Archie show you around before we unload the baby? I enjoy showing off the rescue to fellow animal lovers. And you never know, you could find a small furry you want to take home."

"There's only room for one small furry in Zandra's life. The position is taken, and it's never becoming vacant." I hopped onto Zandra's shoulder and nuzzled her ear with my booping snooter.

"I agree. Although, I wouldn't mind taking a look. I can never resist the cute ones," Zandra said.

"Just looking, no taking."

She grinned at me. "Just looking. Promise."

"I'll lead. I know everyone." Archie dashed to the main barn.

"I have a dozen secure pens inside here. They're for the larger, unpredictable animals. The smaller barns are for those who need a safe space and time to heal from injuries," Finn said. "Just don't poke your head in any pens without checking with me first. There are things in here that'll happily eat limbs as a snack."

"Heard and understood," Zandra said. "This place is bigger than I thought it would be. You can afford all this space?"

"Sure can. I'm a guy with many talents. And I call in a few favors now and again when I need feed or extra land. If space gets tight, I ask Torrin if he's got room, so long as it's an easy animal. He's a simple guy, so I don't want to overtax his scaled brain."

I nodded along, half-listening as I examined each pen with Archie. Several contained foul-smelling beasts I decided not to investigate closely.

"I've even had a few weddings here," Finn said.

Zandra's eyebrows flashed up. "No offence, but it's not the romance capital of Crimson Cove. There are animal droppings all over the place."

He roared with laughter. "Not my idea, and my first happy couple begged me to have their ceremony here. It was easy to get a license, and there's plenty of space. Some people are even animal madder than me and you. Perhaps you'll consider this as a venue when you get married."

Zandra smirked. "That won't happen anytime soon."

"Really? Has Torrin stopped asking you out?"

"Yep."

"There must be some guy in Crimson Cove who's caught your eye," Finn said. "You sure you're not into Torrin? Some ladies like brawn over brains."

My whiskers twitched. Finn was jealous! I knew he had a thing for my witch.

"I've barely seen him since he helped me find out if Adrienne was involved with the Shadow gang," Zandra said.

Finn glanced at me and widened his eyes. I swiftly shook my head. Now wasn't the time to reveal what we'd found at the ghoul factory.

"I lent a hand, too," he said. "I snuck around in Angel Force to check records. Bertoli was suspicious."

"It doesn't take much to make him suspicious."

"True. Even though he pretends he has no problem with my half-demon side, he's always waiting for me to stab him in the back. Probably with the horns that'll sprout from my head as I breathe fire over him."

Zandra glanced at Finn's forehead.

He patted his sandy-blond hair. "Fear not. My demon side doesn't come with horns."

I'd seen Finn in demon mode, and it was scarily impressive, even with no horns. He could obliterate with ease. I used to be able to do that.

"You won't be offering this as an angel wedding venue, then?" Zandra said.

"I hire this space only to the very special witches in my life." Finn winked at Zandra. "Let me know if you ever want walking up the aisle. I look amazing in a white tuxedo."

Although Finn was doing some heavy flirting, Zandra wasn't reciprocating. When they'd met, I thought she'd been interested, but the flirting was now all one-sided. Perhaps Zandra was more interested in Torrin. Or was there somebody else? I hadn't noticed her talking about anyone in particular, but I'd been preoccupied.

I needed to pay better attention to my witch to make sure things didn't go sideways. Her lack of experience with serious relationships could get her in trouble if I wasn't around to lend a guiding paw.

Finn did a slow turn once we reached the last barn. "That's the end of the tour, unless you want to see what I do with the animal waste. It all gets recycled."

Zandra grimaced. "I'll pass. Thanks. This place is great. You undersold yourself."

"I don't want to gather too many adoring fans by bragging all the time. Let's bring in your load. How's Diggers doing?" Finn directed us back to the front of the barns.

"Sleeping, so he won't be trouble to move," Zandra said. "What got him so riled he had to escape?"

"He lost his sucky blanket."

Archie grumbled a laugh. "It's a gross bit of cloth Diggers has always got hanging out of his mouth. And it stinks."

"Be nice. It's his comfort blanket. One of the other animals pinched it from his pen," Finn said. "I got there a few seconds too late to calm things. Diggers started shooting flames at anything that moved then broke through the magic surrounding his pen. I didn't realize he was such a powerful dragon."

"Did you find the sucky blanket?" I said.

"It's back in his pen, ready for him to drool all over."

Zandra and Finn took a moment to get the van open and inspect Diggers, while I stood back with Archie. Once they were happy, Zandra used a floating spell to maneuver the dragon out of the van and back into his pen.

"He won't get out again," Finn said. "I've put double strength magic around his pen and moved the critter who caused the trouble. He's not a bad baby. He just got frustrated."

"Where are his parents?" I watched from a distance with Archie, not keen on having my fur singed again.

"No idea," Finn said. "Someone left two unhatched eggs at the barn gate. Dragon eggs are expensive to buy, so I don't know why anyone would ditch them. I asked all over and used every contact I had to see if anyone knew why they'd been abandoned, but I drew a blank. In the end, the responsible thing to do was keep the eggs warm and hatch the babies."

"You've got two dragon hatchlings here?" Zandra said.

"Sure. The other one is in a different barn. They hate each other, so it's easier to keep them separated."

"I thought you said this was a small animal sanctuary." Zandra rested her hands on her hips.

"It started that way, but nearly every day, I'm getting someone turning up with an unwanted animal or one they found abandoned. The problem is getting worse, and I can't figure out why."

"Barney said the same thing when we joined animal control," I said. "Could it be a disturbance of the magic upsetting the animals and their magic users?"

Finn lifted his hands. "If it is, I'm out of that loop. Thanks for bringing Diggers back unharmed. If Oleander had hunted him, there wouldn't be much left of his little guy."

We all nodded in agreement. Oleander didn't turn into a sweet marshmallow like Zandra or Finn around animals.

There was a crash, and snarling came from another pen. I hopped up to check where the noise was coming from.

"Careful, Juno." Finn locked the dragon's door and hurried after me.

"What have you got in here?" I stopped by a closed door and sniffed the tiny gap at the bottom.

"An angry honey badger. Mack. Mean as a stepped on King Cobra."

There was a thud on the other side of the door, and claws raked down the wood.

"What's gotten into him?" Zandra joined us.

"It's an interesting story." Finn tapped on the door, and the snarling and scraping stopped. "Mack, if you behave, I've got visitors out here. Would you like some company?"

"Let me out," growled a low, angry voice.

"I can't do that. But back away from the door, and we can have a chat."

There was some scuffling, and after a moment, Finn inched down a viewing window and peered inside. "Jeez! You've made a mess of the place again. Stop doing that. I'm not the enemy. I'm also not your maid."

I hopped onto Zandra's shoulder to get a better look. Inside was a stout black and off-white honey badger. He had a long snout, a bit like a fox, and he exposed needle-sharp teeth when our eyes met.

"Greetings. I'm Juno, and this is Zandra Crypt, the most incredible witch you'll ever meet. Finn is a friend to the animals, so you should take better care of your accommodation."

Mack growled.

"Mack's not here because he wants to be," Finn said. "He's a murder suspect."

My head whipped around at the same time as Zandra's.

"I didn't know honey badgers could kill," Zandra said.

"They're mean little suckers when loose in the wild," I said. "I've not seen many with powers, but I've encountered a few over the years. Who did he kill?"

"Not me. Blood sucker meat. Never do that," Mack said.

"Blood sucker meat?" I cocked my head.

"Mack's under house arrest as part of my Angel Force responsibilities," Finn said. "He was found with his dead owner. Unfortunately, by the time

Mack had eaten his fill, there wasn't much of his owner left to identify."

"He ate his bonded magic user?" What kind of monster was this honey badger?

"Not me. Just hungry. Not a killer." Mack raced to the door and head-butted it several times.

"That's enough!" Finn said. "You're only hurting yourself. You're not getting out until there's been a proper investigation. The crime scene was a mess," he muttered to us.

"He scares me." Archie whimpered, his head down. "Mack's always ranting about vampires."

"Mack's victim was a vampire?" I said.

"Dorian DeAngelo," Archie said.

"Never heard of him," Zandra said.

"You may not have come across him." Finn kept a close eye on Mack. "He was one of the oldest vampires around here and looked after a hive on the outskirts of town. He lived in an enormous old mansion called Bronze Acre. Everyone thinks it's haunted but only because the vamps always skulk in the shadows and flit around the roof in bat form. Dorian became a recluse over the last few years."

"He only wanted to spend time with me," Mack said. "My friend. Would never kill him. Blood sucker meat tastes gross." He head-butted the door so hard he dazed himself. He staggered back and flopped onto his side.

Finn groaned. "Not again. Give me a second." He hurried off and came back with a small dart and a long, thin tube. "I can't get near enough to Mack to treat him every time he hurts himself without risking injury. I'm having to use healing magic from a safe distance." He popped the dart into the end of the tube and blew through it. The dart embedded into Mack's leg, and his labored breathing eased and his eyes fluttered closed.

"He's a mess," Zandra said. "Are you sure he killed Dorian, though? Old vamps are almost impossible to kill."

"It's very likely he was involved." Finn closed the viewing hatch and gestured us away from the door. "The entire investigation is a mess."

"What happened?" Zandra said.

He grinned. "I'll be breaking the rules if I share information on an active investigation."

"We saved you from being turned into a ghoul not so long ago," I said. "We also solved a difficult murder and cracked open a ghoul turning ring. And all you bought Zandra as a thank you was a cactus."

"Which is dead," Zandra said.

He mock gasped. "What did you do to it?"

"Ignored it. That's what Sorcha and Vorana told me to do. It just wrinkled up and died."

"Such an insignificant gift for all our hard work." I licked a paw. "And I got nothing."

Finn chuckled. "You got me. And since I owe you a favor, I'm happy to share. I trust both of you."

"So..." I snuggled close to Zandra's ear, always interested in the gossip.

"Dorian was found inside a locked room in his mansion. It was his sleeping quarters, where he kept his coffin full of grave dirt. Mack was in there with him. We're still picking apart the details because the scene was so chaotic, but it appears Mack overpowered Dorian, killed him, and ate several parts of him, including his face."

"Impossible. An ancient vampire could easily overpower a honey badger," I said. "What powers does Mack have?"

"He absorbed some of Dorian's vampiric abilities since they've been together for such a long time. He's what we call a drone of last resort."

Zandra wrinkled her nose. "I've heard about that. They're animals kept by a vampire, so they always have a tasty snack close by."

"From what I'm figuring out, Dorian and Mack had a special bond. Mack wasn't just a food source. And he has some power of his own. He's old and super strong. I wonder if Dorian was tinkering with Mack's magic, trying to get him to live longer. Vampires get attached to their drones, and it breaks their heart when one dies."

"It would still have taken significant power for Mack to kill Dorian," I said.

"You said your regular honey badger can be as mean as a cap full of trapped hornets."

"I'm confused. When a vampire dies, they turn to dust. How was Mack able to eat Dorian?" Zandra said.

Finn raised his hands. "As I said, this is one messy mystery. However Mack did it, he messed up. He killed Dorian then found himself in the room with no way out, so he had to use Dorian for food."

I stared at the pen door. Something felt off about this murder. Was Mack the killer or another victim?

"That's enough talking about eating vampires and angry honey badgers," Finn said. "How about I show you a cute basket of tiny horned kittens? They're the most adorable fluff balls you'll ever see. If you don't take one home, I'll pluck out my feathers."

"Then prepare to be bald. I already have the perfect fluff ball in my life." Zandra petted me, looking like she wanted to stay and learn more about Mack, but she eventually followed Finn.

I hopped off her shoulder and stood with Archie, looking at the closed door and listening to the snuffled, unsettled snores of the honey badger.

"What do you think?" I said to Archie.

"I'm glad he knocked himself out. Mack is terrifying."

"He's also freaked out and scared. I think there's more to Dorian's murder than meets the eye."

"You do?"

"Yes. Let's see if Mack is a cold-blooded killer or a misunderstood furball with an attitude and a dead vampire on his mind."

Chapter 3

A magical malfunction and a pancake probe

"That's the spot. You always know which bits need attention." I lounged bonelessly on the front porch of Vorana's house as my new furry honey, Sammy, groomed behind my right ear. It was a new relationship, but so far, it was going well. I was enjoying getting to know Sammy, while getting used to dating someone with so much fur.

After indulging in Sammy's over enthusiastic licking for a few more moments, I rolled onto my belly and gently licked his cheek. "I met an interesting honey badger this afternoon. He's a suspect in Dorian DeAngelo's murder. Have you heard anything about that?"

Sammy's eyes were half-shut, a goofy smile on his fuzzy face as I groomed him. "Sure. Everyone's talking about it."

"I know nothing about Dorian or Mack, so it was a surprise."

"Unless you've lived in Crimson Cove a long time, that's no surprise. Dorian had that big ole haunted mansion on the edge of town. If you'd been here fifty years ago, you'd have seen him out most evenings with Mack. Dorian loved flamboyantly colored suits and top hats. His favorite color was puce. It's a cross between purple and pink."

"I heard he'd become a recluse. Why was that?" I moved onto Sammy's other ear.

"No one knows. Although I've heard people say Dorian wanted out. It happens to the ancient vampires. I guess, when you've lived for almost five hundred years, things get jaded. There's nothing new, and you've seen the same trends come around so many times, you're tired."

I paused my grooming. "He was considering a sun step?"

"It's one way for an old vamp to go out. Although, not all vampires are so badly affected by the sun anymore. Maybe someone as old as Dorian was different. It's all the new-fangled sun blocking clothing and UV blocking shades, you see. They've adapted."

"Sorcha isn't bothered by the sun," I said.

"She's not a full vamp. The old ones stick to traditions and don't tinker. Dorian would retreat during high sun, so I guess it still messed with him."

"When was the last time you saw him?"

"It's been months. His retreat started slowly. He used to come into Crimson Cove every night but then cut down his trips."

"Did he always have Mack with him?"

"Sure. Those two went everywhere together. They were best friends."

"Then why has Mack been arrested for Dorian's murder?" I said.

Sammy shook his head. "He'd never do that. Mack adored Dorian. Dorian even made a honey badger backpack, so he could carry Mack around when he got tired."

"That must have been a sight."

"It was cute. But if Mack ever heard you making fun of his custom backpack, you saw his sharp side. Honey badgers are mean."

"Was Mack ever mean to Dorian?"

"Never. They looked out for each other. I know some people think Mack was involved, but I don't believe it. Mack is intimidating, but he has a soft side. He reserved it for Dorian."

I shifted around and checked Sammy's tail for knots and burrs. "Did Mack become Dorian's main source of food and friendship in the last few months of his life?"

"I guess. He was a drone of last resort. Although Dorian wouldn't have fed from him too often."

"He's a big honey badger."

"Yeah, he's huge. And it's mainly muscle. But if Dorian fed on Mack every day, he'd have gotten sick. Drones need time to recover, lots of sleep, and food, or they wither and die."

"What about the rumors Dorian was tweaking Mack's magic? And Finn said he might have been extending Mack's life using magic, too."

"That's interesting. I'd love to know if it was true. It's so heartbreaking when you lose someone and have to go on alone." Sammy hid his nose under one paw.

I shuffled around and rubbed my face against his until he chirruped. "It must be hard with Rachel gone, but think of the good times you had with her."

"I do, but it doesn't always help. I'm still lonely." He lifted his head. "Although not so much, now I have you. I know this is all new, and I don't want to rush things, but—"

A squeak popped out of my mouth as a shudder ran through me, and my legs stiffened.

"Juno, what's wrong?" Sammy was on his paws, looking down at me. I hadn't even realized I'd fallen onto my side.

"It's nothing." A sharp pain stabbed through me, and another shudder hit.

"You're sick! Why didn't you say something? We could have had our date another night."

I gritted my teeth and squeezed my eyes shut. I'd had this feeling before. It meant there was an imbalance in my magic.

"Should I get Zandra? Or Vorana? They're inside."

"No! I'm fine. Just a tiny headache." Even though I had my eyes closed, I felt Sammy's warm, reassuring presence. I was glad he was here. I usually endured these pains on my own because I hated Zandra to see me suffering. She'd only worry.

"What can I do to help?" Sammy said.

"Sit with me until the headache passes. That's all I need. Some quiet company."

He snuggled next to me, and his warm breath huffed across my ears. "I hate to say this, but you should see the vet."

I grimaced. "No vet required. The pain is already easing."

"Are you sure I shouldn't get help? You're usually so strong."

I hissed at him gently. "I'm still strong. Don't make the mistake of underestimating me. You don't know me that well."

He snuffled my ear. "I think you're magnificent. Ever since we met, I knew there was something special about you."

It felt like I'd known Sammy a lot longer than a few weeks, but things moved quickly in Crimson Cove, and I felt settled. This was home, and I couldn't let my annoying magical malfunction mess with it.

After taking several steadying deep breaths, I opened my eyes. "I have an idea."

"Something to make you feel better? I could get food. Would that help?"

"No, not that. An idea about your lack of bonded magic familiar." As my pain eased, I wanted to distract Sammy. I couldn't have him worrying about me.

His face grew concerned. "Go on."

"Have you considered a bond with Barney Hoffman?"

Sammy wriggled back a few inches, his eyes wide. "No. Every time I wonder if there's someone out there for me, I keep thinking of Rachel. No one will ever replace her. I thought Zandra might, but you're right. We wouldn't work together."

"We never replace those we've bonded with, but we can find alternatives who fit neatly into our lives."

He was quiet for a few seconds. "Do you think about the magic users you were bonded with before Zandra? Do you miss them?"

"My situation is different from yours. I voluntarily severed those bonds. They weren't right for me, and that was partly my fault. Their power and influence dazzled me, so I didn't spend enough time exploring their goodness and motivations and ensuring they were decent."

Sammy cocked his head. "You didn't just know they were right for you?"

I ran my tongue along the back of my teeth several times. Very few people knew my origin story and how I'd once ruled as a demi-goddess, before my humiliating encounter with a goblin jerk who thought I'd wronged him. When you were turned into a magical familiar, rather than being born one, you received no instruction manual, so I'd made a few mistakes.

"Some of us aren't as intuitive as others," I simply said.

"I assumed everyone got that feeling, deep in their stomach. I got it the day I met Rachel. It was a bit like falling in love but different. I got tingly and happy and didn't want to leave her side."

"I had that with Zandra. She met me when I was bonded to someone else. A deeply unpleasant dark magic user. Unfortunately, she had siren abilities, so I'd become beguiled. I'd lost control and was dangerous to be around. It wasn't until I met Zandra that everything changed."

"It's amazing, isn't it?" Sammy sniffed at my side. "I'm not sure about another bonding. What if I don't get that feeling with Barney? I mean, I kind of know him, but I don't get tummy shivers when I'm around him. I've always been nervous of him because of his role in animal control."

"Have you had any one-on-one time together? That could change everything. If you put yourself in the right mindset to find someone new, it could open things up for you."

"I hadn't thought about that. I'm still not sure, though. What if he doesn't like me?"

"The pairing has potential. Barney is lonely after losing his familiar so tragically, and you need a gentle, easy-going partner to bond with."

"I'll think about it." Sammy's gaze ran over me. "How are you feeling?"

"I'm back to my usual perfect self." I nuzzled him. "Now, how about you help me get more information from Mack about Dorian, and I'll fix you up on a bonding date with Barney?"

Sammy considered the options before nodding. "I'll give it a go. And after that, we could go to the vet together. I always shake when I'm there, but I'd go with you and hold your paw to make sure you're well."

"Don't worry about me. You focus on having an open mind with Barney. Everything else will sort itself out."

Sammy looked like he wanted to say more but then snuggled against me and closed his eyes.

Maybe my distraction techniques hadn't been as successful as I'd thought.

"These pancakes are the best you've ever made." Zandra was on her third cherry and dark chocolate pancake. We were at the table in Vorana's kitchen the next morning, and as usual, she was the perfect host as she freshened coffee and added a few extra salmon treats to my plate.

"I enjoy trying new recipes, and I always need a taste tester. Before you and Juno moved into the basement, it was just me and Sage, and although I love sampling my food, my waistline thinks it's a terrible idea." Vorana settled into a seat and helped herself to a pancake.

I glanced at Sage, Vorana's ancient, grumpy familiar, who was half-chewing, half-sucking a long strip of dried fish.

"We're always happy to be your taste testers," Zandra said. "And I've got a crazy busy day, so need all the fuel I can stuff in. We may not have time to stop for lunch."

"We always have time for lunch," I said.

Sage huffed out an agreement as she finally beat the dried fish and slurped it down.

"Did you go on any fun visits yesterday?" Vorana said.

"One stands out. We met a honey badger at Finn's animal rescue. He's a murder suspect."

Vorana's eyebrows flashed up. "Mack? Everyone's gossiping about what happened to Dorian. I knew Dorian wasn't happy, but to lock himself in a room and get his drone of last resort to kill him. It's shocking."

"Is that what everyone's saying happened?" Zandra said.

"I've heard different variations. I was in Bites and Delights yesterday talking to Sorcha. You know how the customers love to gossip in there. Anyway, someone said Dorian stopped feeding and collapsed, another customer reckoned he'd staked himself, but most people were saying it was Mack. Something about Dorian being partially eaten. Is that true?"

"Apparently so," Zandra said. "The crime scene sounded messy, although Finn didn't go into much detail."

"Mack is protesting his innocence," I said. "And Sammy told me Dorian was considering taking a sun step."

Vorana's mouth dropped open. "That's dramatic, even for Dorian, and he loved anything theatrical. But Dorian had become a hermit. I thought nothing was horribly wrong with him, though. He just seemed sad. What made him want to end things?"

We all looked at each other.

"I think Mack is innocent," I said. "The more I find out about his situation, the more it makes no sense that Mack killed Dorian and then ate him."

Zandra set down her fork. "Juno, I'm not sure I like where this conversation is heading."

"It's heading into trouble," Sage grumbled. "Any more dried fish?"

"Of course, angel." Vorana filled Sage's plate. "Need any help? I can cut it into tiny pieces for you."

"I'm not a baby."

Vorana kissed Sage's fluffy head. "You're my baby."

"When we met Mack yesterday, he said blood sucker meat tasted gross." I tried not to be envious of how full Sage's plate was. "He wouldn't have tucked in unless he had no choice. Everyone knows how awful vampire tastes."

"I don't," Sage said. "Never bitten one."

"Err... same here." Vorana stabbed at her pancake. "Zandra, any experience with vampire steak?"

She poked out her tongue. "Gross. Never had vampire rare, medium, or chargrilled."

"You're not missing anything," I said. "Mack would only have eaten Dorian if nothing else was available. He must have been desperately hungry, trapped in that room."

"Huh! So what happened?" Vorana said.

"My money's on Mack. Never trust a honey badger," Sage muttered around a mouthful of food. "Mean little critters."

"Everyone says that." Zandra sipped her coffee. "And Mack was feisty when we talked to him."

"He was distressed because he's being accused of a crime he didn't commit. We should look into it," I said.

"I knew you wanted to poke around," Zandra said. "Are you worried Angel Force won't do a good enough job?"

"We know how Angel Force operates. It's always best to double-check their workings. They've been known to miss things."

"Finn didn't seem to think Mack was guilty," Zandra said.

"He also didn't say he was innocent."

"You've been spending more time with Finn?" Vorana grinned. "He's a good-looking guy."

"That he is." Zandra stuffed half a pancake in her mouth and chewed.

"What about Torrin? Been seeing him, too?"

"Can't say I have. Work keeps me busy. Aren't you going to be late opening the bookstore?"

Vorana chuckled. "Being the boss has its perks. I just wondered if you'd decided about who you wanted to spend more time with? Finn or Torrin?"

"I have. I pick you, Sage, and Juno. That's enough for me."

I shared a knowing look with Vorana. We were keen on improving Zandra's love life, and I considered Finn and Torrin suitable partners. Neither was perfect, but they didn't seem like guys who'd run from a challenge. And Zandra always offered that.

"I know they're single, and they've been asking about you," Vorana said.

Zandra ate more pancake.

I studied her carefully. Zandra didn't have a type, and it was hard to figure out when she was interested in somebody. She could be playing it cool with Finn and Torrin.

"If we're looking into what happened to Dorian, we need to move quickly," Zandra said. "From the way Finn was talking, they don't have any other suspects for the murder."

I allowed her to change the subject to the deceased vampire, since it was a topic of interest to me. "Agreed. Mack was distressed, and I hate to see any animal suffering."

"We could drop by Angel Force and see how the investigation is going."

"And see Finn again."

Vorana waggled her eyebrows. "Excellent idea, Juno."

Zandra rolled her eyes but then grinned. "Fine. We'll go after work. But you two have to stop matchmaking. I can figure out my own private life."

"With a little help from me," I said under my breath. "Oh, and Sammy is dropping in at the end of the day. I have plans for him, too."

"Juno, you keep meddling in other people's lives and you'll get in trouble," Zandra said.

Vorana collected the empty plates. "Meddle away. Otherwise, I'll have to keep answering questions from Finn and Torrin about Zandra. I've had both of them in my store last week, and they're not exactly raging bibliophiles."

"That sounds rude," Zandra said.

"It's accurate. Torrin looked at the comics for half an hour." Vorana placed the plates in the sink, turned, and winked at me.

I winked back. I had everything planned. Fix my witch up with a gorgeous guy, get Barney and Sammy bonded, resolve my magical malfunction, and solve Dorian's murder. What could go wrong?

Chapter 4

First date nerves and car swerves

"Are you sure this is a good idea?" Zandra cleaned out the work's van at the end of our shift. "I'm not sure Barney is ready for a new familiar, and Sammy has always seemed nervy to me."

"Barney's lonely, and so is Sammy. Their personalities are a great fit. What's the harm in getting them to meet and talk through the possibility of becoming bonded?" I sat on the step of animal control, watching Zandra work.

She straightened the equipment in the van, climbed out, and secured the back doors. "Barney's still grieving, and I can tell Sammy is, too. They should work this out on their own, without your interference."

"It's not interference. It's help. And Sammy agreed to it." I turned as a familiar musky scent filled my booping snooter. "And here he is. Right on time. Always so reliable."

Sammy hurried to the van. He was hunkered down, his belly almost touching the ground, as if he was avoiding being noticed.

"What's the matter with you?" I said.

"I'm not sure I can do this. What if Barney doesn't like me?"

"He'll adore you almost as much as I do. Don't be so nervous." I booped the end of his nose with my paw.

"You don't have to do this, Sammy." Zandra walked over and joined us. "Juno has a way of convincing people to do anything, but that doesn't mean she's always right."

"It usually does, though," I said. "I get things right nearly one hundred percent of the time."

"I don't want to be a disappointment," Sammy said.

I shook my head. "That would be impossible."

"If this is happening, I'd better tell Barney, so he doesn't get a surprise." Zandra hurried into the animal control office.

"Wait! Barney doesn't know I'm visiting?" Sammy backed away.

I circled him and nudged him in the butt, back to the office. "He will in a second, thanks to Zandra." Barney could get almost as twitchy as Sammy, so I'd decided ignorance was bliss until the very last second. "And this way, you'll see his genuine reaction to the news he could soon have a new familiar."

Sammy gulped. "I suppose. I spent ages grooming this afternoon, so I'd look my best. Rachel liked it when my fur felt silky."

"It's great you've made the effort, but Barney will be more interested in your connection and not how soft you are." I slid along his silky side. He felt delicious. I was getting used to all the fur. "Just be yourself, and it'll be fine."

"I will. I trust you, Juno."

We had a brief nuzzle, then I led Sammy into animal control and through to Barney's office at the back of the building.

Barney looked pale as we entered, and he gripped his coffee mug. This wasn't the start I'd hoped for.

I pressed on. "Barney, you know Sammy."

Barney cleared his throat. "Of course. I thought you were attached to Sorcha, but Zandra just told me you're looking for a bonding."

"I... well, maybe. And I'm not Sorcha's familiar." Sammy gulped again and looked at me before continuing. "Tinkerbell won't allow that. Sorcha lets me stay in the café most nights, since I don't do well outside. Not on my own, anyway."

"Ah, I'm sorry to hear that. It's not nice to be on your own." Barney shifted in his seat. "I'm not sure how this will work, though. I... I'm not looking for a bonding. I... it's too soon."

"You don't want me?" Sammy shuffled to the door, and only my paw on his back, claws extended, stopped him from escaping.

"Oh! I didn't mean that. It's just I've only ever had one familiar, and when we bonded, it was so simple. I've never actively looked for another familiar to bond with." Barney's forehead grew shiny. "Is there something special we have to do to see if we have a connection?"

"How about you take the pressure off and don't rush this?" I said. "Spend time together this evening, find out if you have anything in common, and go from there. You don't have to bond instantly. Think of this more like a first date."

"I guess we could try that," Barney said. "But I should warn you, my life isn't exciting. It involves a lot of paperwork and meetings. Izzie never used to mind those. She'd usually fall asleep on my lap."

"You go outside, though?" Sammy said. "Rachel loved the outdoors."

"I remember. She was always collecting herbs. She gave me a wonderful balm when I had a knee injury. It cleared the problem overnight."

"Yes, she was wonderful."

"Izzie was just as special," Barney said.

Sammy's nose crinkled. "Not as special as Rachel."

"How about you stop comparing the specialness of your former partners and focus on the now?" I said.

Barney sighed. "My office feels like it's missing something." His gaze went to the empty cardboard box in the corner of the room.

"Then help each other," I said. "Get to know each other. That's the first step. You're committing to nothing by doing that."

"That doesn't sound so bad." Sammy's expression brightened, although Barney still looked nervous.

I was about to suggest they plan something fun together, but Zandra scooped me up and settled me on her shoulder.

"We'll leave you to it," she said. "It'll take the pressure off if it's just the two of you without us watching your every move."

"It might help." Barney still clutched his mug, looking like he wanted to be anywhere else than in the same room as Sammy.

"I'm not sure that was a great idea," Zandra whispered as she hurried away from the office. "Barney was shocked when I suggested he meet Sammy. I reassured him, but it's a big deal for both of them."

"I know what I'm doing. I'm great at putting people together." I peered over Zandra's shoulder to see if Sammy and Barney were talking.

"You mean matchmaking, and that's a different thing. You know how tough it is when you get the familiar bond wrong. People get hurt, and familiars are mistreated."

"Neither Barney nor Sammy have a mean bone in their bodies. They're sweet and kind, and putting them together will double that. Everyone will adore them."

"Or exploit them because they're too trusting." Zandra rested her head against me. "Let's head to Finn's and see how Mack's doing. Then we're eating. Lots. I'm starved."

We climbed into the van and headed to the edge of town. It was getting dusk, and the streetlights were coming on. Zandra flicked on the van's headlights and drove through the light traffic toward Finn's animal rescue.

"You were elusive over breakfast when Vorana questioned you about Finn and Torrin," I said.

"Was I?"

"You've lost interest?"

"What makes you think I was interested in the first place?"

"They're good-looking, single guys, and you have plenty in common with them. They both love animals."

"In case you forgot, Torrin ate the hedgehogs we were tracking the first time we met him. That's hardly a high standard of animal welfare."

"It was a misunderstanding. And he regurgitated them. Nobody got hurt."

"Not the point." Zandra drove in silence for a moment. "I don't mind either of them. And you're right, they're cute and want the best for Crimson Cove. They have decent jobs, their own hair and teeth—"

"A ringing endorsement."

She laughed. "They have nothing wrong with them. I should want to date one of them."

"I'm sensing a but."

"It's nothing. Maybe it's me. I've got a lot on my mind. It's hard to focus on relationships and getting to know people when I'm distracted."

"Your mother?"

Zandra sighed. "The trail on Adrienne has gone cold. Colder than it was before we looked into it. It's been over three weeks, and I've had no news. She hasn't gotten in touch, and no one else has heard from her. It really is like she's vanished."

I shuffled about in my fluffy bed. I needed to come clean with Zandra about discovering Adrienne's purse at the ghoul factory. It would make her sad, but she had to know the truth. Or the possible truth. It was only a purse. It didn't mean Adrienne was a ghoul.

"Zandra, I may not have been—"

She shrieked and slammed on the brakes, sending the van into a sideways slide. "What was that?"

The flash of movement in front of the van had been so fast it was a blur. I placed my paws on the dashboard and squinted into the gloom. "It's a person, and they're holding something. It looks heavy, and it's moving."

"There are few magic users who can move so fast. That was a werewolf or a vampire." Zandra pulled the van to the side of the road, unclipped my harness, and we got out.

The second the door opened, high-pitched squeals filled the air.

Zandra looked one way and then the other. "Whoever that is, they came from Finn's land. His barns run parallel to this road. The entrance is up ahead on the left."

The squeals continued, but the noise was getting quieter. "You think they stole an animal from the rescue? Why do that?"

"I don't know. Can you still see them?"

"They've slowed. Whoever was taken is putting up a fight."

"Then let's go get them."

We sped off after the magic user and their mysterious, squirming bundle.

I lifted my booping snooter and inhaled deeply . "It's not a werewolf. There's no smell of damp fur or poorly contained rage and testosterone."

"Vampire?"

"The distinct absence of any smell suggests that possibility."

"Let's slow them down." Zandra pulled an amulet out from under her shirt. It glowed in the gloom when she touched its center.

"What have you got there?"

"Something from the chest Adrienne left me. I've been practicing with it." She aimed the amulet at the fleeing stranger, and a blast of orange light slammed into their back and sent them to the ground.

"You got them!" My witch was so clever.

Zandra grinned as we raced over to the fallen magic user. They'd dropped whatever they were holding, and now I was closer, I could see the wriggling critter was in a sealed bag, writhing on the ground, squealing and cursing.

The magic user flipped over. Her eyes were black, her fangs exposed, and her skin pale. She wore a catsuit that accentuated her delicious curves.

"Stay where you are unless you want to be zapped again," Zandra said.

The vampire hissed.

I hissed back just as fiercely. "Who are you?"

"None of your business." She moved slowly until she was sitting, her gaze on the amulet Zandra held.

"Why did you run out in front of my van?" Zandra said.

"I didn't see a van."

"Huge white thing with blazing headlights. Hard to miss. You scared us half to death."

"Shame I didn't get you all the way to death's door. Although that can still be arranged. And I am hungry." The vampire hissed again.

I growled at her and extended my claws, showing off my impressive murder mittens. "Who's in the bag?"

"Also not your business." The vampire reached for the bag, but a warning blast from Zandra's amulet made her recoil. Her glare turned icy. "Walk away if you know what's good for you."

"I can't do that, and this is our business. We work for animal control, and if you're kidnapping animals, we're stopping you."

I nudged Zandra's leg in approval. She was an amazing witch, always looking out for others.

The vampire sniffed and rolled her shoulders. "It's my animal. It was in the shelter, so it has no owner. I plan on taking care of it."

"If you've stolen one of Finn's animals, he'll be mad. And I've seen him when he's angry. It's not pretty," Zandra said.

She was right. Finn's half-demon side was scarily impressive.

The vampire leaped up, but Zandra zapped her with the amulet, and she crashed to the ground. The amulet's power impressed me. Adrienne had left some special treats for Zandra to use before she went missing.

"You're going nowhere," I said. "Not until we get our questions answered."

The vampire glared, so I glared back. She sighed and looked away. "This is vampire business. We deal with things in a certain way. You have no power over us."

"Once again, I draw you back to our roles in animal control," Zandra said. "If we think anyone is harming an animal, we have the authority to stop them, ask questions, and take away the animal."

While Zandra reprimanded the angry vampire, I edged away and sniffed the bag. There was something familiar about the smell. The noises the creature made were muffled, suggesting it had a gag in its mouth, so asking questions was pointless.

"This is your last chance." The vampire shot me a filthy glare. "Turnaround, take your mangy cat with you, and leave. Forget you saw me."

"There's nothing mangy about Juno. And I'm only leaving once you've been arrested, and I've taken this animal off you." Zandra loomed over the vampire.

"I think I know who's in this bag," I said.

Zandra glanced at me. "Who?"

The vampire lunged and knocked Zandra off her feet. Fangs flashed as the vampire pulled back her head to sink needle-sharp teeth into Zandra's neck.

I screeched a battle cry, dug into the ancient well of sluggish magic inside me, and launched at the vampire. I hit her square in the face, slamming into her fangs. One fang pierced my side, but I had to keep that ferocious mouth away from Zandra. I bit the vampire's forehead and sank my claws into her cheeks.

The vampire gave a muffled yell against my belly and reared back. A second later, she was flying back as another blast from Zandra's amulet slammed into her chest.

I held on as she hit the ground and more blasts of magic pounded into her.

"Let me out. I'll kill that monster." Mack's distinct voice could be heard from inside the bag.

"Mack? Is that you?" Zandra stared at the bag.

I extracted my teeth from the vampire's forehead. "I've got her. You get Mack free."

"One wrong move, vampire, and you'll get another blast from my amulet." Zandra crouched and opened the bag.

Mack sprang out and tossed a shredded gag to one side. Sparks of green magic fired off him, causing Zandra to duck. He growled and lunged at her, punching into her chest.

"Mack, stop! We're friends." I jumped off the vampire and raced to protect Zandra.

His head swung my way, his eyes glazed. "Tyrants! You took me."

"No! That vampire did. We were getting you free."

"Mack, we mean you no harm." Zandra used her special quiet voice she only brought out when encountering a distressed animal.

He twisted and glared at the vampire. "You! You took me?"

The vampire was on her feet and backing away, her hands up. "I just wanted to have a friendly chat."

He growled so low the ground shook. "Lies! I'm going to kill you."

Chapter 5

A honeyed call to action

Mack was almost as quick as the vampire, their movements a blur as he attempted to body slam her into the dirt.

She did an impressive back flip, narrowly avoiding being squashed by a chunky, angry, honey badger, who had a single-minded focus to destroy.

For a second, the vampire looked like she'd fight back. Her fangs were out, a thin, high hiss shattering the quiet, but then she turned and sprinted into the darkness.

Mack chased after her.

I looked at Zandra. "We have to help him."

She groaned. "We'd better follow and make sure they don't tear themselves to pieces."

I raced ahead, impressed by how quickly Mack was gaining on the vampire. The magic Zandra had slammed into her must have weakened her vampire mojo.

Just as Mack pounced, the vampire turned and grabbed him in midair. He squealed when she sank her fangs into him and then tossed him toward us.

I dug into my magic and thrust out a spell to soften his fall, but my magic wavered, and it failed. Mack crashed to the ground.

I stopped beside him. His breath heaved out, and blood trickled down his fur from the vampire bite.

"Give me a minute, and I'll get her," he grunted out. One beady eye shifted to me. "Who are you again?"

"Greetings. I'm Juno, and the wonderful witch by my side is Zandra Crypt. Do you remember we visited you at the sanctuary?"

He wrinkled his nose. "Thought you looked familiar. Give me a paw up. I have a vampire to destroy."

"You're going nowhere." I placed a restraining paw on his side. "You're fortunate that vampire didn't drain you dry."

"She wouldn't have dared."

Zandra helped Mack onto his paws. "Let me heal the bite. It looks painful. She sank her fangs all the way in."

"I've had worse." He grunted again. "But I ain't feeling good, and I'm not skilled with healing magic."

"You sit still, and I'll get to work." Zandra placed a hand over the holes in Mack's side, and a wave of orange magic flowed over him.

I also kept a paw on Mack and calmed him with my magic. At least that was working.

After a moment, we'd gotten our breath back, and Mack's injuries were healed.

"Do you feel up to walking to my van?" Zandra said.

Mack's snout pointed into the darkness. "What about Little Miss Vamp? I need a word with her."

"She's long gone. It's warm in the van, and there's food in the glove box. Juno won't mind sharing her treats."

I very much minded sharing treats, but now was the wrong moment to object.

Mack considered the options as he tested each limb, twisting his paws left and right and then flexing them. "That doesn't sound terrible. These old bones thought my fighting days were over. It shook me up being grabbed."

"Then let's get food and take some time out," Zandra said.

Mack nodded.

We walked slowly back to the van. Zandra opened the passenger door, and while I hopped in, she assisted Mack to get into the foot well. I'd share my treats but not my seat.

Once we'd had something to drink—I had water, as did Mack, while Zandra sipped from a thermos of coffee—the treats were distributed. Mack ate six of my finest fishy treats in thirty seconds. The shock must be making him stress eat.

"I could have taken her down, you know," Mack said. "I almost had her when you arrived."

"You're a brave fighter," I said. "That vampire knew she'd taken on too much when she stole you."

He grunted. "I know vampires. I'd been with Dorian for almost a hundred years. You learn a thing or two when you spend every day with a vampire."

"I didn't realize honey badgers were so long-lived," I said.

"Have you met many of us?"

"A handful. Of course, having a full familiar bond with a magic user increases our life span, but I didn't realize vampires could achieve such a feat."

"Dorian was special. Unique. There was nothing he couldn't do if he set his mind to it. Our bond was special."

"I'm sorry for your loss," Zandra said. "And it was under such sad circumstances."

Mack gulped down the fishy treats he'd been chewing. "I keep having nightmares about it. It doesn't seem real, and I expect I'll wake and he'll still be here. We'd get snacks, snuggle in his coffin, and watch a movie, just like we always did. Or play a board game. Dorian loved board games."

"It sounds like you had an amazing bond with him," I said.

"It was the best. When you find the right one, you just know."

I nodded. I felt exactly the same way about Zandra.

"Do you mind me asking what happened to Dorian?" Zandra said.

Mack stopped chewing on yet another treat. "Why the interest?"

"Because his death is odd," I said.

"Odd, like I had something to do with it? Angel Force thinks I killed him. Everyone does." Mack growled.

"Tell us your side of the story." I nudged another treat his way. It was a small sacrifice if it got Mack talking.

Mack lowered his nose and looked at his paws for a long, silent minute. "I held out for as long as possible, but I was hungry. I didn't want to eat Dorian."

"How long were you trapped in the room with him?" I said.

"Seven days."

I shuddered, and Zandra grimaced.

"Was it usual for him to lock himself in his bedroom?" Zandra said.

"Yeah. He hated to be disturbed. Dorian would gather the supplies we needed, lock the door, and forget about everything else."

"What did he have to forget about?" I asked.

Mack lifted his head, anger glinting in his eyes. "I've heard the rumors about him. I used to go out more than Dorian toward the end of his life. Everyone thought he wanted to end things. He was an old vampire, and he'd done enough living."

"It's true older vampires can get like that. And Dorian was incredibly old," Zandra said.

Mack bared his teeth. "He was reclusive, not crazy, and we still had fun together. He didn't want to die."

"You were a friend to Dorian and a food source?" I said.

"That was our agreement. By forming an alliance with Dorian, I was safe from trouble. It was a solid deal. He didn't feed from me often, about once a week, and never much because it made me tired. And his appetite had gone south recently. He said every time he ate, it gave him indigestion."

"What trouble do you need to be protected from that required a vampire bodyguard?" I said.

"Life is complicated. And my fur is magnificent, so I was always someone's target."

I inspected Mack's mottled, coarse fur. I couldn't imagine anyone turning that into a hat or a pair of mittens.

"What happened to Dorian?" Zandra said. "You were trapped in the room for seven days before you got free, but you haven't said how he died."

Mack shuffled around on the floor. "I'm ashamed to say I was asleep when he passed."

"Was there someone else in the room with you?" I said. "They attacked Dorian?"

"No! Well, if they got in, I didn't see them. And they must have been quiet. We're talking ghost quiet. Not a sound."

"And the room was locked from the inside?"

Mack nodded.

"Were there spare keys for that room?"

"No, Dorian only made one set of keys. It was his exclusive domain, and no one else could enter without his permission. Of course, I was excluded from that. Where Dorian went, I went, too. He was happier when we were together."

"You woke to find him dead?" Zandra said.

"It was the thump that woke me. Dorian hit his head. There was so much blood. At first, I thought someone had done it to him, but I tried to get out, and the door wouldn't budge. It was then I realized it was still locked. No one had come in."

"Could someone have been hiding in the room?" I said.

"No! I'd have sniffed them out. We were alone. But even if they were hiding, and I didn't notice, where did they get to when I woke up?"

"You tried to save Dorian?"

"It was too late. He was gone, and there was nothing I could do. It was a mess, and I was panicking. I know basic healing spells, but nothing that would have fixed his head wound. He hit the edge of the marble plinth his coffin rests on. Left a big old dent in his skull."

"That must have been horrible to discover," Zandra said.

Mack's head dropped, and his nose touched the floor. "It haunts me."

"You said you were stuck in the room for a week. Why not use the keys to get out?" I said. "Or contact someone on a snow globe."

"Dorian locked the keys in a cabinet with a combination code. I don't know the code, so there was no way of getting inside the box. I worked on it for hours, but I couldn't get it open. And as for a snow globe, Dorian hated those things. He only had one in the entire house, and he never took it into his bedroom. Once we were locked in, he wanted to make it as difficult as possible to get out. He said it was our haven, and no one should intrude."

"What about the rest of the vampire hive? They must have been worried when you didn't appear after a day or two," Zandra said.

"It wasn't unusual for Dorian to stay in his room for at least a week. As I said, he took in everything he needed and said he wasn't to be disturbed. The other vampires knew better than to go against his orders."

"You must have knocked on the door to raise the alarm," I said.

"Dorian had the room soundproofed decades ago. He didn't want noise getting in or out."

"Dorian sure liked his privacy," Zandra said.

"He thought most people were idiots. He tired of the way the world was changing and didn't want to be a part of it. He spent a lot of time talking about the past and how he wished he could go back." Mack sighed. "Maybe he was thinking about ending things, but he'd never do that and leave me behind. He loved me."

I twitched my booping snooter. "Maybe he planned for you to go out together, but something went wrong."

Mack snarled at me. "Dorian would never abandon his hive. He loved them, too. He was a perfect master."

"Of course he loved them. We're just exploring the possibilities, so we can figure out what happened." Zandra gently rested a hand on Mack's head.

I tensed, but he made no aggressive move toward her.

"I didn't mean to offend you with that comment," I said, "but it's so odd that he died from hitting his head. Even a thwack against a marble plinth shouldn't kill a vampire."

Mack shrugged. "That's the only explanation I got. And I thought I'd die, too. I held out for as long as I could, but I was starving and half out of my mind. In the end, I figured Dorian wouldn't want me to die, and if I could survive by eating a small part of him, he'd approve."

"We heard you ate most of his face," I said. "And some other extremities. Fingers? Or..."

"I started on his injury. I figured it would be easier than gnawing on a tough, shriveled part. He tasted so bad, I almost couldn't do it. But I kept focused on what Dorian would have wanted. For me to live. I plugged my nose and got eating. It was the worst thing I'd ever tasted. Like death, garbage, and old pizza. Really old, moldy pizza."

I poked out my tongue. "How did you finally get out?"

"It was the smell that alerted the rest of the vampire hive. The stench of decay seeps through anything. It took them the best part of a day to work up the courage to open the door, and I could do nothing but wait," Mack said. "They finally ripped the door off its hinges and got me out. Well, restrained me. The vampires were crazed with grief when they discovered Dorian had gone. And, of course, I was the only one in the room, so I was automatically guilty of murder."

"You're fortunate the vampires didn't kill you on the spot," Zandra said. "They hand out justice in a unique way."

"I know it. But they knew how much I loved Dorian. That fact saved me. I told them he'd fallen. I showed them the injury on his head, although it was messed up because of all my chewing."

"Had Dorian been suffering with any illnesses?" I said.

"No illness, but his behavior had been weird for months. He withdrew from everyone, moaned about a strange taste in his mouth, and his vision kept going blurry."

"You've told the angels this?"

"I told them everything several times, but they're still dumb enough to want to charge me with murder. I didn't do it. Something else is going on."

"I agree," I said. "Dorian's death is strange. What about his decay? How fast did he disintegrate? Perhaps he had something in his system that prevented him from turning to dust."

"It happened slowly. He just lay there, looking at the ceiling. Most vamps poof out of existence when they die. He didn't. Probably because he was so old."

I considered all this information. "The fact you were stolen from the animal sanctuary suggests something else is going on. Who was the vampire who grabbed you?"

"No idea. But there's one thing I know for certain: the vampire vultures are circling. They want this territory," Mack said. "There's a power vacuum in Crimson Cove because of Dorian's murder, and it'll bring trouble to town if it isn't filled quickly."

"A vampire war in Crimson Cove? We can't allow that." This town had just become my home, but I was already protective of it. No vampire skirmish was messing things up for me and Zandra.

"You think a vampire from another hive took you to get information about what happened to Dorian?" Zandra said.

"Maybe. Or maybe they think I did it. It would be a bonus if they recruited Dorian's killer and would make other vampires pause before challenging their claim over this territory." Mack's gaze shifted from Zandra to me. "I am innocent, but I don't know how to prove it."

"We can help with that," I said. "We're experienced crime fighters."

Zandra just about kept a smirk off her face. "Not exactly, but we can poke around and ask a few questions."

Mack grumbled to himself. "I'm not some pity badger who doesn't know what he's doing."

"No one said you were. You look like a fine figure of a honey badger to me. Best I've seen in years," I said.

He grunted some more. "I won't go down without a fight. I'd rather chew off my face than go inside for murdering Dorian."

"You won't need to chew off any part of your anatomy. Not with us helping you."

Mack snuffled the floor for crumbs. "Then I guess, if it's no hassle, I could do with help to figure out what happened. And a place to stay. And more of those treats."

I exchanged a look with Zandra, and she nodded.

"You can stay in Vorana's basement with us. But you need to keep quiet and stay out of the way until we figure things out," Zandra said.

"I can do that. I'm no trouble."

I patted his back. "Consider us on the case. We'll solve this in no time."

Chapter 6

Interview with the vampire

"This sweet omelet is amazing." Zandra sat at a small table in Bites and Delights with our landlady, Vorana Stowell, and the café's owner, Sorcha Creer, the next morning. "I'd never have thought to make a sweet omelet."

"Why not? You put eggs in cakes, and it's not as if they taste of anything. Eggs are just a binding agent. It's the flavors you add that make the difference." Sorcha grinned as Zandra helped herself to another omelet. "And they're proving popular with customers, so they'll be a regular feature on the menu."

I happily accepted a small piece of omelet from Zandra from my position on her lap.

Vorana had Sage in her papoose, and she was being hand fed small pieces of buttered toast, which she seemed to enjoy. I always found toast a little crunchy for my delicate mouth.

Tinkerbell, Sorcha's grumpy sort of familiar, sat at a distance, looking on with disdain. I could hear her muttering but paid her no attention. Tinkerbell was an embarrassment to the familiar community, and I wanted nothing to do with her.

"What's so urgent we needed a get-together this morning?" Sorcha said.

"I need to know about vampires, and I figured you'd be the lady to see," Zandra said. "Plus, your food is incredible."

"Hey! Keep talking like that and the breakfast pancakes will come with a side order of burn," Vorana said.

Zandra laughed. "I'm spoiled for choice. Your pancakes are great. I could eat them three times a day and never get bored."

Sorcha flashed her fangs. "But my sweet omelets are better. It seems Zandra picks friends based on their ability to feed her." She winked at Vorana.

"There could be worse criteria," Zandra said.

"So, what do you need to know about vamps?" Sorcha said.

Zandra took a bite of her omelet. "You've both heard about what happened to Dorian, right?"

"Of course. It's such a sad way to go. Although Dorian's reign has been fading for a long time. That hive was overdue a change of leadership. It's such a shame it happened that way," Sorcha said.

"Why was his reign fading?" I accepted another piece of omelet from Zandra.

"Dorian had lost interest in looking after the hive and making sure Crimson Cove didn't have problems from other vampires. In the last year, there were two takeover attempts from rival hives. The most recent one almost succeeded." Sorcha sipped her coffee. "If it hadn't been for Mack rallying the vampires, we'd have had troublemakers moving into Crimson Cove."

"Mack saved the day?" Zandra said.

"He did. Which is why this situation is even sadder. If the rumors are true, Mack killed Dorian." Sorcha shook her head. "I've heard it from numerous sources."

"Do you think he did it?" I said.

Her nose wrinkled. "I like Mack, but he has a messy past. Do you know who he was bonded to?"

"I figured he'd always been with Dorian," Zandra said.

"They've been together the longest, but Mack got tangled in dark magic. He bonded to a nasty piece of work when he was a young familiar, and they dabbled in shady magic. It changed Mack."

"He's rough around the edges, but I didn't detect darkness in him." And I had experience with dark magic, so I knew when I was exposed to it.

Sorcha leaned closer and glanced around to make sure no one was listening. "Mack was bonded to a necromancer. Those guys love twisting the natural order. This necromancer did something to Mack. It meant he'd live a long time, like hundreds of years beyond his natural lifespan."

Vorana whistled. "Whenever you do deals like that, it comes with a cost. You don't use powerful magic without paying for it."

"I thought it was Dorian who did something to Mack to make him live longer," Zandra said.

"Nope. It was the guy before him," Sorcha said.

"And you think the price Mack paid was being turned into a cold-blooded killer and eating Dorian's face?" I said.

"It could be. Mack is intimidating. Whenever he came to town with Dorian, people kept out of his way," Sorcha said.

"Dorian helped Mack," Vorana said. "He softened him up. I've heard tales of when they first got together. Mack would attack people for no reason. That behavior stopped after they formed their alliance. Vampires often get a bad reputation, but Dorian was a good one, and his goodness rubbed off on Mack."

"I think all vampires are amazing, but I'm biased." Sorcha's smile faded. "Zandra, I know you stick up for the little guy but don't automatically trust Mack. With his shady past, maybe something snapped. He could have fought Dorian and killed him. Being bonded to a necromancer would have given him access to terrible magic. Some of that could have stayed inside him."

"I'm keeping an open mind about Mack," Zandra said. "Innocent until proven otherwise, even though the angels think he's guilty."

"You've been working with Angel Force on this?" Sorcha said.

"Not yet. Maybe not at all. We're just asking questions to make sure an innocent honey badger doesn't get charged with something he didn't do."

"I admire you for prodding at the angels," Vorana said. "Have you met Finn's boss yet?"

"No. Is there something wrong with Finn's boss?"

"Um... well, Cythera is a special case. You'd have to meet her to understand. Just stay on her good side. She knows all the rules and laws dating back centuries, and if she doesn't like you, she'll stamp them on your head."

"How very un-angel like." A weird green creature scuttling along caught my attention beside Sammy. I blinked. My eyes weren't malfunctioning. The green creature was Elijah wearing a dinosaur costume with spikes on his back, and he didn't look happy about it.

I slid off Zandra's lap while she chatted about Cythera and hurried over to Sammy and Elijah. "What do we have here?" I tweaked Elijah's back spikes.

"Not a word. Don't smile, laugh, or smirk. This is so humiliating," he said.

I looked at Sammy, who appeared gloomy and not enjoying seeing Elijah in a dinosaur onesie. "I have to ask why you're dressed like that."

"This is Sorcha's fault. She took me in as a foster. I didn't like the sanctuary, so she let me have a bed until I find a permanent place."

"Okay, but why the dino costume?" I couldn't resist another spike tweak.

He batted away my paw. "Sorcha thinks I get cold because I don't have fur! She bought all these dumb outfits and makes me wear one every day. I've been a T-Rex, a hippo, a dragon, and now this! I'd rather sleep in the gutter than endure the embarrassment."

I lowered my ears, not impressed by his rudeness. "So leave."

Elijah huffed out a breath. "I'm tempted, but the food here is amazing. And the bed she gave me is so soft."

"Worth the humiliation?"

"Almost." Elijah nudged Sammy. "Cheer up. He's been like this ever since he woke."

I tilted my head as I regarded Sammy. "Maybe he doesn't like the company he's keeping."

"We're over that. Sammy's my friend now, right?"

Sammy nodded but didn't seem convinced. I needed to find out what was wrong with my furry love interest, but I had to get back to my witch. "Don't get in any trouble, you two. Sammy, I'll see you later?"

His head lowered. "Sure. Later."

What could be wrong with my handsome hunk of fluff? I dashed back to the table to rejoin the conversation.

"The weird thing is, Mack's uncertain what killed Dorian. He was asleep when Dorian died and could only say for certain he fell and hit his head," Zandra said, as I settled back on her lap.

"Dorian's not been well for a long time," Vorana said. "It was the reason he stopped going out. I saw him not so long ago staggering along the street. I stopped to help because I was so concerned. He looked thin and pale, as if he hadn't fed for months. When I asked him what was wrong, he said he felt sick."

"Could it have been infected blood?" I said.

"From where?" Zandra said.

"Not possible. His vampires supplied him with the best food sources," Sorcha said.

"He fed from Mack," Vorana said. "Would Mack deliberately taint his blood to injure Dorian?"

"I can't see that happening," I said. "And Dorian would have tasted any poison or pollutants."

"Dorian could have had a rogue vampire in his hive," Zandra said. "Someone wanted to make a power grab."

Sorcha shook her head. "I'd know if anything like that was going on. Vampires never work alone, and they're a close-knit bunch who love to gossip. If anyone wanted to go after Dorian's position, it wouldn't be a secret for long. And Dorian was adored. He was one of the oldest and most respected vampires around."

"So we're looking outside the hive for his killer?" Zandra said.

"It's a good place to start. But other than the two attempts this year to remove Dorian, the vampire community has been quiet. The peace in Crimson Cove was because of him. It was only as his star faded that rival hives wanted in on the action."

"I still think you should take a closer look at Mack," Vorana said. "Honey badgers are mean."

"Everyone says that about them," I said. "But once you get past Mack's gruff exterior, he's a decent guy. He wants what we all want. A safe place to live, a warm bed, decent food, and a lifelong bond with the perfect magic user. That's been taken from him, and he's been framed for murder, so he is angry."

"Don't forget his necromancer past," Sorcha said.

I rested my head against Zandra's stomach. Perhaps I'd been too quick to believe everything Mack had told us. Everyone kept saying honey badgers were mean, but just like my witch, I was keeping an open mind.

But that went both ways. Perhaps Mack had turned bad again and eaten his vampire. Reluctantly, for now, I wasn't ruling Mack off the suspect list.

"Which vampire hive has their fangs poised over Crimson Cove?" Zandra said.

"That would be Remus Salamander. The last two attempts to take over were by his hive," Sorcha said.

"And where would we find him?"

"Remus lives two towns away in Oak Park Ridge."

"Do you consider his hive a serious threat, or are they friendly vamps who like to chat to witches and their familiars?" I said.

"They're decent, but there's enough of them to put up a fight if it comes to it," Sorcha said. "I know a couple of vampires in the hive, so I can put in a good word for you if that would help. They rarely talk to strangers. All introductions need to go through the proper channel, or you won't get anywhere."

"Set it up, and we'll go there this evening after work. See if they've been poking at Dorian," Zandra said.

"I'll send you a message if I have success," Sorcha said. "But be careful questioning them. Crimson Cove is open for business as far as they're concerned. With Dorian dead, a new hive will force its way in, and they won't play nice if you accuse them of murder."

"We'll accuse nicely," I said.

We had our first suspect and were on the road to figuring out what happened to Dorian and clearing Mack's name.

❧❧❧ ❧❧❧

After a hectic day at animal control, I was ready to put my paws up and relax, but Sorcha had sent through a message an hour ago. Remus was prepared to meet us, and that meant a trip to Oak Park Ridge.

We headed out of Crimson Cove on the main road toward Remus's hive in the work's van.

"I noticed Sammy didn't stick around this morning at the café," Zandra said. "And Barney barely said two words to me today."

"I noticed that, too."

"Is there trouble in paradise?"

"I don't understand."

Zandra pursed her lips. "I told you not to push a bond onto them. They're not ready."

"I didn't! They gave up too quickly. I'll try again."

"Keep your cute little nose out of it."

"Sammy told me he's ready to find someone."

"Maybe so. But Barney isn't. His familiar has been dead for years, but he's not over losing her. You're scratching open old wounds by forcing this match."

"Let's focus on the vampires and Mack." I'd fix any problem between Sammy and Barney. I knew they were perfect for each other. I just had to get them to see that.

After driving for thirty minutes, we arrived in the pleasant, tree-lined town of Oak Park Ridge. The houses were large and detached, the front yards neat, and the place had an established air of refinement. Typical vampire land. You'd never catch a vampire slumming it.

Zandra followed the directions until she pulled up outside a picture perfect detached house with an immaculate lawn and marble statues framing the entrance.

We climbed out of the van and headed to the front door.

A pale, beautiful brunette wearing a formfitting red dress that trailed on the floor opened it. "Good evening."

"Hi. We're here to see Remus. I'm Zandra Crypt, and this is Juno."

"Come in. He's expecting you." Her voice was like warm honey.

She led us along an extravagantly decorated hallway with expensive red silk wallpaper and a thick dark carpet underfoot. It was a perfect combination to hide blood splatter if the feeding got out of control.

"Remus will receive you in his private parlor." She opened an ornately carved door and stood back to let us in.

An exquisitely dressed blond vampire with movie star looks and shoulder-length hair stood from a pink chaise lounge. He wore an immaculate three-piece soft gray suit.

He walked over and shook Zandra's hand. "Right on time, Miss Crypt. Welcome to my home."

"Call me Zandra. Thanks for seeing us so quickly."

"Sorcha is a sweet lady, so I can never refuse her. When she said you needed to talk to me as a matter of urgency, I was intrigued and had to know more." His ice-blue eyes sparkled under the chandelier. "And who is this magnificent creature?" He crouched and held out his hand.

I set my paw in it, and we shook. "Greetings. I'm Juno."

"Ah, a splendid familiar. Your fur shines. And your power, most intriguing. I've felt something similar, but it's been many years. How long have you been bonded?"

I pulled back my paw, not wanting Remus to reveal too much about my ancient power. "We've been together for over a decade. It's a successful partnership."

"I should say it is. Your power, combined with a Crypt witch legacy, must mean you two are unstoppable. I'm almost afraid." Remus chuckled softly to himself.

"You know about the Crypt witches?" Zandra said.

Remus stood from his crouch and smoothed his waistcoat. "I keep abreast of all influential families. The Crypt witches are up there with the elite."

"Then I hope I don't disappoint. I got the surname because my dad married into the family. I'm not a real Crypt witch."

I glanced up at Zandra. She was giving away a surprising amount of information. She usually kept her cards close to her chest when meeting new people.

"Even more intriguing. I sense I'm in for a most stimulating evening." Remus clasped Zandra's hand again and pulled her close. "Tell me more. Tell me everything."

My eyes narrowed, and my fur bristled. Uh-oh! Vampire power simmered in the air, and it was directed at my witch.

Chapter 7

Beguiled by a blond

"Hey! Fang Boy. If you don't stop that, you'll be eating stake for dinner. And I don't mean the medium rare variety." I hissed and raked my claws through the lush carpet.

Zandra turned her head slowly toward me. "Juno! What's the matter?"

I stalked toward Remus, my fur bristled and my cheeks puffed out to display my magnificent whiskers. "Don't play your vampire games with us."

He simply smiled. "Games! What are you suggesting?"

"Zandra, move away from the sneaky vampire."

"Why?"

"He's using parlor tricks to get you to talk." I hissed at Remus. Some vampires could influence people when they made eye contact with them. I'd always thought it a deceitful talent and, even more so, given it was being used on my witch.

Zandra blinked, confusion on her face. "Remus wouldn't do that."

"Unless you've turned into Miss Chatty in the last ten minutes, it's exactly what he's doing. He's lowering your inhibitions. If you're not careful, he'll have you dancing on the table while you reveal your secrets, and we'll leave with no information."

"You speak ill of me." Remus flipped his hair and pouted. "Providing you give me a few tasty treats to excite my cerebellum, I'm happy to talk to you. And please, put away those claws. I'm a vampire, so you won't shred me to pieces with those tiny things."

"Never underestimate a familiar's murder mittens when you're threatening her witch." I raised a paw. "Let go of Zandra's hand and get away from her."

Zandra stood there, not seeming able to move.

Remus finally relented. He took a dainty step back and released Zandra's hand. "I meant no harm. But I'm always curious to know more about new people. When you've lived as long as I have, things get boring. When I meet a fascinating individual, I want to learn all about them."

"Then ask questions. Don't beguile them," I said.

Zandra shook her head, and her eyes narrowed. "Trick me again, and you'll regret it."

Remus didn't seem perturbed by the threats shimmering from us. Instead, he sighed. "There are so few magic users who can challenge me these days, but I have a feeling a Crypt witch with such an interesting familiar would be a worthy contestant."

"We're not here to entertain you." Zandra still looked dazed, but her usual suspicious character was settling back into place. "Did Sorcha tell you why we wanted to speak to you?"

"She did. Please, take a seat, and I'll call for refreshments."

"We don't want anything," Zandra said. "We're not staying long."

"Your familiar's delightful stomach just growled, and you'll want the delicious cakes my chef made. It's so rare he sees anyone eat his food. I try a few morsels out of politeness, but he's not challenged here. He's been baking ever since I told him of your visit and has even made special treats for Juno. I trust you like fish, my *petit ange pelucheux*."

My stomach growled my answer. Treacherous stomach.

"Since he's gone to so much trouble, we could eat," Zandra said.

"Perfect. And my apologies for using my ability. I forget myself, but there's no reason for bad manners. Refreshments and stimulating conversation are all I'm offering from this moment forward." Remus extended a hand to a large, well-rounded couch in a pale green crushed velvet.

I hopped up and had to repress a sigh of contentment. It was so soft under my paws, like walking on clouds touched by angels. I turned in a circle three times and settled, keeping a watchful eye on Remus to make sure he didn't try more beguiling.

Zandra perched next to me. She rested her hands on her knees and took a moment to look around the room, while Remus sent a message on his globe for refreshments.

Remus studied her once he was finished. "I know what you're thinking. I'm an ostentatious fool who has more money than sense."

"It crossed my mind," Zandra said. "I doubt those are replica antiques dotted around."

He indulged her with a smile, giving just a hint of fang. "I've been alive for over three hundred years. If you fail to amass a fortune after three centuries of existence, you're doing something terribly wrong with your assets. I've invested wisely, and I like pretty things. There's no reason for me to scrimp or save. And beautiful things give me pleasure."

I rested my head against a silk cushion. As much as I didn't like this vampire, I couldn't disagree with his love affair with silk.

Remus settled in a matching seat opposite us. "I struggle to find beauty anymore. It's difficult to come by when you've lived through so many rinse-and-repeat cycles. The same fashion trends, the same political lies, the wars over the same cause that rumbled around a hundred years ago."

"I've heard it said older vampires lose their lust for life," Zandra said.

"If you're referring to the tragic events that led to Dorian's demise, I cannot dispute that. He had almost two hundred years on me and lived through three magic uprisings. He even saw a vampire queen beheaded. Of course, not all of history is tragic and violent, but an alarming amount is." Remus tilted his head. "Here are our refreshments."

A tall man with bright blue eyes wearing chef's whites strode in, carrying a gilded silver tray. He set it down on the table in front of the couch and stepped back. "May I present my offerings? Summer fruit fondant fancies, strawberry custard creams, salted caramel loaf cake, and red velvet cheesecake cupcakes. And cream cheese and salmon puff soufflés for your familiar."

It was hard not to drool, and a quick glance at Zandra showed she was just as impressed with the delicious delicacies on display.

"It looks incredible. This is for us?" she said.

The chef nodded. "I've been waiting for an opportunity to try my new recipes."

"You shouldn't have gone to so much trouble."

"It was my pleasure. Please, try it all. And you're welcome to take leftovers." The chef nodded eagerly, his gaze flicking to the food.

"You don't mind if my chef watches you eat, do you?" Remus lounged back on his chair, amusement dancing in his eyes.

Zandra already had half a fondant fancy in her mouth, so she could only shake her head.

"Wonderful. It makes him happy when people enjoy his food. He's a feeder. He loves to fatten up his victims." Remus laughed. "Much like I do before a bloodletting feast."

Even Remus's ghoulish talk wasn't putting me off the delicious, light as air soufflé I inhaled. I devoured three whilst barely pausing for breath.

"These are incredible." Zandra held out a red velvet cheesecake cupcake.

The chef's face glowed with pride. "You're so kind. Remus gave me everything I needed in the kitchen to create a feast fit for a king. Or a queen."

"The best for the best, my dear boy." Remus's head tilted again. "Here's the tea. It's a wonderful Indian infusion I have shipped over every month. It's one of the few beverages, other than blood, I enjoy. And you must allow me to pour. I like to spoil my guests."

I was so distracted by the food, I'd almost forgotten the reason we were here. I wrinkled my booping snooter. More tricks from this slippery vampire.

I finished my last mouthful of soufflé and forced myself to hold back from eating another. "You talked about Dorian losing his lust for life. Perhaps he grew tired of battling for his place in Crimson Cove."

Remus's gaze briefly lowered as a willing drone placed the tea on the table. "Ah, my subterfuge has barely distracted you. You may both go," he said to the chef and the drone.

They nodded and backed away, closing the door softly behind them.

Zandra looked at me and winced. "Another trick?"

"Not by my power. My chef really is most excellent," Remus said.

"Still trickery." I kept my gaze averted from the table.

"Taste bud trickery." Zandra licked her fingers clean.

"Tell us about your attempts to snatch Crimson Cove," I said.

Remus poured Zandra's tea. I declined the offer of a drink, so he settled back in his seat with a flowered patterned cup. "I've had my sights set on Crimson Cove for some time. It's a marvelous location and attracts a surprising number of powerful magic users, including yourselves. It's only natural I paid it attention."

"You're not denying you had a problem with Dorian?" Zandra said.

"I had no problem with him personally. Over the decades, we've shared feasts and even been on a few hunts together before they became illegal. I liked him, but I wanted what he had more than his friendship."

"So you decided to take it by force?" I said.

"Not by force. I tested the water to see how he'd react to stepping back."

"You were surprised he fought back?"

"I underestimated the loyalty of his vampires. Although Dorian barely fought in either of the skirmishes, his vampires were faithful. We were bloodied and quick to retreat. Now, however, there is a power gap in Crimson Cove." Remus set down his cup and steepled his fingers together. "Add in the tricky situation that the Shadow gang is no more, and there is little stability in the area. I didn't approve of their methods, but they stamped on any criminal activity that wasn't of their making. You need a powerful, organized group willing to keep the town safe."

"You know the Shadow gang?" Zandra sat tense in her seat.

I flicked my tail. Having tangled with that unpleasant gang and being aware of their involvement in Adrienne's disappearance, I was unhappy to hear them being mentioned.

"I wouldn't be doing my job if I didn't know all the troublemakers." Remus arched an eyebrow. "I believe you had something to do with their downfall."

"They were doing something we didn't approve of, so we told them so," Zandra said.

"Excellent work. I never trusted them. Anyone who did business with the Shadow gang made a deal with the devil."

"Did you ever deal with that particular devil?" I said.

Remus pressed a hand to his lifeless heart. "Juno! You think little of me to believe I'd do something like that."

I simply shrugged.

He chuckled. "Crimson Cove is without a vampire master, and that makes it vulnerable. There are much fouler vampires than me out there already making plans to take over."

"None have been cocky enough to attack Remus and his hive," Zandra said.

"Naturally. I'm the closest competitor, and in our society, it's deemed impolite to go after a territory of interest to another vampire. I have first rights to a claim because of my geographical location. It's old fashioned etiquette alive and well and working in my favor."

"Do you intend to take over Crimson Cove now Dorian is dead?" I said.

"Why not? I can make it magnificent again. Dorian had gotten lazy. He was barely siring any new vampires. Of course, we live an extraordinarily long time, but you need new blood coming up from behind." Remus inspected his perfect fingernails. "Before I become as disaffected as Dorian, I'll tutor the next leader. He should have done that. He should have created new vampires and taught them how to lead. Instead, he shut himself away with his curious drone of last resort and refused to acknowledge any issues. That's bad leadership. Dorian should have been ashamed of himself. Maybe that's why he gave up."

"You think his death was by his own hand?" I said.

"Partly, although I believe he used his four-legged drone to finish him off." Remus reclined in his seat and crossed one leg over the other. "Dorian was world weary. It was long overdue he moved aside and let someone who cared about Crimson Cove take over."

"Are you the vampire who cares enough to do that?" Zandra said.

"I would, if it was my territory."

"And it will be now Dorian is dead," I said. "How convenient."

"Ah! And now we get to the heart of your visit."

The door opened, and two striking dark-haired male vampires walked in. They nodded at Remus and stood as if on guard by the door.

Zandra glanced at me but said nothing about the new arrivals. "We're looking into Dorian's death because we don't think he did this to himself."

"Intriguing. I heard the angels arrested his drone of last resort. Some kind of badger, isn't it?"

"Mack is being questioned. He was trapped in the room when Dorian died," I said. "He's a honey badger."

"It's extraordinary that such an insignificant creature could destroy a master vampire. Unless..."

I flicked my ears. "Unless what?"

"They came to an arrangement. Our drones will do anything for us. Dorian could have decided it was time to turn up his toes and shrivel into insignificance, so he ordered his badger to finish him off."

I hadn't thought about that. It was true drones would do anything they were told. Their behavior was partly motivated by a steadfast admiration and devotion to their vampire, but the majority followed orders because they wanted to be turned into a vampire. But why would Mack want that? He was genuinely distraught about Dorian's passing and hadn't mentioned a desire for immortality.

"Has someone from Angel Force questioned you about Dorian's death?" Zandra said to Remus.

"Why would they do that?"

"To get your alibi."

"I'm happy to tell you my alibi, but the angels haven't talked to me."

"You're kidding?" I said.

"My understanding is they're not looking for anyone else. They know what happened to Dorian."

"Idiots," I muttered under my breath.

Remus laughed softly and took a sip from his china teacup. "I don't mind the angels, providing they stay out of my way, but I wouldn't want them to focus on me in a criminal investigation. Their investigative skills are less than exemplary."

"Which is why we're here," Zandra said. "We've spoken to Mack, and we're not sure he's guilty of anything other than being loyal to Dorian and trapped with him after he died."

"And you're looking at me as a murder suspect?" Remus shook his head. "I hate to disappoint, but I was here when Dorian died."

The door opened again, and two more male vampires stepped inside. They joined the others but didn't speak.

Even though Remus looked the picture of relaxed vampire refinement, the fact he was calling for backup revealed his nerves. We could be on to something with this line of questioning.

Zandra set her plate to one side. "I haven't actually told you when Dorian died."

Irritation flickered across Remus's face, but it was gone in a second. "I'm aware of the approximate date and time. It was a week ago, wasn't it?"

"Something like that."

"Well, I was here. And my drones will testify to that. My vampires, too. We were together. Much like Dorian, I'm particular about the company I keep. So many people tire me with small talk about the weather or gossip about neighbors, and all I hear when they open their mouths is an unpleasant squeaking. There is only so much pointless waffle one can stand. My household understands that."

Zandra looked at the four vampires standing by the door. "Is Remus telling the truth?"

Unsurprisingly, they all nodded.

"You see, I have nothing to hide," Remus said.

"You also have drones and vampires who'd agree if you claimed fuchsia pink flares were coming back into fashion," I said. "Your alibi is worthless."

"Until a moment ago, my adorable little bundle of prettiness, I wasn't even aware I needed an alibi." Remus's smooth façade was back in place. "If Angel Force doesn't see me as a suspect, then I'm not one. And I mean no offence, but I know your backgrounds, and I know where you're employed. Animal control has no power to arrest me. You also have no right to question me, but I like to help my friends, which is why I agreed to this meeting."

I was unhappy with Remus's alibi or his condescension, but there was little we could do. "If it wasn't Mack, and it wasn't you, who wanted Dorian dead?"

A smile lit his blue eyes. "Now you're asking sensible questions. You should speak to the Shadow gang. They're bullying thugs, and intensely jealous of anyone more powerful than them."

"The Shadow gang is out of commission. They have been for weeks," Zandra said. "You know this."

"Only the members you know about are behind bars," Remus said. "That gang is sneaky, and their pockets are deep. Even though they're no longer actively working in Crimson Cove, they can contact people in the outside world. For all you know, they may have had loose ends to tidy. Dorian could have been one of them. He'd had trouble with the gang but had always scared them off. Maybe he wasn't successful this time."

So, we were back to the Shadow gang. This information was an unwelcome addition to the investigation. The last time Zandra and I had gone up against the gang, I'd opened dark magic to defeat them, and still felt flickers of it inside me.

"Now, if there's nothing else, I have a dinner party to prepare for," Remus said. "You'd be welcome to join me, but the guests are all vampires, so you may find the food a little bloody for your tastes."

"We'll pass, but thanks for the invite." Zandra grabbed another cake and stood.

"My chef will send you the rest of his creations, so there's no need to hurry. Call it my way of showing no hard feelings, despite your unwelcome interrogation."

Zandra paused, the fondant fancy halfway to her mouth. "We'd appreciate that. He's amazing. And since I have no hard feelings about you beguiling me, it makes us even."

Remus inclined his head. "My friends will see you off the premises. It's not that I don't trust you not to snoop on your way out, but... I don't. Have a pleasant evening."

We left the room, closely followed by the four vampires, who stuck to us like new, menacing shadows.

I hopped onto Zandra's shoulder. "What do you think about the Shadow gang connection?"

"It's one I don't want to explore, but we have to."

"Remus has a strong motive, though. If he gained control of Crimson Cove, he'd massively expand his power base."

A vampire behind us snarled. I wasn't apologizing. If he disliked what he was hearing when nosing into a private conversation, it was his concern.

"We should pursue the connection to the gang," I said. "Even if it's to rule them out. Then we can return to Remus and question him again."

The vampires all snarled this time. It was fun riling them.

"I agree. Tomorrow, we'll speak to Finn, see if we can get a meeting with Anan Shadow, and talk to him about if he's been committing even more murder."

I wrinkled my booping snooter. Whenever we dealt with the Shadow gang, trouble loomed.

But I wasn't afraid of a little trouble, and neither was my wonderful witch.

Chapter 8

Not an angel delight

The next morning arrived too soon, especially since we'd made an early start so we could get to Angel Force before work.

Zandra yawned as she strolled through the doorway of Bites and Delights, causing me to yawn right in her ear and make her wrinkle her nose.

Sorcha raised a hand. "No breakfast with Vorana today?"

"She was still in the bathroom when we left. I'm here for treats, as well as breakfast," Zandra said.

"Oooh! Who's the lucky person getting my treats?" Sorcha presented her delicious glass-fronted cabinet of tasty delights with a flourish of one hand.

"Angel Force. I figured bribery with your delicious muffins would soften them up."

"It always works for me. How many do you need?"

"I'll take a dozen of the cherry and dark chocolate, a dozen triple chocolate, and some vanilla and caramel toffee."

"You mean business. What do you want from the angels?" Sorcha got to work boxing the muffins.

"I'm still looking into what happened to Dorian. I have a new lead, but I need access to a criminal who's behind bars. I figured the angels had the right contacts to make it happen."

She glanced over her shoulder. "Before you do that, I've got someone you need to talk to about Dorian. Have you got the time now? He's here."

My sleepy eyes opened. Had a new piece of the puzzle just been revealed to us?

"Sure. Who is it?" Zandra said.

"Bryce Ottoman. I have a dark room at the back for the vampires who come out in the daytime. Not all of them flame in the sun, but it's never pleasant for them to sit in brilliant daylight and sip a mocha blood latte. So I designed the dark room. They can visit anytime and relax. And right now, Bryce is in there. He was one of Dorian's drones."

"A drone? Not a vampire?" I said.

"No, he just behaves like one. Now, the poor guy will never be turned." Sorcha pressed her lips together. "I felt so sorry for him when I found him in the alley behind the café this morning. I gave him a free mug of coffee and a toasted sandwich. He said he only drank blood, but I can guarantee there'll be no sandwich when I check to see how he's doing. You should talk to him. He was with Dorian for years."

"He could give us an insight into Dorian's mood or if anyone was giving him problems just before he died," Zandra said.

Sorcha placed the boxes of muffins behind the counter. "I'll leave these here, and we can go straight through. Bryce was a loyal drone. Once he knows you're working on finding out how Dorian died, I'm certain he'll talk to you." After a quick check to make sure her customers needed nothing, Sorcha led us along a corridor and into a room on the right. The window was covered with thick, dark curtains, and there were two table lamps on.

Sitting by himself at a circular table was a tall, dark, classically handsome man who looked to be around fifty. He was short but had an air that made me pay attention. He wore his white shirt unbuttoned almost to the waist, displaying a disturbing amount of chest hair, with an amber pendant nestled among it.

He looked up as we entered the room.

"Sorry to disturb you, Bryce, but this is Zandra Crypt and Juno. They're investigating what happened to Dorian."

His forehead wrinkled. "Are you with Angel Force?"

"No, we work in animal control," Zandra said. "We've spoken to Mack about Dorian's death and have a few questions."

Bryce scowled when she mentioned the honey badger's name. "That monster. You're on his side?"

"No one's side. We just want to get to the truth," I said.

"Zandra is a good one, and she's not sure Mack killed Dorian," Sorcha said. "Listen to what she has to say. You wouldn't want Dorian's killer getting away, would you?"

Bryce looked at the crumb-covered plate in front of him. "Of course not. I... I thought it was strange Mack killed Dorian, but I can't see who else could have done it. That beast was with Dorian for a week. Mack had time to figure out how to destroy him."

"Hey, any chance I can get more coffee?" a customer called along the corridor.

Sorcha ducked into the corridor. "Be with you in a sec. I'd better go. You all okay if I leave you to it?"

"Thanks. We'll be fine," Zandra said.

Sorcha dashed out and shut the door.

Bryce sighed. "Take a seat, but I'm not sure I can tell you anything helpful. We all know what happened."

Zandra settled in the seat opposite Bryce, and I remained on her shoulder.

Although Bryce was handsome, from the circles under his eyes, he'd not been sleeping. His demeanor looked shut down, and his broad shoulders were slumped forward.

"I'm sorry about what happened to Dorian," Zandra said.

"I'm still in shock. I wish I'd been there to help. I'd have convinced the vampires to open that room earlier. But that's the trouble. When they had an order from Dorian, they obeyed it. It wasn't until one of the other drones smelled Dorian that it stirred them to action."

"You weren't there when they discovered his body?" I said.

"No. When Dorian wasn't around, I'd get restless, so I went to see a friend. I was devastated when I got back later that day."

"Which friend?" I said.

Bryce pursed his lips. "Does it matter?"

Zandra rested a hand on my side. "We don't think Mack murdered Dorian, so we're looking at anyone else who had a motive."

"Don't look at me! If Mack didn't kill Dorian, Dorian killed himself."

"Why do you say that?" Zandra said.

"He'd been considering ending things for ages. I tried to get him engaged in the hive business, especially with his rivals circling, but Dorian had lost interest. All he cared about was spending time with that honey badger and pretending the rest of the world didn't exist." Bryce hunched forward in his seat. "It was hard to accept. I tipped my world upside down to be with Dorian. He'd promised me a life of immortality and joy, but every time I asked to be turned, he found an excuse not to do it."

"You sound bitter," I said.

"I have a right to be bitter. He refused me. He couldn't be bothered to go through the effort of transforming me and taking care of me."

"The feeding and training?"

"Sure. It's not as if he'd bite me and that was it, I'd become a perfect vampire. I'd need to feed from him and have a source of fresh food for a month. After I got stable, I'd need training to control my urges, so I could live safely among the community. Turning a drone into a vampire needs focus and dedication, and Dorian lost those a long time ago."

"So why stay with him?" Zandra said.

"Because I was loyal, and I loved him. I'd have done anything for that vampire." Bryce's gaze lowered, and he placed his hands around his empty coffee mug. "Now he's gone, I have no opportunity to fulfill my lifelong ambition. I used to be an actor. That was how Dorian found me. He watched one of my early movies and sought me out."

"That's unusual. Most drones go to the vampire and beg to be a part of their hive," I said.

"Dorian wasn't like most vampires. He enjoyed looking for people he thought would be a good fit for his family. At first, I was stunned by the offer and turned him down. I have some magic, but it's not great. In truth, I barely use it. But Dorian saw something in me. He told me I'd make an incredible vampire."

"What did he do to make you change your mind?"

Bryce pointed at his face. "In the acting game, your looks only take you so far. When they fade, the plum jobs go, and I wasn't ready to play someone's grandfather when I was still in my forties."

"So you agreed to become a drone in waiting?"

"Yes, and the terms were simple. Dorian would pay for everything I needed, provide me with a home, allow me to keep acting, and feed from me once a week. I also had to attend the functions he hosted and be there whenever he needed me. But with five other drones in the house, as well as me, those tasks weren't hard. And who doesn't love a party?"

"And in return, he'd change you into a vampire?" Zandra said.

"Yes. I was to stay with him for five years. After that, I'd be turned."

"How long were you with him?"

A soft grunt slid out of Bryce. "He found me when I was thirty-five. I'll be fifty on my next birthday."

"Wow! Why stay if Dorian didn't follow through with his agreement?"

"Because I kept hoping he'd change his mind. But he'd lost interest. It got pretty dark in that hive, and I had to talk him around when he wanted to end things."

"You stopped Dorian from ending his own life?" Zandra said.

"He kept asking me what the best method was, and I kept telling him no method was a good method. I begged him not to do it. He couldn't leave the family he'd created."

"What did he say?"

"He'd tell me he was joking and would never do that. But by then, the doubt set in. I was even talking to the other drones about what we should do. Then the fateful day came." Bryce blinked away tears. "Perhaps Dorian arranged with Mack to assist him. Dorian was a troubled vampire, and if I'm being honest, I resented him toward the end. He behaved as if he didn't care about anyone but that honey badger. For me, Dorian died a long time ago." A tear slid down his cheek.

Bryce seemed sad, but maybe he was crying because he was about to be found out, not because he missed Dorian. And he was an actor. They could turn on the waterworks anytime they liked.

"It would be helpful if you told us who you were with when Dorian was found," Zandra said softly. "Just so we can rule you out."

Bryce sniffed. "Sure. I have nothing to hide. I was with Marcus Blackwell. We'd gotten together to have a drink and a catch-up. Ask the other vampires and drones, though. I wasn't in the house when they found Dorian. I'd never hurt him, even though he didn't look after me. I was loyal. Everyone in the household was. None of us wanted Dorian dead."

"Who do you think did it?" I said.

Bryce was quiet for a few seconds. "Mack. Something went wrong with their bond and he attacked Dorian, or Dorian convinced him to help him end things. It was the two of them alone in that room, and the room was locked from the inside. I can't see how else it happened." He covered his eyes with a hand, and more tears appeared on his cheeks.

Sorcha tapped on the door and poked her head around the side. "Oh, Bryce. You poor lamb." She brought in another plate of toasted sandwiches and a fresh mug of coffee. "I didn't mean for you to get upset. Zandra and Juno are helping."

Bryce gulped back tears. "I know. It's just hard to come to terms with what's going on."

"Perhaps you should go," Sorcha whispered to us. "I'll be out in a second."

Zandra nodded, and we left the room and headed back to the café counter.

"For all the tears, Bryce is another one with a motive," I said. "He was sick of being rejected by Dorian. He must have felt used since he'd upheld his end of the bargain and then Dorian didn't turn him."

"It's a decent motive, but he's got an alibi. If he wasn't in the house, he couldn't have done it," Zandra said.

"We should look into that. He could be lying. And there isn't an exact time of death for Dorian."

"Okay, Bryce stays on the suspect list. What next?"

"Buy muffins and talk to the angels?"

Zandra grinned. "Perfect plan."

Sorcha joined us in the café a moment later. She passed over the muffins, and Zandra paid for them. "Don't feel bad about upsetting Bruce. He's a sensitive guy. That's why Dorian liked him. He enjoyed being with emotionally literate people, you know, guys who aren't scared to show their emotions." Sorcha passed back some change. "I'll keep an eye on him and make sure he's fed and not too miserable."

"And I'll get these muffins to Angel Force and see what else I can find out. Thanks, Sorcha." Zandra gathered the muffins, and we left the café and walked to the Angel Force office. "How shall we handle this meeting?"

"Let's start with Finn and work our way up if we have to. As Remus said, if we give them something to titillate the cerebellum, they may do likewise."

She snorted a laugh. "It's worth a shot. Muffin bribery is an effective strategy."

Once we were past the reception desk, we were led along a corridor into a large, open-plan office. There were half a dozen angels sitting around, and several looked on with interest as Zandra walked by with the muffins.

"Hey! I wasn't expecting you, was I?" Finn strode over, a smile on his face.

"No, but we thought we'd drop by and see how things were going. And I got the angels these." Zandra flipped open a box.

Finn arched an eyebrow. "No reason for your visit other than to charm me with muffins?"

She shrugged. "I was wondering about the investigation into Dorian's death."

"You two shouldn't be in here. You don't have visitor badges." Bertoli strode over. "You should have signed in and been given badges. Who knows what mischief you'll get up to?"

"Does wearing a badge stop people from misbehaving?" I said.

"We keep a record of everyone who comes in and out of this building. We have sensitive material everywhere. If something gets stolen—"

I hissed. "Hold up, feathers. We don't steal."

"They brought muffins for everyone. Isn't that nice?" Finn winked at me.

Bertoli eyed the muffins. "How do we know they're safe to eat?"

"Someone got out of the grouchy side of bed this morning," I muttered.

"I got them from Bites and Delights five minutes ago," Zandra said. "And, unfortunately, I left my poison pouch at home, so you won't die if you eat one."

Bertoli reared back. "That was a threat. Who else heard that?"

None of the angels commented.

Finn patted Bertoli's shoulder. "Go grab us all coffees. You haven't had one today, and it's showing."

"I'm not your errand boy. Get your own coffee." Bertoli marched away, muttering to himself.

"He hates us, doesn't he?" I said.

"Bertoli's been grumpy since he got here. I keep telling him to relax and have a strong coffee, but he won't listen. Come this way, you can leave the muffins in the kitchen, and we can talk without being set upon by the badge police." Finn led us into a pristine, gloss white kitchen, and Zandra set down the boxes. "So, what do you want to know?"

"We've been asking around about what happened to Dorian, and we're not sure Mack had anything to do with his murder," Zandra said.

Finn nodded slowly and leaned against the countertop. "Go on."

"I went to speak to Remus Salamander. His name got mentioned as a suspect, especially since he's been trying to take over in Crimson Cove."

"I mentioned that to the boss when we discussed motives."

"Remus said no one from Angel Force had spoken to him, so I guess your boss hated the idea."

"She's only interested in Mack. And given how Dorian was found, I can see why." Finn pinched his chin between two fingers.

"You have your doubts?" I'd given the kitchen a thorough sniff and found no trace of rodent, tasty crumbs, or spiders. The angels kept a tidy place.

"I keep an open mind until evidence points in a single direction. Mack claimed he had nothing to do with it. He admits to eating Dorian because he was desperate and couldn't get out of the room but that Dorian was dead when Mack started eating. Although him escaping from my sanctuary looks bad. It suggests guilt."

Zandra raised her eyebrows at me but kept quiet. So did I. No one else knew where Mack was hiding, and we needed to keep it that way.

There was a swish of air, and a huge angel with impressive wings fluttering behind her stepped into the kitchen. She was so beautiful to look at, it almost hurt my eyes, and I was used to being around extreme levels of beauty since I looked in the mirror every day.

"Cythera, you've not met Zandra Crypt or Juno, have you?" Finn said.

Cythera towered over us at an impressive seven feet tall. She was dressed head-to-toe in white, a gleaming silver badge on her lapel. "Bertoli informed me there were intruders on the premises."

"They're not intruders. I know Zandra. She helped with a previous case. Bertoli just made a mistake." Finn tilted his head. "It wouldn't be the first time."

Cythera's face remained blank as she studied first Zandra and then me. "I also heard Bertoli's account of interference in a previous case by outsiders. That was you?"

"It was. We figured out what the Shadow gang was doing and helped break a ghoul trafficking ring. We should have been given medals of commendation," I said. "We didn't even get a thank you note and a box of Mrs. Meow's Fishy Fancies."

Cythera simply arched an eyebrow. "You need visitor badges if you're staying. If we discover anything missing, we'll know where to find you."

"We're not here to steal." Zandra spoke through gritted teeth. "I've got information on Dorian DeAngelo's murder."

Cythera looked less than impressed.

I decided to be the bigger cat in front of this puffed up mound of feathers and smooth a path with skilled negotiation. Well, bribery. It was almost the same thing. "How about a muffin? Freshly made this morning."

"I don't do carbs. And we don't need civilian involvement in this investigation."

"Are you sure about the muffin? They smell amazing." Zandra opened a box and presented it to Cythera.

"I'll take one." Finn grabbed a muffin.

Cythera continued to stare at us.

I jumped on Zandra's shoulder and nuzzled my nose against her ear. "I could bespell her or obliterate her. She's not very friendly."

Zandra glanced at me, amusement dancing in her eyes. "That won't make a great first impression."

"I don't see you getting your badges," Cythera said. "If you don't follow protocol, you need to leave."

"Sure, we'll leave, if you don't want Dorian's murder solved," Zandra said.

"It's already solved. Everyone we've spoken to has said Dorian was planning to end his life. If you'd seen the evidence, which I'm sure you haven't," Cythera's icy cool gaze flicked to Finn, "you'd have discovered Dorian stopped feeding in his final days. He became confused and collapsed. Then his honey badger finished him off."

"That's the only line of inquiry you're following?" Zandra addressed the question to Finn.

He finished his muffin. "It's heading that way. After searching the room Dorian was found in, there's no way anyone could have gotten in and killed him."

"Who told you Dorian stopped feeding?" I said.

"His drones, the other vampires, even the honey badger. When a vampire's appetite declines, you know they've given up," Cythera said. "Now get your badges or leave the premises."

"I'm not done. What about Remus Salamander?" Zandra made no move toward the door. "He's got to be a suspect. Or the Shadow gang. They have history with Dorian."

"The Shadow gang is no longer operating in Crimson Cove," Cythera said.

"Thanks to us," I muttered.

"They could be. There are gang members and associates who have yet to be arrested," Zandra said.

"That's interesting," Finn said. "Who told you about their connection to Dorian?"

Zandra tugged on the end of her hair. "Remus."

"And how sure was Remus the gang was involved in Dorian's death?"

"No! We're wrapping up this case." Cythera waved a hand in the air. "That honey badger is dangerous and mean. The fact he escaped your custody only makes his guilt more certain. He's our killer."

Finn crossed his arms over his chest. "I don't know how he got out. That pen was secure, and I doubled the wards."

"Mack didn't escape. A vampire took him," I said.

Cythera stared me down, but if she wanted a staring contest, I'd win. I once stared down an ogre for fifteen minutes. Didn't blink once.

She flared her nostrils. "How do you know that?"

"We were there when it happened. Well, we were driving to Finn's animal sanctuary when the vampire ran in front of the van. Zandra almost hit her. The vamp carried something in a bag. That something was Mack."

"You know where the escapee is?" Cythera said.

"Mack's not an escapee. He was abducted." Zandra glanced at me. "And we don't know where he is. The vampire dropped him and Mack ran off," I said.

"Who was the vampire?" Finn said.

I slowly licked one paw and swiped it over my ear. "Neither of us knew her. She wasn't from around here."

"With no name and no honey badger, you have no evidence this vampire took him." Cythera appeared to be sucking a lemon. It made her no less beautiful.

I swished my tail. "Isn't our word good enough?"

Cythera's nostrils flared again. She could make them enormous. I could probably jab a paw right up one.

"Obviously not," Zandra said to me.

"There was evidence of damage to the outside of Mack's pen," Finn said. "I assumed he'd done it. Several of the panels were damaged from the outside. I never thought someone would abduct Mack, though. Why do that?"

"Because there's more to Dorian's death than you realize," I said. "This vampire must be from a rival hive, and those hives are circling, wanting to take Crimson Cove. Remus needs to be on your list of suspects."

"And so does the Shadow gang," Zandra said.

"Our focus is on finding Mack, not on flights of fancy dreamed up by individuals who don't respect rules when it comes to badge wearing. Why didn't you apprehend Mack? That would have been helpful," Cythera said.

"As people often tell me around here, I don't have the power to do that," Zandra said.

Cythera fluttered her wings. "There's no point in complicating this investigation. Mack will be found and charged. We all know how vicious and unpredictable honey badgers can be. He lost control, knocked Dorian to the ground, and ate him while he was still alive. Disgusting behavior."

"That's not what happened," I said. At least, it most likely wasn't. I wasn't accepting a honey badger had duped me.

"I want to hear no more about rival hives or gangs of no consequence. And I don't expect to see either of you back here soon." Cythera swept away, leaving a trail of white feathers.

I looked at Finn. "Your boss is super sweet."

He shrugged. "Cythera loves to follow the rules. She's not so bad once you get to know her."

"We'll pass on that," Zandra said. "And we should go. I don't want you in any trouble because you're associating with non-badge wearing rule breakers."

Finn laughed. "Fair point. I'll walk you out." Once we were outside the building, he caught hold of Zandra's elbow. "I couldn't say anything in there in case any of the angels overheard, but Anan Shadow is in Spring Prison. If you want to find out if the Shadow gang was involved in Dorian's murder, you're welcome to visit him. We can't do anything to stop you from asking questions."

"You sneaky angel," I said. "I knew there was a reason I liked you."

"Just be careful with that gang," Finn said. "They can still cause trouble, even though they're behind bars."

"I appreciate the heads-up," Zandra said. "I'll let you know if I find anything that connects the gang to Dorian."

After we said our goodbyes, we headed in to work.

The interesting turns intrigued me in this case. This was more than a mean honey badger losing control. When vampires and shady gangs were in the mix, it always made a mystery more intriguing.

***

"We're set." Zandra turned away from the snow globe on her office desk. "We're going to the prison tomorrow after work. Although the warden said Anan may refuse to see us."

"That guy's got such an ego, he won't be able to resist talking." I was curled on a pile of papers to make sure Zandra didn't do too much form filling. "And he won't be able to resist bragging if his gang had something to do with Dorian's murder."

"Get out! That's not yours."

We jumped as Barney yelled. I'd never heard him yell before.

"What's wrong with him?" Zandra hopped from her seat and zipped along the corridor with me beside her.

We entered Barney's office and discovered Sammy nestled in a cardboard box. His ears were flat and his pupils dilated.

Barney's face was bright red as he glared at Sammy. "That's not your box!"

"It was empty, and it looked comfortable," Sammy said.

"Get out this instant," Barney roared.

Sammy didn't move.

I attempted to drag up my magic and send out a wave of calming energy, but nothing emerged. My magic was slumbering.

"Everyone, take a deep breath and then exhale," Zandra said. "What's the problem?"

"He's in her box! No one is allowed to touch that box." Barney jabbed a finger at Sammy.

"It's a cardboard box," Sammy said. "You must have realized I'd sit in it, eventually. It's the perfect size for a cat."

"It's not yours. Get out!"

Zandra moved to stand between them. "Sammy, you need to get out of that box. And Barney, you can't keep yelling. It'll only make things worse."

I dashed over to Sammy and rested a paw on his head. "You'd better do as she says. That box belonged to Barney's old familiar. It's a sort of memorial to her."

"Why didn't Barney tell me? I thought he left it here so I could try it for size." Sammy leaped out of the box and ran out of the room.

I dashed after him and found him crying in the corridor, his tail drooping and his head down.

"I'm a failure. I can't move on. I thought this would work, but it's horrible."

"Is it too soon? I thought you wanted this." I rubbed my face against his to soothe him.

"Barney isn't Rachel, and I loved her so much."

"Of course you did, and you still do. There's no pressure to form a bond with Barney. But I thought you'd like it. You keep telling me how lonely you are. I figured this would help."

Sammy sniffed back his tears. "I do want someone to bond with. We're all better when we have a special person to protect."

I wrinkled my booping snooter, and my whiskers twitched.

He cocked his head. "What are you thinking? Should I say sorry to Barney? I really didn't know about the box. I feel awful."

"It's not that. Mack, the honey badger everyone thinks killed Dorian, would never have ended Dorian's life. They had a bond as strong as me and Zandra, you and Rachel, or Barney and Izzie."

"It would be the worst crime to harm the person you're bonded to."

"The real crime is Angel Force wanting to pin this murder on Mack. We can't let that happen."

Sammy rubbed his face against mine. "You're so brave and clever. Of course, Mack couldn't have done it."

"I am both those things. So are you. And a brave, clever cat never backs down from a challenge, does he?"

Sammy went quiet for a few seconds. "I'll try again with Barney. Something worth fighting for isn't always easy to get right the first time."

He was such a wonderful cat when he got over his timidity. "Perfect. And I'll help Zandra solve this vampire's murder, make sure an innocent honey badger doesn't get charged with the crime, and ensure Crimson Cove doesn't become a vampire battleground."

Sammy's chirrup wavered. "Sounds dangerous. Can I help?"

Chapter 9

A close encounter of the unpleasant kind

We arrived at Spring Prison after work the next day, and my tail flipped when I discovered Finn waiting out front, wearing dark jeans and a red sweater.

I checked Zandra's expression, but she didn't seem excited to see him. There was definitely a cooling of interest on her side.

"Hey, what are you doing here?" Zandra headed over to Finn with me beside her.

"I intercepted a message sent to Angel Force about your visit. They monitor all visitors who see any of the Shadow gang members. The prison warden tells us who's coming to see them. It's useful to know who their contacts are and if we can get dirt from them about the Shadow gang."

"That's sneaky," Zandra said.

"The angels aren't as ineffective as everyone believes," Finn said. "If you don't mind, I'll sit in on your conversation. Of course, this is an unofficial visit. I'm not here as a representative of Angel Force."

"Which means your boss can't complain because we're hanging out and discussing a murder."

"Exactly. Shall we?"

We walked through the first set of heavily bespelled gates. We waited for them to close behind us and then went through a second gate and along a corridor. This ended at a large door with two guards standing on either side. They checked we were expected, and we were allowed inside.

The entrance room was bright and airy, and there were tables on either side where we had to put our personal belongings. I had nothing but my fur, so I only had to endure a brief magical scan.

Finn emptied his pockets, showed them his ID, and Zandra did the same with her purse.

"Any sharp objects or unofficial spells or potions in this purse?" the male guard said.

"No, it's mainly old receipts and candy wrappers."

The guard methodically went through each section of the purse. He flipped open the side pocket, froze for a second, then squeaked and leaped back, slamming against the wall.

Zandra peered into the pocket and leaped back. "Juno!"

My eyes widened. I'd left Zandra a treat. It came with fur and a tail and used to squeak.

"Lady, why have you got a dead rodent in there?" The guard stayed well away from the purse.

"Sorry! It's Juno, my familiar. She likes to leave me disgusting gifts."

"You need to remove that gift, or you're getting no farther. Carrying that around with you is a health hazard."

"I never catch diseased creatures. I wouldn't want to make my witch unwell," I said.

"I'm not touching it. Juno, you deal with this." Zandra jabbed a finger at the purse.

I hopped onto the table, removed the mouse, and dropped it on the floor. Such a waste.

"Don't leave it there!" the guard said. "Someone could stand on it. And it stinks."

"I've got this." Finn scooped the mouse in a tissue and placed it in a nearby trashcan. "Juno, maybe stick to gifts that don't rot."

"It's not my fault Zandra didn't find it soon enough to appreciate the meaty delicacy."

Zandra rolled her eyes.

Only when the guard was certain the mouse was gone did he finish inspecting her purse. Once that was done, we headed through a final set of doors and sat at a small table in a featureless room with barred windows that hummed with magic.

"Why the interest in this case?" Finn said. "Did you have a connection to Dorian?"

"Never met the guy. Didn't even know about him until after he died," Zandra said. "Blame Juno for our involvement. She doesn't want to see an innocent honey badger sent down or destroyed."

"Neither do you," I said. "It's always animals first."

"Neither do any of us." Finn rocked his chair back. "I don't suppose either of you have any idea where Mack is, do you?"

I shared a pointed look with Zandra, but neither of us spoke.

He held up a hand. "I get it. Mack is safe, though? That vampire didn't injure him?"

"Mack's fine," Zandra said. "He doesn't deserve to be locked up."

"Cythera will throw the charge sheet at him as soon as he's located."

"Which means we need to find the real killer as quickly as possible," I said.

"Let's see if Anan can help with that." Finn inclined his head, and I looked over to see Anan Shadow heading toward us. He had a guard on either side of him and shackles around his wrists and ankles, meaning he had to shuffle walk.

"You three. I hoped I'd never see you again." Anan slid into the seat opposite us.

"You could have refused the visit," Zandra said.

"I was curious. Why are you here?"

"Because we think you're still being shady even while you're in here," I said.

Anan grinned. "Is that so? That would make me impressive, wouldn't it? Still a criminal mastermind while in shackles. Perhaps you should watch your backs if I really am so dangerous."

"How well do you know Remus Salamander?" Zandra said.

Anan's eyebrows rose. "The vampire in Oak Park Ridge? I know of him. What about him?"

"He doesn't think much of you. And he pointed the finger at you for Dorian DeAngelo's murder."

"Huh! That old, weird vampire is dead. Interesting. What happened to him?"

"You don't seem surprised you're connected to his murder?" Finn said.

Anan shrugged, a shark-like smile on his face. "It won't be the first time someone's called me a killer. And it won't be the last."

"Did you ever do business with Dorian?" Zandra said.

"Nope. And I had no problem with the guy. Although, I know never to trust a vampire. They lie. Remus has just proven that by trying to pin Dorian's death on me."

"Why would he lie about you being involved?" I said.

"He's sneaky, like all vampires. And maybe he wants to take the heat off himself." Anan tried to stretch his arms over his head, but the shackles restricted his movement. "It makes more sense Remus wanted Dorian dead than me."

"That depends on what your relationship with Dorian was like," Finn said.

Anan's expression soured. "If the angels want to frame me for this, they won't succeed. I have no motive."

Zandra sat back in her seat. She looked perplexed.

I was also uncertain about what to say next. Anan, unfortunately, had a point. Remus had suggested the Shadow gang's involvement, and because we had an unpleasant history with them and knew how shady they were, we'd assumed they were involved. Had Remus misdirected us?

Anan chuckled. "Cat got your tongue?"

"I remember you telling me that, as long as the vampires kept out of your way, you wouldn't hassle them. Perhaps Dorian caused you problems, so you needed him gone," Zandra said.

"He was a creepy old dude, who'd lost touch with reality. I don't have time for freaks like that. And he never bothered me. Dorian knew his place in Crimson Cove and would never stand against me. If he did, he'd know there'd be a stake heading his way."

"His behavior had become eccentric," I said. "Maybe you did something he didn't like, so he challenged you."

"Or maybe you're clutching at straws. You're looking for some sucker to pin this murder on, so why not pick me? After all, you reckon you've got a cast iron case against me with those ghouls found outside my warehouse. What's one more charge to add to my rap sheet?"

"We could be lenient if you cooperate in this case," Finn said.

"Sure you would. And I'm about to grow a horn and prance around like a unicorn." Anan shook his head. "You're wasting your time. I'll be out of here soon. They'll drop the ghoul charges any day. My lawyer is working on it."

"That's never going to happen," Finn said. "Other members of your gang are talking, and they're all saying you were the ring leader. None of them wanted to be a part of your sick little ghoul campaign, but you threatened to turn them into ghouls if they didn't cooperate."

"They'd never do that. My gang is loyal to me."

"They're loyal to the idea of shorter sentences and freedom from intimidation."

"There's always a deal to be done." Anan stared at Zandra. "Say hi to Adrienne for me. I miss that cute face of hers."

Zandra sucked in a breath and stood from her seat, a swirl of rage rolling off her. "What do you know about her? Where is she?"

Anan sat forward in his seat, his gaze hazed with insanity. "Wouldn't you love to know? If you get me out of this dump, I'll show you exactly where she is. You can have a family reunion."

"He's lying," I said. "Anan knows nothing about where your mother is."

"If you ever find her, get her to visit me in here. We have unfinished business to discuss."

"He's goading you." Finn placed a hand on Zandra's arm. "This is a distraction. Anan does this every time we interview him. He claims to know something about another case or an unsolved murder but then leads us in circles. Don't believe a word he tells you."

"I only do that because it's fun to mess with the angels. But it's cruel to separate a mother and daughter." Anan flashed up his eyebrows. "Zandra, if you forget what happened in my warehouse and speak in my defense when my case goes to trial, I'll have perfect recall about Adrienne. Wouldn't that be nice?"

Zandra's hands clenched and unclenched several times. She huffed out a breath.

I leaped onto her shoulder and curled my tail around her neck, forcing out a pulse of calming magic. "We don't need help from the Shadow gang to find Adrienne. It'll only lead us into trouble. Listen to Finn. He's the good guy here."

"A half-angel, half-demon is considered good these days?" Anan whistled out a note. "I don't know what the world is coming to. I'm done here. Take me back to my cell."

The guards approached and led Anan away.

Zandra sank into her seat. "That didn't go as I expected."

"Anan is a giant jerk. It's why I joined you," Finn said. "To him, this is a game. He loves to push people to the edge before shoving them off. Every interview we do is the same. And he's so deluded he really thinks he's getting off those charges."

"The guy's lost his mind," I said. "It's because of the dark magic. It changes a person. Turns them, twists their thoughts, and makes them bad."

Zandra rested a hand on my side, her touch shaky. "This isn't over. That sneaky sucker knows something about Dorian, and he definitely knows something about Adrienne. I'm not stopping until I find out exactly what he's hiding from us."

I crept up the stairs of the basement at just past one o'clock the next morning. I hopped over the creaking floorboard and navigated the tricky task of opening the door into the main house.

Once I was through the doorway, I inched along, sniffing for signs of life. I couldn't complete this mission alone, so I had to disturb Sage from her slumber.

I'd seen several cat beds dotted around the house, so I was hopeful I'd find her in one. I checked the bed in the kitchen, the living room, and the one in the hallway. All empty. That meant Sage was sleeping on Vorana's bed, which made this task trickier.

I tiptoed up the main staircase and nosed open the master bedroom door. Instantly, I heard Vorana's soft breathing and, accompanying it, a huffy snort.

Sage's wheels were parked by the bed, and I used them as a stool, so I could see over the edge.

Vorana was on one side and Sage on the other. Her head was on a pillow, and she was flat on her back, her back legs splayed wide. Maybe I should leave her, but she was an old and powerful cat, and I needed a side order of power, especially with mine being so flaky.

I softly hissed.

Neither Vorana nor Sage moved.

I hopped onto the bed and froze in place in case the movement roused Vorana, but she didn't stir. I crept over to Sage and huffed into her ear.

Her eyes flashed open, and she snarled.

I clamped a paw over her mouth, shook my head, and looked at Vorana. Then I lowered my paw once I was certain Sage knew who I was.

"I need you to come with me," I whispered.

"Why? What's going on?"

"I'll tell you everything but not here. I don't want to wake Vorana."

"In case you've forgotten, I don't walk so well. Vorana always lifts me off the bed."

I glanced at the edge of the bed. Her wheels would make too much noise, since one squeaked. "Put your front paws around my neck. Hold on, and I'll jump us off the bed."

"This had better be a matter of life changing urgency." Sage inched out from under the covers, keeping a close eye on Vorana.

I positioned myself by the edge of the bed, and Sage shuffled over, pulling herself along on her front legs. She flopped herself over my back and gripped around my neck.

I leaped, staggering slightly because of the extra weight as I landed. We stayed still until we were certain Vorana was still asleep, then I hurried us out of the bedroom, easing the door almost closed so Vorana wouldn't hear us.

Sage unwrapped herself from around me and balanced on her front legs, her left hip resting on the floor so she was reclining like a Hollywood starlet on a casting couch. "Is someone breaking in?"

"No."

"Your magic playing up?"

"It's not that."

"Zandra sick?"

"No. Shush for a second. I'm going on a kitten impossible mission."

"A what?"

"An impossible mission cat style. Or it would be impossible if it weren't for an awesome bunch of magical familiars I know. I need you to come with me."

Sage cocked her head then looked at her back legs. "I see an instant flaw in your kitten impossible plan."

"Just because you have wheels doesn't mean you're useless. Sage, you have more power than you let on. I don't know what put you in those wheels, but it involved saving your witch's life."

"Well worked out. That doesn't mean you get access to my power. I must be vigilant around Vorana. She needs me close by."

"You don't have to be in the house all the time. We'll put protective wards around the building before we leave. I'm leaving Zandra here, so I need to make sure she's safe, too."

"To do what?"

"Interview a vampire."

"What are you doing chasing after the vampires?"

"I'm saving an innocent honey badger from being charged with a crime he didn't commit."

Sage grunted. "If you mean that badly behaved honey badger, Mack, I'm not so certain he is innocent. We all know how feisty and unpredictable those creatures are."

"Mack adored Dorian. He'd have fought to keep him safe with his last breath, just as we would our bonded witches."

"Their relationship was different. Vampires don't bond with magical creatures, not in the way we do with our witches."

"Perhaps not, but they still had something unique and wonderful. That means Mack would never have killed Dorian."

"It's what his species does. They live to destroy."

"Not every honey badger is malevolent."

"Most of them are, and I include Mack in that. He's a troublesome critter. Stay out of this and let the angels do their jobs."

"They're doing their jobs wrong. And Mack has little time. Please, I need your help. I'm an amazingly awesome cat, but I know my limits. If I go into a hive of vampires, I could end up never leaving."

"And you expect a cat with only two working legs to assist you? You've knocked a screw loose. I'm useless to you."

"You're incredible. You're strong, courageous, and steadfast. You're exactly who I need on my team."

"I'm tired, grumpy, and my back aches from your bad landing. That's all I care about. Now, I'm going back to bed. Although, thanks to you, I'll be sleeping on the floor." Sage turned and dragged herself into the bedroom.

As much as I wanted to convince her she had oodles of value, time wasn't on my side. Sage had issues, but they'd have to be dealt with later. I'd prove to her she was valuable, though.

I hurried out of the house and stopped outside Bites and Delights. I tapped on the window, rousing Sammy from his sleeping spot. He blinked several times, as if not believing what he was seeing. I gestured him outside, and a moment later, he appeared around the side of the building with Elijah.

"Everything okay?" Sammy said sleepily. "I thought I was having a dream when I saw you."

"And I thought he'd lost his marbles," Elijah grumbled. "Don't tell me you're here to have a disgustingly romantic date."

"I'm on an important mission, and I need backup. It involves vampires. Sammy, will you help me?" I said.

"Vampires! What are you doing messing around with the bloodsuckers?"

"Helping Mack. I visited the Oak Park Ridge vampires with Zandra, and their leader, Remus, pointed to the Shadow gang being involved in what happened to Dorian. When we spoke to Anan Shadow, he said he knew nothing about it and suggested Remus was hiding something." My booping snooter twitched. I never liked to admit I was wrong. "I was perhaps too trusting of Remus, so I'm going back in, but in disguise, and I need a team to help me."

"To do what?" Elijah said.

"We're on a kitten impossible mission. We're going in and posing as potential drone pets. It's a hot trend with vampires. They want a devoted animal they can hang out with and feed off when times are lean."

"That's disturbing," Elijah said.

"I figured I'll pose as a drone pet while the other one looks around."

"What are we looking for?" Sammy said.

"Anything that connects the hive to Dorian's murder. It's common knowledge the Oak Park Ridge vampires want to take over Crimson Cove."

"It's a waste of time trying to find a vampire to chat with. None of them will tell us if they were involved," Elijah said. "Vamps stick together."

"So we win them over. We draw them into our trust and then ask for examples of their courageous acts and their plans to expand. If they like us, they'll want to keep us, so they'll start bragging. They could let something slip."

"I'm not sure they'll do any bragging to impress me." Sammy pressed a fleshy part of his front leg.

"They will me," Elijah said. "I'm the most handsome cat in town."

"Shush, both of you. Sammy, you're magnificent, and Elijah, keep your ego in check, or this won't work."

"You're a fine one to talk about ego."

I glared at him until he lowered his head and mumbled an apology.

"No offence to your amazing kitten impossible mission," Sammy said, "but we need muscle on our side."

"You have someone in mind?" I said.

"Archie. We can swing by the sanctuary and pick him up."

"That's perfect. He'll cover more ground because he's so much bigger, and he has an excellent nose for sniffing out problems."

"Dumbest idea ever," Elijah said.

My hackles rose. "We haven't invited you to join us. Go back into the café and do whatever tedious thing you were doing before you poked your nose in."

He sniffed. "I'll tag along. I don't wanna see you get killed."

"When I arrange a kitten impossible mission, it always succeeds. Who's the best with translocation magic? We don't have much time."

"I can do it," Elijah said.

"Then make yourself useful. Everyone join paws. We'll head to the sanctuary, grab Archie, and then go to Oak Park Ridge."

Twenty minutes later, and after collecting an overexcited Archie and explaining the plan, we arrived outside Remus's house. As expected, the inside was brightly lit, suggesting plenty of vampires were home.

"Archie, go around the back and look for a way in while we distract the vampires. Look around as many rooms as possible. See if you can smell anything unusual. We're looking for any clue that could connect Remus to Dorian's murder."

Archie stood tall. "I won't let you down." He bounded into the shadows.

I smoothed down Sammy's fur and gave Elijah the onceover. "Follow me." I marched to the front door with the boys behind me and knocked.

"Wait! If you've been here before, won't Remus recognize you?" Sammy said.

"He would if I didn't do this." I tugged on the strands of my ancient magic and willed a transformation from the tips of my ears to my toe beans.

"Wow! You've turned tabby. Same eyes, but it's cute," Sammy said.

"Don't get any smart ideas about me staying like this. This look is temporary." Mainly because my magic wouldn't hold a glamor for more than a couple of hours.

"I'll always love your pristine white fur. It's so glossy."

I bumped my face against Sammy's.

"When you two have stopped mooning over each other, we need our game faces on," Elijah said.

I shot him the stink eye then focused. It was time for kitten impossible to begin.

The same striking vampire who'd let me and Zandra in opened the door. She looked straight ahead, and her expression grew puzzled until she glanced down. "Oh! Tiny fluffies."

"Greetings. We're here to fill the vacancies of drones of last resort. You have openings."

"We do?"

"That's what everyone's talking about."

"Um... I'm not sure you're in the right place."

"We are. Remus is expecting us." I strutted past her, and the others followed, Sammy scuttling and Elijah striding.

I headed toward loud voices and laughter. It sounded like Remus was having a party. I strode in as if we were expected, and Elijah and Sammy stood on either side of me. He was doing his best not to look nervous, but there was a faint tremor to his legs. Elijah looked on with disinterest, as if he didn't care he was in a room with a dozen vampires and they'd just spotted us.

"Did someone order snacks?" A large, broad-shouldered blond male vampire strode over.

I hissed and whacked him with magic. "Show respect. We're the most magnificent magical animals you'll ever encounter. We're here to see if you're an appropriate hive to join. Prepare to impress us."

The blond vampire rubbed his arm where I'd zapped him. "You lost me."

I hissed again, drawing more attention our way. "We heard the hive is recruiting magical drones, and cats are your first choice. Naturally, I understand why. I'm Jasmine, and these are my companions, Sammy and Elijah. We're healthy, have extensive powers, and have heard good things about this hive." I looked around and wrinkled my booping snooter. "Although, from what I'm witnessing, I'm unimpressed. We should take our offer elsewhere."

"Uh, boss, you need to see this. These little furballs want to join the hive," the blond vampire said.

"What's that, Tobias?" Remus strolled over. He wore a dark red smoking jacket and tailored black pants. He carried a silver goblet in one hand, and from the pungent aroma coming from it, I could tell what it was full of. "How adorable. Fluffies!"

"Not fluffies. Powerful magical familiars. You should bow before us," I said.

Remus's eyebrows rose. "Intriguing."

"I like the look of that one." Another vampire strolled over, his hungry gaze on Elijah. "When I feed on animals, I hate their fur getting stuck in my fangs. It wouldn't be a problem with the bald one."

I pinged him with magic. "We're not takeout!"

Remus's intelligent gaze flickered over us. "She is right. These fine animals aren't food." He bowed. "It's a pleasure to meet you, but I haven't advertised for any drones of last resort, animal or otherwise."

"Damien lost his drone last week," Tobias said. "Maybe he arranged this visit."

"True, but he hasn't come out of his room since then," Remus said.

"That's the name I heard when we were considering a visit," I said. "No one said what kind of drone you wanted, though. Of course, all the finest vampires have cat drones."

"Is that so?" Remus said.

"I wouldn't mind the hairless one," the newly arrived vampire said. "Can I have him as dessert?"

My hackles lifted, and I growled.

Remus shooed away the vampires. "Patience. I want to learn more. You said your name is Jasmine?"

I nodded.

"Well, Jasmine, a clever cat such as yourself will know establishing a bond with a drone is no easy task."

"He looks chunky." Tobias pointed at Sammy. "Why so scared? What's the matter, little fella? Don't like fangs?"

I hissed at Tobias. "Show respect. If we chose, we could destroy this hive. You should be winning us over, not making disparaging comments about our appearances."

Tobias hissed back, but Remus put a hand on his arm. "Let's keep this friendly. I'm intrigued by the proposition." His attention settled on Elijah. "I have concerns about you. I know enough about ghouls to see you've been tainted."

"You've brought some part-ghoul creature in here?" Tobias recoiled.

I glanced at Elijah, whose expression was sullen and his skin tinged with pink. "It's true, Elijah has been tainted, but he's such a strong creature he can hold off the ghoul infliction. Wouldn't you like an animal so powerfully magnificent as a part of this hive?"

Elijah puffed up his chest.

"My little furless friend, has the Shadow gang touched you?" Remus said. "They've been dabbling in the foul business of ghouls for some time."

"They tried to turn me into a ghoul." Elijah glanced at me. "My magic holds it back, though. And I can protect any vampire with my abilities. I'm awesome."

"You're associated with the Shadow gang?" I said to Remus.

"I wouldn't say we have an association, but I'm aware they've been involved in the local ghoul problem."

There was a crash overhead and a growling yelp.

I tensed. Archie had been discovered.

Remus's eyes narrowed. "See what that was."

Two vampires rushed out of the room and returned only a few seconds later with a writhing Archie, his muzzle bound.

"Oh, even more fascinating. Here's another fluffy. Why are you creeping about in my rooms, puppy?" Remus's voice was light, but his gaze was cold.

Archie grumbled his answer, but his words were impossible to understand through the muzzle.

"Put him down and unbind his muzzle if you value your lives," I growled as I stalked toward the vampires restraining Archie.

They exposed their fangs.

Remus walked over too, swirling the contents of his goblet. "Do as she says. The hound won't attack. I don't think we have anything to worry about, do we, Juno?"

I looked up at him and forced my tail not to twitch. "You mean me?"

"Your disguise is excellent, and you make a striking tabby, but I'd know those beautiful eyes anywhere. Once seen, never forgotten."

My whiskers bristled. "Let Archie go, and I'll explain everything."

"I'm interested enough to accept your proposal. Let the hound down and remove his binding." Remus pursed his lips. "Juno, I trust your companions will behave."

"They will. Although, if your vampires don't, we'll show our true strength."

Elijah hissed, and Sammy joined in a second later and sparked magic across his fluff in a show of solidarity.

Remus raised a hand. "Impressive, but we have no desire to fight."

"I have a desire to eat the chunky one," Tobias said.

"Oh, hush. Ignore Tobias. He's greedy." Remus stroked his companion's arm. "Juno, why are you here?" He walked to the couch and settled on it.

I followed him and jumped onto a seat. "Because you weren't telling the truth when I visited with Zandra."

"You suggest I told you an untruth?" Remus hissed softly, and his vampires joined in.

"Enough of that. Cats will always be able to out-hiss vampires. You led us down the wrong path by suggesting the Shadow gang was involved in Dorian's murder."

Remus plucked at a piece of lint on his knee. "Did I suggest that? I can't remember."

"We visited Anan Shadow, and he pointed the finger at you."

"Never trust a Shadow brother."

"He said the same about vampires. So, which one of you is lying?"

Remus leaned back and took a moment to sip his drink. "The familiar bond has always fascinated me. It's something we can't fully achieve as vampires."

"Dorian had something almost as good with Mack." I was a little surprised by the change in topic, but I'd go with it. "They didn't have the magical tie, but they had an incredible bond."

"You do so much for your bonded magic user. Here you are, in the dead of night, surrounded by a hive of hungry vampires, and you're doing it to help your witch. I'd never get that from a drone or a pet."

"You'd be surprised," I said. "Pets form powerful bonds with those they love."

Remus sighed. "I've thought about it, but they die so soon. The bond would barely be there before they were gone. It would break my heart."

"Hellhounds live for a long time," Archie said.

Remus looked up and studied him. "How long do you live?"

"Potentially forever. I'm almost a hundred, but I'm still a teenager in hellhound years. It's the power from the underworld, you see. So long as that's there, I live as long as I like. Of course, if something gross happened to me and I got chopped into tiny pieces or blown apart by a powerful spell and the ash blown away, I might not come back, but I'd figure something out."

"Well now, then I have an interesting proposition for you." Remus leaned forward, his eyes alive with excitement. "Juno, give me Archie, and I'll give you something of interest about the Shadow gang."

Chapter 10

A deal with the undead

My gaze shot to Archie, and he gulped. "I'm not in a position to trade Archie. He's a free living hellhound."

"That's... that's right. I'm a hell living free hound," Archie stuttered.

"Isn't that what you came here for? You were offering your services for information. You can't have truly believed you could poke around without being discovered." Remus gave an almost imperceptible gesture, but his vampires moved to block the way out. "And I've been nothing but hospitable, especially considering you broke in and attempted to deceive us. That calls for flexibility on your part. A gift to show no hard feelings."

"Maybe vampires who kill other vampires don't deserve flexibility." I kept an eye on Archie. He'd gone quiet and was staring at Remus.

"Juno, let's not be cross with each other. I'm aware you're a unique familiar. Our previous meeting showed you have a power not to be trifled with," Remus said.

"Don't make fun of her weird power," Elijah said.

"I'm not. Juno is one of a kind. I'm sure, if you've spent time with her, you're aware of that. She has a special quality to her magic. It's something I haven't felt for decades, perhaps even hundreds of years. Such a unique beauty needs to be cherished and given a healthy amount of respect. That's what I'm doing. And it's why I haven't set my vampires on you." Remus's pink tongue darted across his lips. "But I require a show of respect in return. Juno understands that."

My gaze went to Archie again. He wasn't looking so scared anymore, more curious. "It's okay, Elijah. We broke in and weren't truthful with Remus."

Remus inclined his head. "May I ask why?"

"Because you wouldn't confess to what you did to Dorian, so we had to find evidence to implicate you."

"Or I didn't confess because there's nothing to confess to." Remus shifted in his seat so he faced Archie. "What do you say about spending the rest of your hellhound life in a vampire hive? We host incredible parties, and just last week, we had a hog roast. Of course, as vampires, we rarely eat that kind of food, but if you'd been here, you'd have had a hog to yourself. There was also apple sauce, crusty rolls, sausages, and toasted marshmallows. A treat for such a fine hound, don't you think?"

Archie's stomach grumbled as he drooled on the carpet. "That sounds amazing."

"It was sublime. We had a feast, too. And in the spirit of openness, if you're considering joining us, you must understand there's always blood at these parties. Sometimes, the food runs away."

"I'm not squeamish," Archie said. "I saw my previous bonded magic user lose his head. It exploded in front of me."

I opened my mouth to tell him to be careful, but it appeared Archie wanted to impress Remus. Was he considering this arrangement?

Remus cleared his throat. "How unfortunate. That must have been... sticky."

"It was gross. His brains went everywhere. I still have nightmares about it." Archie lowered his head, and the temporary bond I'd formed with him to keep him alive while he adjusted to life without a magic user warped.

"I could help with those nightmares. Vampires are excellent at removing unpleasant memories."

"And implanting false ones," Elijah muttered.

Remus shrugged. "Perhaps that, too. We have many talents. And you'd learn about them if you joined us. If you became a part of the hive, you'd have a huge family around you. We'd look out for you. You wouldn't be alone."

Archie whined and lowered his head.

"Give me a moment." I trotted to Archie and nudged him to the other side of the room. It was for show. If the vampires chose to, they'd easily be able to listen in to the conversation. "You don't have to do this."

"That head vamp said he's got information about the Shadow gang. It could solve your murder."

"He didn't actually say that. Remus could be tricking us."

"The information will be most useful in solving Dorian's murder," Remus said.

"This is a private conversation," I said.

He held up a hand. "My apologies. I'm just eager to do business together. And my hive would love to have a hellhound around. We could start our own trend. Hellhounds and vampires. Everyone would fear us, and no one would fight us. I'm amazed I've not thought of this before."

Elijah and Sammy joined us, both of them looking worried.

"Don't trust the vampires," Elijah said.

"I never agree with Elijah, but he's right. What if they hurt you, Archie? Or turn you into a vampire hellhound?" Sammy said.

"I don't want that." Archie huffed out a breath. "But it's not the worst offer I've ever had. And I've got nowhere else to go. And they have hog roasts. Did you hear?"

"But you have your new home to go to. You're leaving Finn's animal rescue any day," I said.

He shook his head and whined again. "When they came to see me again, I got excited. I drooled on the nice lady's smart pantsuit. She got upset, and I tried to wipe it off with my tail but made things worse. And then I had gas, an aftereffect of having a diamond in my gut for so long, and let rip in the guy's face. I didn't mean to, but he was bending down, so he got a face full. With the drool and gas combination, they decided I wasn't for them."

"I had no idea," I said. "I'm so sorry. You were excited about the next stage of your life with your new family."

He gave the hound version of a shrug. "It's okay. They seemed too posh for me. I've spent most of my days with guys who play dirty. If you remember, Osorin's house wasn't a palace."

"I know I'm not supposed to be listening, but you'd want for nothing if you joined with me," Remus said. "You'd have your own room."

Archie lifted his head. "With a bed?"

"Yes! As many as you like. You could have a bed in each room or sleep on my bed."

"Oh! I mean, wow! Osorin made me sleep in the yard. He said I was too noisy."

"And I have extensive grounds out the back. Eight acres, all secure and fenced in, so you'd have the free run of the place."

"All for me?"

"You'd share with the rest of us. We run daily. And we have wild deer and rabbits. They're yours for the taking. We often take. It's most stimulating."

"Rabbits! I love rabbits. Tasty!"

I sighed. There was no point in having a private conversation in a room full of nosy vampires, and Remus seemed genuinely keen on selling this option to Archie. There was an earnestness in his voice, suggesting he saw something in Archie he liked. And why not? This drooling hellhound was magnificent.

"What do you say, Archie? A trial run to see if you'd like living here and being my companion?" Remus said.

"Don't rush into anything," I cautioned him.

"I should do this," Archie said. "Finn's been great to me, but I don't want to stay in an animal rescue for the rest of my days. It's boring, and there's not much to do. Most of the other animals fear me. Living with the vampires wouldn't be so bad, and the feasts and rabbits sound amazing. And I love to run for miles and miles. I could be myself living here."

I wrinkled my booping snooter. "Let's see if we can do a deal. One favorable to you. No information is worth sacrificing your freedom." I turned and settled on the plush carpet, my attention on Remus. "Archie is considering your proposal, but we have stipulations."

"I'm listening."

"Archie needs to know he's safe."

"If Archie was under my care, not only would he have my protection, but the hive would look out for him. If they didn't, they'd discover my dark and unfriendly side." His expression blanked, and the cold, undead creature he truly was reared up for a second.

The other vampires cowered and looked away.

"And I... I don't want to be bitten," Archie said. "I don't want to be a drone of last resort. I want to be your pet. I'd make an excellent pet. I'm loyal, fast, and strong. And I'll stand by your side in a fight. I'm amazing when I fight. A true predator." He growled and flashed his impressive fangs.

"I see that. You'd be a worthy pet." Remus considered Archie's comments. "If you don't wish to be fed on, you may be my loyal pet. No biting or feeding. You have my word."

"From any vampire," I said. "Archie is off-limits to all fangs."

"Naturally. He'll belong to me. I'll order the others to leave him alone. They won't go against a direct order."

"Actually, I'd like it if we belonged to each other," Archie said. "If that's okay with you. Partners. Maybe even friends. Best friends."

Remus's expression softened, and his eyes hazed. "That would be delightful. I can think of nothing I'd like more. A true, loyal friend by my side for eternity. Yes, I'd enjoy that very much. What an excellent idea. Partners and friends."

"You're really okay with the no biting clause?" I said. "I figured you'd want to take a nibble from Archie now and again when prey was hard to find."

"No, he'd be a true pet and a friend, with my complete protection." Remus stood and pressed a hand against his heart. "You have my word. And you'd want for nothing, Archie. You'd have a dream lifestyle."

"If you discount the dead bodies you'd have to dig holes for," Elijah said.

"Oh! I love digging holes. Osorin used to yell at me for digging up the yard, but there's nothing more satisfying than getting the earth flying. I'll dig the holes for you. Huge holes."

Elijah sighed. "I'm wasting my time helping this moron."

"Your offer is kind, Archie, but I have people who deal with the disposal aspects of our lifestyle. You won't need to get your paws muddy unless you want to," Remus said.

Archie's tongue lolled out. "I do. I always pick great spots to dig."

"Then you're welcome to dig holes in the grounds for as many hours as you desire."

"Wait, a moment. Let's make sure everything is crystal clear before we make any agreements." I leaned in close to Archie. "You know vampires can be sneaky."

"We also have excellent hearing," Remus said.

"Then hear this. No eating Archie, no draining him and dumping him in a hole dug by one of your people, no using him as a weapon unless he wants to fight, no dry humping—that one's for you, Archie—and no turning him into a vampire hellhound."

Remus drew in a long breath. "I have no problem with those terms. Archie, is there anything else you require to make this arrangement pleasurable for you?"

Archie glanced at me again. "I'd like my friends to visit whenever they want and not worry about being bitten or chased."

"Make a list of names for me, and I'll ensure their safety when they visit. Anything else?"

Archie gulped. "I... I like this arrangement. I think I could be happy here."

"No doubts?" I said.

He shook his head. "Let's see how it goes. I can't believe I get my own room. And the hog roasts! We must have one soon. You'll all have to come."

I nodded. "If this is what you really want. No pressure. You're a free hellhound."

Archie lifted his huge, fuzzy muzzle. "I want this."

"Excellent. Then we'll seal the deal. Tobias, bring steak for our guests and a bottle of the O negative reserve from that supermodel who visited in 2001." Remus rubbed his hands together.

Tobias dashed off while the other vampires clapped Remus on the back and smiled at Archie. Everyone seemed happy to have a new member of the household.

Archie padded to Remus and sniffed him. Remus gently petted Archie's head and examined his paws.

"Such a fine hound. But after our feast, it's bath time. Then you can pick your room."

Archie whined. "Must I have a bath? Osorin never made me take them."

"My adorable creature, vampires have an acute sense of smell, and you smell less than delicious. Call this a tiny compromise on your part. I have a range of wonderful bubbles, so you can choose your scent. And then we'll research collars. You'd look striking in something with studs."

"Or not. Not all animals like collars." I stayed back with Sammy and Elijah to give them a chance to bond. To my amazement, they seemed thrilled to be together. This wasn't the outcome I'd expected from the visit, but I was happy it happened. Archie had experienced a lousy start to his life, so it was time something decent showed up for him. I never expected his perfect place to be in a vampire hive, though.

"We'll find something we both agree on." Remus looked up. "Now, your reward. Ricardo, fetch the red USB stick from my desk drawer."

In the blink of an eye, Ricardo had returned. He gave me the stick.

"What's this?"

"A recording of a conversation Dorian had with a member of the Shadow gang." Remus continued petting Archie, rapture on his face. "It should make everything much clearer about Dorian's murder."

I sniffed the USB stick. "How did you get this?"

He shrugged. "We have our ways. Enjoy."

I planned to. If this led us to Dorian's killer, I may even return to celebrate with Remus and the rest of the fang gang.

Chapter 11

A clue and a return to the gang

I hopped on to Zandra's bed and stuck my cold nose on her cheek.

She grimaced and pulled away. "It's too early. You can't want breakfast already."

"It's almost five o'clock. And I have news."

"Tell me about your dreams in a couple of hours. I need more sleep." Zandra rolled over and pulled the covers up to her chin.

I jumped on her head. "This is about Dorian's murder. I've been investigating. I found a new clue."

Zandra huffed out a breath. "The only other supernaturals who'd be awake at this time are the vampires or the werewolves. Please don't tell me you've been to visit any of them."

"Don't be angry, but I didn't want to wake you, and we needed to learn more about Dorian's connection to the Shadow gang."

She groaned. "Juno! You went to see Remus, didn't you?"

"Get up, make a coffee, and I'll tell you everything. And we need a computer."

"A computer? What have you been doing?"

"Being awesome and solving this case." I jumped up and down on her head. "Let's move."

Zandra grumbled to herself before rolling out of bed. She blinked at me, still looking half-asleep. "Did you get bitten by any vamps?"

"As if."

"And you're not hurt or in any trouble?"

"Never!"

"Good. This had better not be a wild vampire chase. I hate missing sleep."

"You have nothing to worry about. And I took some friends with me, so I had backup. We even found a home for Archie."

"A... never mind. I can't process any of this without caffeine." She shrugged on her dressing gown and shuffled her feet into her slippers.

"I'll wake Mack. He needs to hear this, too." While Zandra shuffled off, I trotted to the box Mack had claimed as his own.

He continued snoring, despite my repeated proddings. Eventually, I nipped him with my teeth.

He snarled and leaped up.

"I have information about Dorian. Follow me." I dashed up the stairs, knowing he'd follow.

Ten minutes later, I was pacing the kitchen, waiting for Zandra to become suitably caffeine fueled and for Mack to finish eating. Zandra had brought her laptop up from the basement, and it sat on the kitchen counter.

She set down her coffee mug. "Okay, hit me. What have you been doing while I've been sleeping?"

"The most incredible kitten impossible mission. I recruited Sammy, Elijah, and Archie to assist."

"And where did your amazing team of magical familiars go in the middle of the night?"

"Back to Remus's house. I knew he hadn't told us everything, and after the conversation we had with Anan, it became clear one of them was lying."

"And you thought the shady guy from the Shadow gang was more reliable than the tricky vampire who's been trying to take over Crimson Cove?"

"Neither are trustworthy, but I had a feeling in my toe beans Remus would be more willing to talk. And I went in disguise, so he didn't know it was me. Mostly."

She arched an eyebrow. "I have a feeling I'm missing parts of this story."

"Only the unimportant parts. I questioned Remus, and he provided useful information."

"In return for what?" Zandra sipped more coffee. "Vampires don't give anything away for nothing. Are you sure I shouldn't check for puncture wounds?"

"No one got bitten, but Archie got adopted. Remus was enchanted by him. So we made a deal."

"You traded Archie for information?"

"No! Archie wanted to join the hive, and Remus was bending over backward to make sure it happened. I always knew that hellhound was something special."

Mack grunted. "I'm kind of lost."

"Me, too, but go on," Zandra said. "Archie is now living in Remus's hive?"

"Yep. He's staying on a trial basis. Although I had my reservations, it could work. And as a reward, Remus handed over a recording of the meeting between Dorian and someone from the Shadow gang. It's on that stick." I pointed my nose at the USB stick on the counter.

"Juno! That was reckless and dangerous. Vampire hives are unpredictable. You could have gotten trapped."

"You underestimate my powers. And with three other incredible magical creatures beside me, I was guaranteed success."

Zandra pursed her lips. "You should have woken me, and I'd have come with you."

I tilted my head. "I suppose you could have turned yourself into a cat, but Remus was astute at seeing through my disguise."

"He figured out who you were and wasn't angry about the deception?"

"He was more fascinated. It seems Remus was lonely and needed a pet to keep him company."

Zandra groaned again. "I know you have nine lives, but you act like you have an infinite number of them." She reached over and scratched between my ears. "I'm glad you got out in one piece."

"Better than one piece. I got a new piece." I scooted the USB stick across the counter. "Plug this in."

Zandra fired up the stick. "It's an audio recording."

"Play it."

Mack shuffled over to hear better.

She hit the play button, and we waited.

"You can't go back on our arrangement."

"That's Anan," Zandra said.

I nodded, my ears forward as I listened.

"I've been hearing worrying rumors about your business practices. I want nothing to do with this if you're hurting innocent people."

"I don't recognize that voice," I said.

"It's Dorian," Mack said.

"There's no such thing as an innocent person. You knew what you were getting into when you agreed to work with us," Anan said.

"I didn't know you'd behave so crassly."

Zandra paused the recording. "Mack, were you aware Dorian did business with the Shadow gang?"

"It never happened. At least, I don't think it did. Although Dorian was having trouble with some other vamps and said he needed to do something about it. They'd approached him with an offer to buy him out of Crimson Cove."

"Remus?"

"No, some slick vamp from out of town. Sebastian something. A slimy creep. Wore too much cologne."

"Was Dorian interested in being bought out?"

"No. He turned down several offers, even though they got bigger every time. His heart was in Crimson Cove, even though he didn't show it. The vamp kept trying to impress Dorian and even arrived in a private helicopter. Why bother? Vampires can move around much faster than helicopters. Anyway, he'd show up, flash money around, and say he'd revitalize Crimson Cove and make it a vampire haven."

"Nothing could tempt Dorian?" I said.

"Turned him down flat. He had no plans to give up Crimson Cove. Even when this vampire challenged him and said how rundown and weak the local vampires were, Dorian didn't rise to the bait."

"Because he lied, and he really was giving up?"

Mack shrugged. "Play the rest of the conversation."

Zandra pressed a button on the laptop.

"I said to make sure he backed off. I didn't expect anyone to die."

"That's Dorian again," Mack said. "He sounds tired."

"Then you needed to be clearer when we made our arrangement. You said that vampire was being a problem, and you wanted him dealt with. I dealt," Anan said.

"I told you to make sure he didn't come back to Crimson Cove."

"Why are you so concerned if a little vampire blood got spilt? It got rid of your problem."

"You made another hive angry. And Sebastian is devastated. You murdered his beloved companion."

"Not my problem. The shot went wide, but the stake found a target, and you made your point. You owe us."

"You're getting nothing else from me. You didn't do the job I wanted you to do."

Anan growled. "You'll pay the rest of the money. No one backs out on a deal with us."

"You've been paid plenty. You were meant to intimidate, not murder. Now leave, before I call in the rest of my vampires."

"They don't scare me," Anan said. "Neither do you. You're washed up and past your prime. You're an embarrassment to the vampire community. It's no surprise they're circling and wanting a piece of this action."

"You'd be wise not to say another word if you value the blood in your body. You may consider me past it, but I still give a nasty bite."

A chair scraped across a wooden floor. "You're a joke and an embarrassment. I will get my money. You'll be sorry if you don't pay."

A door slammed, and a second later, the recording ended.

"I'll kill him," Mack snarled. "That scummy Shadow gang member threatened Dorian, and now he's dead. It was him! He got into Dorian's bedroom and murdered him while I was asleep."

"But how?" Zandra said. "The Shadow gang aren't stealthy. They love to destroy. It's often messy."

"We need to go back and ask Anan that question," I said.

"I'm coming too," Mack said. "When I see Anan, I'm tearing his head off and using it as a pillow."

"Bit gross," Zandra said. "You'll stink out the basement if you do that."

"You need to stay out of sight," I said to Mack. "You're still the prime suspect in Dorian's murder. The angels want to charge you. Keep quiet and let us handle this. Anan knows us."

"You'll handle it today, though? No messing around."

I placed a paw on his side and pulsed calming magic into him. "We'll get a confession out of Anan. We have this recording, so he can't keep lying to us."

Zandra stifled a yawn. "I can't go back to bed now, not after hearing that. I'm grabbing a shower and getting dressed. Then I'll put in a call to Angel Force and let Finn know what's going on."

"I can't sit around and do nothing," Mack said. "I want to help."

"Help me by hunting out breakfast," I said. "Then I'll go with Zandra, and we'll solve Dorian's murder for you."

After much grumbling from Mack, and me promising him all my fishiest treats for breakfast, we struck a deal.

This mystery was almost over.

We crammed in a full day of work in four hours then drove to the prison to speak to Anan.

"I'm about to give up on Finn," Zandra said as she pulled into the parking lot. "I've been trying to reach him all morning, but I'm not getting any reply."

"We don't need the angels. We've got the evidence to show Anan was involved. We'll have him listen to the recording and then get a confession. Case closed," I said.

"Hopefully. I'll leave Finn a message, so he knows what we're doing." Zandra left a short message via her mobile snow globe and forwarded a copy of the conversation between Anan and Dorian. "That's the best I can do. Now, let's go talk to a killer."

Five minutes later, and once we were through the security checks, we sat at a table in the visitor area, waiting for Anan.

He strolled in, still in shackles, and accompanied by two guards. "No smug angel with you this time? Did I scare him off?"

"He's on his way. While we're waiting for him to arrive, why don't you tell us about the arrangement you had with Dorian to murder his rival?" Zandra said.

Anan's jaw dropped for a second, but then he snapped it shut. "No clue what you're talking about."

"I have a recording of a conversation you had with Dorian. He was angry you killed someone on his behalf and was refusing to pay you. Want to listen?" Zandra said.

"There was no recording. I wouldn't allow it."

"You must be slipping," I said. "Dorian recorded your last conversation, and you made several clear threats. You murdered Dorian, didn't you?"

The door opened, and Finn dashed in, looking unusually rumpled around the edges. He also had a bandage on his hand, and I could smell fresh blood. "Sorry I'm late. I got your message, but I was dealing with a situation at Angel Force."

"You need to rein in your witch and her dodgy cat," Anan said. "They just about accused me of murder."

Finn sat in a seat. "Then they're doing my job for me. Thanks for a copy of the conversation, Zandra.

It filled in the blanks about Dorian's murder. So, Anan, how did you do it?"

Anan hunched forward in his seat. "I want to hear this conversation. I won't believe it's real until I do."

"We figured you'd say that," Zandra said. "I checked with the guards, and they said it was okay for you to listen on a laptop."

One of the guards brought over a laptop, and the conversation was replayed.

Other than the muscles in his jaw flexing, Anan kept his feelings to himself.

"It's clearly you on that recording," Finn said.

"I wasn't with Dorian when that conversation happened. It's been faked."

"We didn't tell you when that recording happened," I said.

"Whatever time and date you tell me, I'll be with my gang. That's how we roll. We look out for each other."

"Not anymore," Finn said. "We collected the last statement from the final gang member last night. They've abandoned you. They're all singing to save their necks, so they won't save you. Give us a confession. How did you get inside and kill Dorian?"

Anan rubbed the back of his neck, his shackles making the movement difficult. "I didn't."

"But you know something?" I said.

"Maybe I did a job for him, and it went sideways. It was his fault. He wasn't clear enough about what he wanted."

"You're admitting that was you on the recording?" Finn said.

"Yeah, sure. That was me."

"And you threatened Dorian, and now he's dead."

"Also true, but you're missing one important point. I was behind bars when Dorian was killed."

"You got someone else to do it for you," I said.

Anan's top lip curled. "Like your angel friend said, I have connections, but they've gone to ground. Everyone is turning against me. I've called around and tried to get a few favors done, but I've met blank walls. I might have wanted to kill Dorian, but I didn't have the resources to do it from in here."

As painful as this was to admit, Anan was making valid points. He had been behind bars when Dorian was killed, and if everyone was turning on him, he was friendless and his connections gone.

Zandra and Finn glanced at each other. They seemed as concerned as me.

"I know my word means nothing, but I didn't kill that vampire, and I didn't pay anyone else to do it." Anan stretched out his legs. "If it wasn't Remus, you need to look at that crazy woman with the enormous..." He held his hands out in front of his chest.

"Dorian had a girlfriend?" Zandra said.

"I don't know if she was a girlfriend, but she was always hanging around. Her name was Nadina something. She was a looker. The kind of woman who made you do a doubletake because she was so hot. Tall with black hair and bronzed skin, and she had huge green eyes. And of course, those huge—"

"We get the picture," Finn said. "Where can we find Nadina?"

"No clue. I asked her out once, but the dumb broad only had eyes for that vampire. I guess it was her kink, loving the undead." Anan shuddered.

I wove around Zandra's legs. This conversation had taken an interesting turn. I'd expected Anan to confess, but we had a new suspect. Unless Anan was lying again.

I glared up at him. "Does Nadina even exist?"

He smirked. "You don't trust me? Ask around. Everyone knows her."

Finn looked at Zandra. "I think we've got everything we need."

"I don't suppose you'll say sorry for accusing me of something I didn't do," Anan said.

"You suppose right. We have this recording, so you're still a suspect." Finn gestured for the guards. "We're done here. Thanks."

With a scowl on his face, Anan skulked away.

"Have you interviewed anyone who claimed to be Dorian's girlfriend?" Zandra said.

"Dorian didn't have a girlfriend. He had lady friends he spent time with, but no one named Nadina came up when we were gathering information." Finn stood from his seat. "I'll look into it, but it could be another of Anan's misdirections." He inspected the bandage on his hand.

"What happened to you?" I said. "You usually look artfully disheveled, but you're more hobo than hot today."

Finn smirked. "Thanks. We've had trouble at Angel Force."

"What kind of trouble?" Zandra stood from her seat.

"We got a visit from Mack. It's why I was late getting here." Finn looked down at me. "Juno, I need your help."

Chapter 12

Mack attack

"Mack came to Angel Force?" I said.

"He did. And the results weren't pretty. The place has been in chaos all morning because of his unexpected visit." Finn flexed his bandaged hand and winced.

"Let's get out of here, and you can tell us all about it." Zandra led the way out of the room. We gathered our belongings and went outside to the van.

"Where's your ride?" Zandra said.

"I flew. It was the quickest way to get here. I'd appreciate a ride back, though."

"Juno has the passenger seat. You're welcome on board, but you'll have to accept a cat on your lap," Zandra said.

"That rather depends on whether I'm accepting an angel as my seat." I looked at Finn and gave him the cat version of a smile. "But I don't mind this angel, so I'll allow my bed to be moved and my seat temporarily taken over. No leaving feathers behind, though."

"Thanks, Juno. I owe you one," Finn said.

After the adjustments were made, and I was settled on Finn's comfortable lap, Zandra drove away from the prison.

"So, what did Mack do?" I said.

"He charged into Angel Force and demanded answers. He was blasting magic in every direction, and anyone who got too close got bitten." Finn held up his hand.

"Why did he attack?" I made biscuits on Finn's stomach. It was too flat, and there wasn't enough fat to get a good biscuit motion going, but I worked with what I had.

"Mack wants to know who killed Dorian. It took six of us to subdue him, and three angels needed medical attention."

"We told Mack to lie low." Zandra glanced at Finn. "As you've probably guessed, we've been hiding him since he was taken from your sanctuary. Mack didn't run off, We kept him safe. He's in Vorana's basement. At least, he was."

"I figured as much, although I deliberately didn't ask too many questions. If I don't know the truth, then I can't lie to my boss. And she's a stickler for honesty."

"There's nothing wrong with that," I said. "Where's Mack now?"

"He was arrested and put in a cell. He's refusing to talk, though. Well, he's refusing to talk to us. But he said he'd talk to you, Juno."

"We formed a bond after helping him with the whole vampire abduction issue. He must trust us," I said.

"Whatever the reason, I need you on this case."

"Is your boss okay with us getting involved?" Zandra said. "It doesn't sound like she's much of a rule breaker."

"Cythera hates the idea, but having seen what Mack did to the place and how powerful he is, she's desperate. Mack kept saying he'd only speak to Juno, and the boss wants answers. So here I am."

"We have to get back to work and make sure there aren't any last-minute jobs," Zandra said. "But we can stop by Angel Force later, around six."

"That would be great. This case is such a mess, and I don't want us making a mistake and charging the wrong individual with Dorian's murder. That's where this is headed if Cythera has anything to do with it."

"We can ask Mack about Dorian's girlfriend," I said. "He'll know if she exists."

"And I'll check the records to see if there's any mention of a Nadina," Finn said.

After we arrived in Crimson Cove, Zandra dropped Finn at Angel Force, then we headed into work. We had two urgent retrievals to deal with, but before that, I wanted to check on Barney and Sam.

"I'll get the van ready," Zandra said. "You go see how the grumpy couple is doing."

I dashed off and paused outside Barney's office. The door was slightly open, and I could smell Sammy in the room, along with Barney. There was an unsettling silence.

I poked my head in and discovered Sammy curled in a tight ball by the window. Although he feigned sleep, tension radiated off him, and his ears kept flicking. Barney had his head down and was scribbling on paper, but his tight shoulders and hunched manner suggested he was equally uncomfortable.

I sighed as I backed out of the room. Maybe I'd made a mistake about their compatibility. They were both such sweet, laid-back guys, so I'd assumed the match would be perfect. Could this be one of the rare times I was wrong?

I heard Zandra's familiar footsteps getting close. My focus needed to be on work for now. I'd deal with Barney and Sammy later.

Once the retrievals were completed, and the animals safely in cages and settled, Zandra washed up, and we headed to Angel Force to meet Finn and talk to Mack.

I stepped through the reception doors and stopped. One wall was scorched black, and the air smelled of burned wood and charred feathers.

There was no one on the reception desk, and a shimmer of magic in front of the entrance door to the office showed there was no way in without angel approval.

"The angels have taken Mack's attack badly." I sniffed the magic barrier.

"I'm not surprised. I had no idea he had so much power. It'll take days to fix all this." Zandra lifted a chair that was missing two legs. "Since Mack's been hanging out with shady magic users and a powerful old vampire over the years, it's no wonder he picked up a dangerous trick or two."

"That doesn't make him bad, just misguided."

Zandra prodded the magic barrier, and it shimmered a warning. "That should get someone out here to check if another honey badger is forcing its way through to wreak havoc on the angels."

I snickered. "You're enjoying this."

"Of course not." She chuckled. "Maybe a little. Who'd have thought one honey badger could whip a squad of angels?"

A moment later, Finn appeared. He grinned. "Just the witch and her familiar I hoped it would be. Come through. I told Mack you'd be dropping by this evening, and he finally stopped growling and even ate something, rather than hurling it at the wall."

We headed through the smoke damaged office. There were several desks missing, not many angels about, and the ever-pervasive smell of burned feathers.

"You'll have to interview Mack in his cell," Finn said. "The boss isn't prepared to let him out. He's considered too dangerous."

"That won't be a problem," I said. "Just show us where he is."

Finn unlocked a secured door and led us along a white corridor. There were four cell doors, and Mack was in the cell nearest to me. There were bars on the door, but it was the magic wards around the cell preventing him from escaping. It was powerful angel magic holding him in. It even made my skin tingle when I got close.

"Mack, your visitors are here." Finn leaned against the wall.

Mack was flat on his side with his back to the bars. He rolled over slowly, his glare on Finn. It softened a fraction when he saw us.

"Hey, Mack. I guess you didn't understand the concept of keeping a low profile," I said.

He heaved out a sigh and dragged himself to his feet. "I couldn't stay hidden in your basement any longer. I was getting cabin fever. And I needed answers. I didn't mean to get you tangled in this."

"We were getting answers for you," Zandra said. "We've even got a new suspect to look into."

"And murder investigations take time," Finn said.

"Which is why I visited you. And you must see how this attack proves my innocence even more. I'd have hardly dropped by Angel Force if I was guilty," Mack said.

"You could be bluffing," Finn said. "Or gone rogue."

"That's not helping," Zandra muttered.

Finn held up a hand. "That's what the other angels are saying. Cythera is determined to convict you. She thinks it's only a matter of time before you confess."

"She'll be dead before that happens," Mack said. "I've got nothing to confess to."

"So talk to us," I said. "Tell us what happened on your final day with Dorian. If we know his exact last movements and mindset, it could give us a clue as to what happened." I settled on the floor outside the cell, and Zandra leaned against the wall near Finn.

Mack also made himself comfortable on the floor in the cell. "You know the basics."

"But that last day, the day Dorian died, how was he behaving?"

"Honestly, I was worried about him. I'd even asked if I could leave because I wanted to get him help." Mack lowered his head.

"What had you worried?" Zandra said.

"Dorian seemed weaker than usual and confused. He was forgetting words or making them up because he couldn't remember the real one. I thought he was sick."

"You mentioned he'd not been feeding much. Could that have been the reason he was confused?" I said.

"Possibly. He even sent away his favorite drone, Bryce. Bryce still came back daily to see if he could encourage Dorian to feed, but he wouldn't eat."

"We've met Bryce. He said the same thing," Zandra said.

"The guy was a poser, but he cared about Dorian. He kept showing up, even though he got rejected. That takes courage."

"From Dorian's behavior, it suggests he wanted death," Zandra said.

"No. Well, maybe. I don't know what he wanted. We were happy together most of the time, but there was little else that pleased Dorian. He hated dealing with the world and all the people who hung around with their hands out. Everyone wanted something from him. They were never content simply to enjoy his company. Or, if they did, it was because they planned to exploit him." Mack growled softly.

"That's why he liked me. I wanted nothing. He was a kind vampire and looked after me. I considered him my best friend." He snuffled around the floor for a moment.

"This new suspect I mentioned," Zandra said, "her name is Nadina. Apparently, she was Dorian's girlfriend. Do you know her?"

His nose wrinkled. "Sure. She was a crazy piece of work."

"They were together?" Zandra said.

"Yeah, on and off for a long time. They met when she was in her twenties. She's a good-looking woman if you're into tiny waists, silky black hair, and big pouty lips. Nadina used to do some sort of modelling. Catwalk. That kind of thing. Recently, things turned sour, though."

"What went wrong between them?" I said.

"Nadina started begging Dorian to turn her into a vampire. She said she wanted them to be together forever, but I knew the truth. She was getting old and wanted to be turned before her looks faded." Mack licked his side. "Her work's been drying up, so she needed to change fast."

"How long had she been with Dorian?"

"Twenty years."

"She's in her forties! No wonder she was desperate. Dorian didn't want to make her his immortal eternal?" I said.

"Not a chance. Doing that was a huge deal, and Dorian didn't want to be with Nadina forever. He confided in me she was too intense and focused on superficial things. She kept wanting to update the mansion and said Dorian's antiques were ugly and needed to go. They had a fight a few months ago, and she left."

"What happened to her?" Zandra said.

"She probably hunted for another vampire, hoping to get turned. She most likely ended up as a meal and her body was dumped."

I looked at Finn. "Any reports of that happening?"

"I'd need a more detailed physical description and her full name to be certain. We don't get many reports of missing persons around here, though."

"Because the vampires are too sneaky to be caught," I said. "What's she look like, Mack?"

"She's tall, model looks, very whiny. She was in that ad for Bitten. You know, that weird lip plumper," Mack said.

"Oh! Her! You mean Nadina Hendrix. Everyone knows that ad," Finn said.

Zandra tilted her head. "They do?"

He blushed. "I mean, most guys do. Nadina wasn't wearing much, and that mouth... anyway, I can find out if she's a missing person."

Zandra smirked, and I chuckled.

"But.. if she was a vampire victim, we'll never know. They're great at hiding evidence of their feeds," Finn said.

"Or maybe she's in hiding for another reason," I said. "What if Nadina figured out how to kill Dorian and is keeping her head down until the heat fades?"

"She's crazy enough to kill," Mack said. "And she knows all the back ways into the mansion. She'd sneak in sometimes and surprise Dorian in the bedroom. Or the kitchen. Or bathroom. Anywhere, really. When that happened, I went to my room and slept. No one needs to see two people naked and getting busy. It's revolting. They have no fur. Well, a little fur. Nadina had no fur, though. And no inhibitions."

"Nadina was desperate for immortality," I said. "Maybe Dorian promised it to her and then went back on his word. She was terrified about losing her career and everything she'd worked for, so she got her revenge."

"If that's true, we still have the problem of how she got into that locked bedroom," Zandra said. "Even if she knew all the sneaky ways in and out of the mansion, there was only one way in and out of that room."

Finn pinched his chin between two fingers. "Yeah, that has everyone stumped. Which is why most of the angels think it was Mack."

"I hold my paws up to the face eating part, but that's it. And after that gruesome dining experience, I'm seriously considering turning vegetarian."

We both shuddered at that unappetizing prospect.

"Now Mack's talked to us, will you let him go?" I said to Finn.

"I promise, I'll behave," Mack said.

"Sorry, buddy. I can't let you go anywhere. You've got to stay in a cell. You must know you've done wrong," Finn said.

I swished my tail. "Mack attacked you because he's grieving. He's not thinking straight. He needs answers about what happened. We all act irrationally when we're grief struck."

"There's being a bit of a jerk and then there's almost burning down a building and seriously injuring three angels. And I haven't forgotten about this." Finn held up his wounded hand.

"You grabbed me from behind," Mack said. "I reacted on instinct. Any honey badger worth his salt would have done the same."

"You could get that bite healed with magic," Zandra said.

Finn shrugged. "I enjoy having a battle injury. It makes me look like a hero."

I rolled my eyes and shook my head. "Mack isn't a threat. He'll behave, won't you?"

"Yep. I'm on my best behavior from now on."

Finn considered the options. "I'll talk to Cythera and see if I can get Mack put under my care, so long as you promise not to go on the attack again."

"You have my word," Mack said, "but on one condition."

"You're not in a position to make conditions," Finn said, "but I'm listening."

"I want Juno and Zandra in on this investigation. They're the only ones open-minded enough to consider me innocent."

"I never said you were totally guilty," Finn said.

"You kind of have," Zandra said.

Finn shrugged. "It's been on my mind. Maybe Juno and Zandra don't want to be involved in a murder investigation. Murder is messy."

"We definitely do. We like mess," I said. "We'll help find the actual killer."

"Err... we will? Aren't we busy dealing with our own things?" Zandra gave me a pointed look.

"We have time."

"If they don't stay on the case, I'm not talking. And the second I get the chance, I'll burn this place to the ground," Mack said.

"Threats won't get you anywhere." Finn scowled at Mack then sighed. "But it's fine by me if Zandra and Juno want in on this case. We'll have to keep it unofficial. I can't make it public knowledge you're working on this investigation, but I can pass on information and leads, so you have the information you need to solve this."

"Works for me," Zandra said. "I'm no fan of hanging out with the angels any longer than I have to."

Finn pouted. "I hope you don't include me in that."

"We'll make an exception for you," I said.

He arched an eyebrow. "So, now what?"

"We have a new suspect to tackle," I said. "It's time to find our supermodel and see what she knows about murder."

Chapter 13

A me time moment

"And then Archie knocked over a vase upstairs, and the vampires found him. For a moment, we thought we were about to become vampire kebabs." I regaled Vorana and Sage about our kitten impossible mission over breakfast the next morning.

Zandra had heard it all before but was happy to listen again. After all, it had been a successful mission. Although she looked worried about the vampire kebab reference.

"Remus has always had an interest in the familiar bond," Vorana said. "He often asks Sorcha how she manages with Tinkerbell."

"Vampires are almost as curious as cats," I said. "And I think things could work out between him and Archie. I checked in with Archie first thing, and they had a successful night. The trial is going well, and Archie got a steak for breakfast."

"That hellhound will get fat," Zandra said.

"Fat and happy," Vorana said. "Nothing wrong with that. Archie hasn't had the greatest of opportunities in life, so why not be overindulged by a ridiculously wealthy vampire? Especially if there's no chance Archie will get nibbled."

"You'll hear no complaints from me." Zandra eyeballed me. "I just wish Juno had told me what she was planning."

"Our wonderful familiars have minds of their own." Vorana planted a kiss on Sage's head. "You're quiet this morning, sweetie pie. Not feeling too good?"

Sage grunted. She'd been pushing her food around her plate since we settled in for breakfast.

While Vorana and Zandra talked about how amazing their familiars were, I shuffled closer to Sage. "What's wrong?"

"Nothing."

"You're not eating. If you don't want it—"

She swiped away my paw. "I do."

"So..."

"Not here."

"What do you mean?"

"Follow me. We'll be back in a moment." Sage cleverly hopped into her harness and trundled off, not waiting to see if I'd follow.

I grabbed my last mouthful of breakfast, jumped off the seat, and wandered into the hallway.

Sage was waiting, her expression even grumpier than usual. "You should have taken me with you."

"Where?"

"On the kitten impossible mission."

"You said you didn't want to come. You said your wheels would hold you back."

"I have a disability. I'm not dead."

"I never said you were. I wanted you there."

"That's not how I remember the conversation. And you only said those things because you felt sorry for me."

My ears lowered. "Sage, I didn't. And you don't know me at all if you think I'd give empty platitudes and pity you. I recognize a powerful familiar when I see one. I asked you on that mission because I knew you'd help me. You were the one who made excuses about not being useful."

"No! It was the other way around."

"Maybe you're losing your memory. Remind me how old you are again?"

"Now you think I'm going senile?" She hissed at me.

I lifted a paw and zapped Sage with a tingle of magic. Not enough to hurt but enough to bring her to her senses. "Maybe that'll jog your memory. You definitely said no. I tried to talk you around, but you dug in your paws. You missing out on an excellent mission is on you, not me."

She rubbed her side where I'd zapped her. "Maybe... maybe I didn't want to get in the way. You're so fast and strong on your paws. And I'm... this. A broken old mess."

I walked over and touched my booping snooter to hers. "Sage, you'd be an asset to anyone on any mission. You have power, wisdom, and experience. You just need to believe in yourself a little more."

She huffed out a breath. "I... I didn't mean to snap. I'm just jealous. I've handled vampires before. I could have dealt with Remus and his hive. It sounded like you had fun. And there was steak. I love steak, but Vorana doesn't eat much red meat. She says it's bad for the colon."

"It was a fun adventure, and I know you'd have whipped those vamps if needed. But do you believe you could, really?"

Sage stepped back. "I'm so used to being pampered and coddled by Vorana, I forget what I can do."

"Next time, you're in on any future kitten impossible missions. Got it? Even if I have to drag you out by your wheels, hissing and scratching."

"Yeah, got it. Thanks, Juno."

We headed back into the kitchen and were delighted to discover Vorana had filled our dishes with more eggs and salmon.

"I was just asking Vorana about Nadina, Dorian's girlfriend," Zandra said.

"She is crazy and beautiful," Vorana said. "Her beauty is off the charts incredible and all natural. She's got power, too. Her mother was a siren and her dad a warlock. A stunning combination."

"Finn was drooling over some ad she was in," Zandra said.

"I expect he was. Even I drool over her ads. Nadina's a stunner. She's been modelling since she was a teenager. She does less now, given people's daft belief that when you turn a certain age, you become invisible to the world."

"Any idea where we might find Nadina?" Zandra said. "Finn knew little about her, but he was going to do some digging. I've not heard anything from him, though."

"Then you're in luck. The best place to look for Nadina is at the Woodville Day Spa. In return for being in their ads, she gets free treatments. She's usually there, having a massage or procedure to look even more amazing. I walked past her once after I'd been in the steam room. Even with no makeup on, she looked gorgeous." Vorana munched on her toast. "Not that I'm jealous. It's what's underneath that counts."

Zandra bumped her mug against Vorana's. "I second that."

"I love a spa," I said. "We could go today. It's the weekend."

Zandra wrinkled her nose. "We could. I'm not a fan of having strangers rub strange smelling oils into my skin, though."

"You don't have to have a treatment," I said. "Although I wouldn't mind having my claws polished."

"How far is the spa from here?" Zandra said to Vorana.

"Half an hour's drive. It's an exclusive place, though."

Zandra arched an eyebrow. "You're saying we don't pass for exclusive?"

Vorana chuckled. "I'm just saying you might like to wear a top that doesn't have strawberry preserves down the front."

"Oh!" Zandra scraped at her shirt, smearing the preserves even more. "I'll get changed then we'll drive to the spa and find Nadina."

Forty-five minutes later, Zandra pulled the van into one of the few empty spots in the parking lot at the Woodville Day Spa. The building was three stories of amber stone brick. There were six chimney stacks on top of the roof and what looked to be a viewing platform looking out over the woodlands surrounding the spa.

We got out and headed through large glass front doors and into a world that smelled of cedarwood, expensive perfume, and money.

I lifted my head and inhaled deeply. The hackles on the back of my neck lifted. It felt like someone was watching me. It was so intense it made my spine shiver. I looked around, but there was no one else waiting in the reception area.

My gaze went outside. I couldn't see anyone out there, but that's where the feeling was tugging me. I wanted to go in that direction and seek the source of such intense scrutiny.

"Hey, something wrong?" Zandra said.

"No, nothing. Just had a weird feeling."

"What kind of feeling?"

I took another look around. "Nothing important. Let's find Nadina."

An immaculately dressed receptionist in a white pant suit with her hair slicked back in a neat bun greeted us with a smile. "Welcome to Woodville Day Spa. Do you have a reservation?"

"No, but I'd like to know if Nadina Hendrix is here," Zandra said.

The receptionist's smile flickered. "May I ask the reason?"

"I need to speak to her."

She made a point of closing the visitors' book in front of her. "We take our clients' confidentiality seriously. We have several well-known public figures who use the spa. We can't allow them to be pestered by the media."

"I'm not a reporter. And I don't care which famous person is currently having a massage. I just need to speak to Nadina." Zandra spoke through clenched teeth.

"Are you a family member?"

"No, but I'm... with Angel Force. This is official business."

The disbelief on the receptionist's face was clear. "You'll forgive me for saying this, but you're clearly not an angel. I know they've relaxed their recruitment rules, but from the familiar beside you, you're a full witch. Therefore, you can't work for Angel Force."

"Not in an official capacity, but I'm friendly with them." Zandra leaned over the desk. "All I want to know is if Nadina is here. I don't even want to go inside."

"And all I can suggest is you wait outside to see if she comes out."

"It'll take you thirty seconds to check your records. Help a girl out."

"Even if I did, and I discovered Nadina was here, I wouldn't tell you. Our customers come here for complete relaxation. If we let anyone in to bother them, our reputation will be ruined."

"I won't tell if you don't."

"No."

They glared at each other for several seconds. It was clear the receptionist wasn't backing down.

I head-butted Zandra in the calf, and after sighing, she turned and walked away from the reception desk.

"You keep her distracted, and I'll sneak in and look around for Nadina," I whispered.

"You don't know what Nadina looks like."

"Look around. Vorana said Nadina does all the ads for the spa, and I'm seeing the same gorgeous face in all the pictures."

Zandra glanced around. "Oh, well-spotted. Okay, I'll antagonize the receptionist and play see who blinks first. You sneak off and nab Nadina."

While the receptionist dealt with another customer and Zandra lurked in the background, I crept off, hid in a corner, then ducked through the entrance door to the spa when someone walked out.

The smell of expensive oils grew stronger as I hurried along the corridor. I peered into several treatment rooms, but there was no sign of Nadina.

The door to my right opened, and I dashed through. I blinked several times. It was an enormous steam room. This was the last thing my beautiful white fur needed. It got fuzzy if exposed to steam for too long.

I turned to leave, but the door had closed and the handle was too high to reach. "Hello, is there anyone in here?"

No one answered.

"I could do with help to get out. If you wouldn't mind opening the door, I'll be on my way."

It seemed I was alone in the steam, and it was getting hotter by the second. I padded around, checking all the benches. There was no one here.

A powerful gust of steam filled the room, and I coughed. I needed to get out of here before I passed out.

I stumbled toward the door or at least in the direction I thought the door was located. I was overheating, panting, and my toe beans were damp and squishing on the floor.

I pressed a paw against the glass and attempted a spell. Nothing manifested. My magic was asleep and had no intention of waking to help me.

"Come on, don't fail me now." I tried again but only got a trickle of power.

I slumped down, panting, feeling the urge to close my eyes.

"Stupid magic." I could no longer rely on my power, and that was distressing. I had to be able to defend myself but, most importantly, defend my witch. Zandra often found herself in dangerous situations, and if my magic floundered, I was no good to her.

"Water," I whispered. "Need water. And salmon."

The door opened and bumped into my side.

"Juno!" Suddenly, I was lifted, and Zandra's face was in front of mine. "What are you doing in here?"

"Can't breathe. Too much steam. Fur ruined. Help. Dying."

Zandra hurried out of the steam room and closed the door. I gasped in air, and a quick glance at my fur showed it was indeed beyond repair. It would take more than a deep condition to remedy this fluff.

"Juno, you're worrying me. Say something."

"I got trapped inside. It got boiling."

"Why didn't you use your door opening trick?"

My ears flicked as I continued deep breathing. "You know about that?"

Zandra cocked her head. "There aren't many things you can keep secret from me. Don't think I haven't noticed how quickly your tin of treats goes down. You sneak out and have secret midnight snacks."

"I had to learn how to open the door so as not to disturb you at two in the morning when I got the munchies." Now I was coming back to my senses, I noticed Zandra was wearing a towel. "Why are you dressed like that? Or rather, undressed like that?"

"It was how I beat the snooty receptionist. She refused to give me information on Nadina, so the only way I could get in was if I paid for a session. I booked the cheapest option I could, which wasn't cheap, but it got me access to the steam room and sauna for forty-five minutes." She stroked a hand down my damp fur. "You sure you're okay? We can leave if you're feeling bad."

"I just got overwhelmed and couldn't see a way out, so I panicked." I couldn't tell Zandra about my misfiring magic. "Let's hunt around and find Nadina."

After Zandra had gotten me water and toweled me off, we hurried around the spa.

Five minutes of searching led us into a semi-dark room with whale music being piped in. There were salt lamps and lots of soft towels.

And draped on a heated, self-massaging bed was Nadina. She was as beautiful as her pictures. She didn't have on a scrap of makeup, and her hair was pulled off her face, but she had the cheek bones of a goddess. And that mouth was everything Finn had drooled over.

The bed next to her was empty, so Zandra climbed on. She looked at me and shrugged.

There was no subtle way of doing this, and we had little time. I was certain the receptionist would be watching out for us, and if she realized we'd gone into the wrong room, we'd be kicked out.

"Greetings. Sorry to disturb you, but you're Nadina Hendrix, aren't you?" I said.

Nadina kept her eyes closed, but a small smile crossed her face. "That's right. I'm not giving autographs today. I'm here to relax."

"You were friends with Dorian DeAngelo, weren't you?"

Her head jerked up, and she stared at me. "How do you know that?"

I looked at Zandra, who appeared to be struggling to get comfortable on the massage bed as it vibrated underneath her. I cleared my throat.

She stopped squirming. "Hey, I'm Zandra, this is Juno. We're sorry for your loss. I'm working with Angel Force to investigate what happened to Dorian. We've been trying to find you, but you're not an easy lady to track down."

Nadina sat up straight. "I'm not that difficult to find. Everyone knows me. You knew Dorian?"

"Not really. But we have concerns about how he died. I figured you might have information to solve those concerns."

Nadina clutched a towel against her chest. "I'm confused. You're investigating his death, but you aren't an angel. Why are you here?"

"It's a complicated story. I'm not sure if you know, but one suspect in the case is Mack, Dorian's honey badger companion," Zandra said.

"I heard." Nadina's bottom lip jutted out, and her eyes widened. "How did you know Dorian? You still haven't said."

"I didn't know him." Zandra glanced at me.

Nadina's eyes narrowed, and her gaze ran slowly over Zandra several times. "How close were you to Dorian?"

"Not close at all."

"Did you date? He liked brunettes."

"No, I've only recently moved to Crimson Cove. I never dated Dorian."

"Dorian traveled. Not so much toward the end of his life, but perhaps you met somewhere else."

"He could have traveled wherever he liked. We've never met."

"You're sure you didn't have a relationship with him?"

"I promise you, I didn't."

Nadina was silent. "So why the questions about his death? What do you do for Angel Force?"

"We handle the tricky cases," I said. "Zandra is an incredible witch."

Nadina blinked twice. Was she doubting my witch's ability?

"And we don't think the right person is being focused on in this investigation. Mack didn't kill Dorian," Zandra said, after giving me the side eye and a small shrug.

Nadina licked her lips. "Oh! Right. They've charged him?"

"The angels are about to, but Mack is protesting his innocence. I'm talking to everyone closely connected to Dorian to see if they know what happened."

Her expression became smug. "I was closest to Dorian, other than that honey badger. We did everything together. And, as I'm sure you're aware, we intended to spend the rest of our lives together. An immortal life, if you understand me."

"We do. Which means you must be even sadder about what happened," I said. "Your true love and your chance at immortality have been taken."

"Of course. Devastated. I loved Dorian. He was my everything. It's a tragedy what happened to him."

"Do you even know how he died?" For someone so devastated, Nadina looked the picture of serenity now she'd stopped interrogating Zandra over her relationship status with the deceased.

"I know Dorian's dead. And I know he shut himself away and refused help. Dorian was sick and isolating himself." She leaned closer. "Is it true that Mack ate him?"

"Yes, but that wasn't the cause of death."

"Oh! How can you be certain?"

"Because I trust Mack, and he's trying to get to the truth just as hard as we are."

Nadina adjusted her towel. "I don't know what to think. I'm so overcome with grief, I'm barely functioning."

"You don't appear grief stricken."

She waved a finger at each eye. "I had my tear ducts frozen, so I never spoil my makeup."

"You can do that?" Zandra stared at Nadina's flawless face.

"Oh, yes. It's not a difficult spell. I don't sweat, either. It makes life so much easier when you haven't got liquid leaking out at inappropriate moments." Nadina lifted a perfectly bronzed shoulder. "So forgive my lack of tears, but I am genuinely shattered to have lost Dorian. Our relationship was idyllic."

I wrinkled my booping snooter. That was a different story to the one Mack had told us.

"Where were you when you found out what happened to Dorian?" Zandra said.

"Here. I'd been trying to get in touch with Dorian for days, but he hadn't returned my messages. I was stressed, and stress is terrible for the skin, so I booked in for a whole day. I was getting ready to leave when I heard two women gossiping about Dorian. It was the worst news. I'll never find another man as magnificent as him."

Zandra slipped off the bed. "Well, sorry again for your loss."

I felt as dejected as Zandra looked. Nadina had an alibi, and it would be simple to check if we could get a look at the receptionist's appointment diary. "Can you think of anyone who wanted Dorian dead?"

Nadina let out a little sigh. "I can't. He was the best of vampires. A true gentleman. Yes, he had become eccentric, but it was a phase. And those dreadful gossips who told me the news of his death said he'd done it to himself. I was so furious I slapped one of them. Dorian would never end his own life. Not when he had me."

"Thanks for your time. We'll leave you to relax." Zandra gestured at me with her head, and we left the room.

"She lied," I said. "Vorana and Mack said Nadina was crazy and obsessive. And Dorian had ended things between them because he no longer wanted her."

"Yet she's making out they had a wonderful relationship and everything was on track for her to become immortal." Zandra strode along the corridor. "We need to check with the receptionist to see if Nadina was here all day when Dorian died."

"She was a guard dog when we asked about Nadina. She won't let us see her oh-so confidential calendar."

"I need to get changed, but then we'll work out a plan," Zandra said. "You wait at the reception desk, see if you can get a glimpse of the schedule. Maybe she'll leave it unattended, so you can take a peek."

"I'll meet you out there." I returned to the reception area, but there were several customers waiting to be seen, and the receptionist was going nowhere.

As I got closer to the main doors, that strange tugging sensation reached for me again. I had an overwhelming urge to go outside and locate the source. After another check on the receptionist, I did just that.

The air felt wonderfully crisp after the stifling warmth of the spa, but I barely paid it any attention as a deliciously familiar pulse of magic pulled me to a grassy mound close by.

My limbs shook. It couldn't be. I hadn't sensed this power in over thirty years. My body pulsed along with the hidden magic. I didn't want to believe what I was experiencing, but what else could it be?

I walked around the large mound. The energy was there, and it was constant. It called to me like a siren song on a wild, stormy night. And I couldn't resist it any longer. I found a soft spot in the earth and dug. The soil was a sticky red clay, and my beautiful white fur quickly became a mess, but I didn't care. I had to get to that source of power. I needed it. It was mine.

A faint cry for help filtered into my ears, but I was so intent on getting the power, I ignored it. My front paws were a blur as I continued to dig, covering myself in mud as I made the hole bigger.

Whoever buried this power made sure it was deep in the soil. Maybe the magic triggered when it sensed my presence. It had been waiting for me to get close before calling.

I couldn't focus on the whys and hows. I needed that magic in my paws immediately.

"Juno, help!"

My head shot up. That was Zandra.

I looked at the hole, one paw raised. No, I couldn't abandon my witch. What was I doing?

Horror gripped me by the throat as I raced back to the spa just as Zandra smashed through the glass doors. She landed on her back but was instantly on her feet and firing her own magic at whoever attacked her.

I dug into my ancient well of power. Don't fail me. My witch was in danger, and it was my fault. I'd abandoned her when I'd made a solemn vow to watch over her. I was a terrible familiar.

My magic wouldn't cooperate. It swilled inside me like a toxic sludge but refused to fire to life.

Nadina appeared through the broken doors, magic simmering around her, still wearing only a towel and a bitter smile. She aimed her spell at Zandra, and the blast took her off her feet. The receptionist stood behind her, her face as white as her uniform. After a second of staring, she turned and raced inside.

"Leave my witch alone." I launched into the air and landed on Nadina's face, raking my claws repeatedly down her cheeks.

She shrieked and grabbed me, trying to pull me off, but there was no way I was letting her touch my witch again.

"He was mine," Nadina screamed. "You had no right to touch Dorian."

"No one touched him." Zandra had blood running down the side of her face, but her power simmered strong on her fingertips. "That's not why I'm here. I never dated Dorian."

That's what this fight was about? Nadina was jealous and thought Dorian had dated Zandra? I clung on, claws dug in deep and moving every time Nadina so much as flinched.

"I loved him." Nadina made a sobbing sound, but, of course, no tears came out.

Zandra approached her slowly. "I was never involved with Dorian. I really am investigating what happened to him."

"You're lying! He was always seeing other women behind my back. I'd beg him not to and told him how much it hurt me, but he didn't care. He was a cruel vampire, not a kind one."

I sank my fangs into her ear, and she shrieked. My paws were coated with not only sticky red clay but also Nadina's blood. It was getting harder to hold on, but I wasn't letting go.

"Juno, that's enough. Nadina knows we mean no harm." Zandra was using the soft voice she reserved for troubled creatures who didn't want to be captured.

"Stop your attack on my witch," I growled in Nadina's ear.

She stopped yanking at me and dropped her hands to her sides. "Dorian was mine. All mine. He promised I'd be his, too. He lied to me. I have a right to be angry."

"Not at my witch." I slowly withdrew my claws and, after a check on Zandra, dropped to the ground.

Zandra scooped me onto her shoulder. "You okay?"

"I'm fine. Sorry I wasn't there when you needed me. I... I got distracted." My gaze flicked to the mound. The power still called to me, but I had to ignore it. For now.

Her expression was full of concern and questions, but she focused on Nadina. "Why attack me?"

"The receptionist said you've been asking questions. I knew you wanted Dorian, you hateful witch. You don't care about his death. You came here to gloat. But I'm better than you. I had him in my life the longest."

"I'm not arguing that point, but I will deny any romantic involvement with Dorian." Zandra pressed a hand against my side, but I couldn't feed her comfort. I was failing in my duties again. "I don't know how many times I have to say this or how many ways, but I really didn't know Dorian. We never dated."

Nadina sniffed. She adjusted her towel, which was in danger of slipping off. "You really weren't in a relationship with him?"

"No, I have much more interest in the animals I work with than the people they're associated with. Animals are much less complicated," Zandra said. "When we learned Mack was about to be charged with murder, we got involved."

"Mack is innocent," I said. "Which is why we're questioning anyone who could have wanted Dorian dead."

"People like me?" Nadina dabbed at her bloodied cheeks with her fingers. She didn't seem bothered I'd ruined the source of her money and influence.

"Yes. You didn't tell the truth about your relationship with Dorian. We know you'd separated because he refused to turn you into an immortal," Zandra said. "You must have been angry."

"Of course I was angry. Dorian had been promising me for twenty years that, when the time was right, he'd turn me and we'd be together forever."

"What went wrong?"

"Dorian withdrew. He stopped loving me. The only creature in this world he truly loved was that wretched honey badger." Nadina scowled at no one in particular. "He'd snuggle with that creature and ignore me. I was jealous. I wanted that kind of relationship with Dorian. We used to have that in the early days. He told me I was a bewitching siren and too good for him."

"What changed?" Zandra said.

"I wish I knew. Some people said Dorian had grown tired of the world and found pleasure in nothing. I couldn't understand that, because I offered him a world of pleasure. I'd have done anything for him. I adored that vampire. But it wasn't enough."

"When was the last time you saw him?" I said.

Nadina's tongue traced across her bottom lip. "I... I asked him to turn me, but he said he needed space. He didn't know what the future held, so he didn't want me by his side in case things went wrong."

"What kind of things?"

"I don't know. That honey badger knows more than me. They were always talking and whispering. I felt like an outsider." Nadina sighed again. "But... Mack didn't kill Dorian. That creature adored him almost as much as me. It should never have happened. Not like that."

"Miss Hendrix. I've called Angel Force. They're on their way." The receptionist remained inside the building, for all the protection it would offer her if the fighting started again.

For a second, Nadina's expression creased into anger, but then a weary acceptance erased the rage. "Thank you."

Zandra moved nearer to Nadina. "You were close to Dorian, so you know his contacts. Who wanted him dead?"

Her gaze went to the sky. "I can only think of one person."

My ears flicked. "Who?"

Nadina drew in a shaky breath. "It was me. I murdered the love of my life."

Chapter 14

We have a winner

"You killed Dorian?" I stared at the quivering mess of a former supermodel in front of me.

Nadina nodded and wiped her nose on the back of her hand. "It was me. I feel like I'm about to explode if I keep it hidden any longer."

"Why kill him?" Zandra said.

"Because of everything you said. I was angry. I'd spent my best years with a vampire who had no intention of following through with his promise. He led me on and pretended we had a future, but it was a lie. I could have had my pick of men. Princes and movie stars romanced me, but there was something about Dorian that drew me to him."

"The fact he could give you immortality, so you never grew old?" I said.

Nadina sniffed. "The idea of immortality and ensuring my looks never faded was almost as attractive as I am. Why shouldn't I want that? Other magic users get to live a long time and still be beautiful."

"You have your own power. I've experienced how strong you are. That would mean you already get a longer life than most," Zandra said.

"It's chaos power! If I let it loose, it destroys and injures. I'd have been dead years ago if I allowed my full power out. It's why I rarely use it. I don't trust myself. Becoming a vampire would have quietened the chaos."

"Or turned you into a dangerously chaotic vampire who couldn't control her urges," I said.

"I was willing to take that risk. I thought Dorian was, too."

I curled my tail around Zandra's neck. "How did you kill Dorian when he was inside the locked room with Mack?"

"I'm not sure I understand. I was never in a locked room."

"Dorian and Mack were locked in his bedroom. That's where he was killed. You must have gotten inside," Zandra said.

Nadina sighed. "Take me to Angel Force, and I'll confess. I'll be glad to get the secret out. I've been feeling terrible ever since I did it, and no amount of massage or meditation has helped me feel any less guilty."

I tilted my head. Why wasn't she telling us everything?

"You'd better get dressed. Juno will go with you while I wait for the angels," Zandra said.

I looked over my shoulder. I was still distracted by the pull of power under that mound, but I'd failed Zandra once, and she'd gotten hurt. It wouldn't happen again.

I trotted inside with Nadina, avoiding the broken glass and smashed furniture, and we went into the changing rooms.

She stood in front of the mirror and touched her damaged face. "I deserve this. After what I did to Dorian, my most prized possession deserves to be taken."

"You'll heal with magic," I said.

Nadina dropped her towel, grabbed her clothes, and pulled them on. "No, I'll let them heal naturally. The scars will be a reminder of what I did and what an unpleasant person I've become."

"It's probably best you don't rely on your looks when you're inside. You might end up with a lot of girlfriends."

She shrugged. "I don't care what happens to me. I let a moment of madness and chaos overtake me, and I must live with the consequences."

Chaos magic was never fun, but I felt we were missing something.

We headed back outside, and I was pleased to see Finn had arrived. He was talking to Zandra and the receptionist. When the receptionist saw us, she backed away and ran inside.

"You're not on the exclusive client list anymore," I said to Nadina.

"So what? I never liked this place. They took advantage of our deal. I agreed to one photo shoot and half a dozen pictures, yet they splash my face on every surface as if they own me."

Finn's expression was serious as he nodded at Nadina. "Miss Hendrix, I hear there's something you need to confess to."

"Yes. I won't fight you. I want this finished."

"Finn will fly you to Angel Force," Zandra said to Nadina.

She paused. "Okay. Will you both be there, too?"

Zandra looked at Finn, and he nodded. "Sure, we can be there. But why?"

"I want to make sure everything is done right. You're looking out for Mack, and he needs to be released. I may not like the scruffy little creature, but he gave Dorian endless amounts of happiness. It was something I could never do. I'm not bitter enough or crazy enough to ruin Mack's life, like I did to Dorian. Will you see he's released and looked after?"

"Of course. As soon as we can, we'll get Mack out," Zandra said. "Animal control will find him a home."

"That's good. Dorian would like that. Find Mack somewhere nice, where he'll be pampered." She looked at Finn. "Do you want my confession?"

"Let's get everything on the record back at Angel Force." Finn extended his wings behind him. He wore a harness across his shoulders. "Have you ever flown with an angel?"

"Of course. I've had many angels court me over the years."

A smile tugged at the corner of Finn's mouth. "I'll attach you to the harness with a strap, so there's no chance of falling."

"Whatever you think best."

"And I work a little different to other angels, so the ride will get hot. I run on demon power."

Nadina took a second to process the information. "Whatever works for you."

Finn attached Nadina to the harness. "Hold on tight." He sprung into the air with Nadina clasped against him, and they disappeared.

"Well, that was fun. Case solved." Zandra brushed down her jeans.

"Almost. I still want to hear how Nadina did it." I took one last long look at the mound thrumming with power. I'd come back for that later.

"We'll soon know the truth. Then we can get back to doing more normal things, like dealing with angry familiars and figuring out where my annoying parent is hiding."

Zandra may have broken one or two speed limits as we raced back to Crimson Cove and parked outside the Angel Force building.

We hurried inside, and I could hear several voices talking at once as we entered the open plan office.

Bertoli saw us first and strode over. "I should charge you."

He was looking at me. "For what? Being fabulous?"

"Attacking Nadina. She's badly injured. Her beautiful face... why do that?"

"You'll have to arrest us both, if that's what you're planning." Zandra lifted me onto her shoulder and stepped into Bertoli's personal space. "Neither of us attacked Nadina. We were defending ourselves from her assault. Nadina threw the first spell. What were we supposed to do, let her hit us because she's cute?"

"I only have your word for that. I know you. Of course, you threw the first spell," Bertoli said.

"Not true, sweet angel." Nadina's voice rang out across the office. "I attacked Zandra without provocation. She'd been nothing but polite when asking questions. My chaos magic ensured I struck first. This is all my fault."

"This witch shouldn't have been asking you anything." Bertoli hurried back to Nadina and hovered around her like an anxious gnat.

"I was happy she asked me questions. I'm sorry to say, I let my jealousy get the better of me. I thought Zandra had done me wrong, but she hadn't. She was helping Mack and getting justice for Dorian. This is all my mistake. Zandra and Juno are innocent."

"We could still charge the cat for inflicting those injuries on you. And from what you've said, Zandra pretended she worked for Angel Force so you'd speak to her."

"No! There'll be no charges brought against Zandra or Juno." A shimmer of Nadina's chaos power drifted across the room. "If you arrest them, I'll use my significant wealth to ensure they get the best legal help. I'll tangle Angel Force in legal battles for years as punishment. Do not test me."

"But... your face. Your beautiful face." Bertoli raised a hand as if meaning to stroke her cheek.

"It's just that. My physical appearance. And it wasn't enough for Dorian to love me and keep me by his side forever, so I'm not worthy. I want it gone. I want people to forget this face. I only want them to know me as a killer."

"Everyone settle down." Finn gently touched Nadina's arm. "Let's clean those wounds if you don't want magic to heal them. Then we'll get you something to drink and do the interview. How does that sound?"

"Give me your guarantee Zandra and Juno will not be in any trouble."

"You have it." Finn didn't hesitate.

Nadina sighed and then nodded at us. "Then let's get this over with."

"Five minutes, then we'll get started. Bertoli, will you help Nadina?" Finn said.

"It would be my pleasure." Bertoli puffed out his chest and led Nadina away.

Finn joined us by the door. "Ignore Bertoli for trying to get you in trouble. He has an enormous crush on Nadina. He's got a picture of her inside his locker, but he thinks I don't know about it. He almost fell off his seat when I arrived with her and has been trying to help her ever since."

"No wonder he hates us," I said.

Zandra lifted me off her shoulder. "You did a number on Nadina's face."

"She hurt you. It was no less than she deserved."

It looked like Zandra had more questions for me, but she turned to Finn. "Can we listen in on Nadina's interview?"

"I can't let you sit in, but we've got a room next door with one-way glass, so you can watch while we interview Nadina. It's old-fashioned, but it helps when the tech breaks during a confession. We always have witnesses watching."

"That works for us."

"Did Nadina tell you how she did it?" I asked.

"She didn't speak, other than to say she was sorry and wished she'd never done it. Follow me." Finn led us into a small room with a large window that looked in on an empty interview room. "I'll grab you some drinks then make sure Bertoli isn't being too much of a creep. Be back in a minute."

Zandra settled in a seat, and I hopped onto her lap.

She petted me for a minute. "I've got to ask, where did you go when we were at the spa?"

"Just outside." I inspected my ruined fur, which still had large clumps of dried red clay in it.

"Did the receptionist catch you snooping at the guest list and throw you out?"

"No. I... I thought I saw someone I knew."

"Oh! Who?"

"It was no one. I made a mistake." A mistake that led to my witch being hurt.

"Okay." She stretched out the word. "How did you get in such a mess?"

"I stepped in a muddy puddle."

Zandra gave me a long, steady look. "What's going on? Your mind's been elsewhere recently. And why attack Nadina with your claws and teeth rather than magic?"

"I reacted on instinct. And it worked, didn't it?"

"Sure, but it was risky. Nadina has power and was blasting it in all directions. You could have been injured."

"I won't ever come to harm, not with you close by." I leaned against her as she gently plucked pieces of dried clay out of my fur. "I'm sorry I let you down. I should have been by your side and protected you from Nadina."

"I wasn't worried about her. I've gone up against worse. But I am worried about you. You need to let me know if something is going on. I can help. We're a team, so we look out for each other."

My ears flicked, and I turned to the glass. "Nadina is coming in with Bertoli and Finn. Now, we'll get answers."

Zandra's sigh made me sad, but she didn't ask more questions about my inexcusable lack of judgment.

A second later, Finn came in with a coffee for Zandra and water for me. "I'm interviewing with Bertoli. I don't think this'll take long. Nadina just keeps saying she wants to confess."

"Thanks. We won't hang around and get in the way. We're just interested in how Nadina killed an ancient vamp."

Finn grinned at Zandra. "You're never in the way. I like having you around. Stay as long as you like." He left us to it, and we settled in with our drinks and waited for the show to begin.

Bertoli went through the formal process of starting the interview and getting Nadina's details. Once that was done, he sat back. It looked like Finn was the lead questioner. Good. He was better at his job than Bertoli.

"You're here to make a confession regarding Dorian DeAngelo's death," Finn said.

Nadina's face was still red, but the wounds on her face were clean and no longer bleeding. "That's right. I confess to killing him. I did it."

"What was your relationship to Dorian?"

"We were a couple. Well, until recently. He no longer wanted to be with me. I tried to find out why, but he'd simply lost interest. He promised we'd be together forever, and he'd turn me into an immortal. He lied, so I killed him."

"When was the last time you saw Dorian?" Bertoli said.

"It was the day he went into his bedroom with Mack. We'd had a fight a few days before that, and I'd begged him to turn me, but he refused. He barely had the energy to argue. He simply said he needed to be on his own. I was so desperate, I went on my knees and literally begged in front of him. He walked away. He didn't care." Nadina's voice hitched, and she looked away.

"How did that make you feel?" Finn said.

"At first, I was devastated. I'd believed Dorian. Then I got angry, so angry, I'd felt nothing like it. Nothing I did kept me calm. So, I snuck into his mansion and waited for an opportunity. I hid in a closet and watched as Mack and Dorian gathered supplies. Mack kept asking Dorian if he was okay, but Dorian kept saying he felt fine. He sent Mack in first and asked him to pick a movie to watch. Just before Dorian went inside, I stepped out from my hiding place."

"How did Dorian respond when he saw you?" Finn said.

"He was surprised but then told me to leave. He said I no longer had a place in his home. That's when I attacked. I'd brought a stake with me, and... and I hit him with it." She placed a hand over her heart.

My ears flicked. I hadn't expected that to be the cause of death.

Zandra leaned forward in her seat. "How did the angels miss a stake wound to the heart during the autopsy?"

"Even Bertoli's not that incompetent," I muttered.

"You staked Dorian?" Bertoli's tone revealed his surprise. "Directly in the heart?"

"I thought I had. That's what I aimed for, but he staggered away. He was in pain but still alive. After a second, he stood straight and acted like nothing had happened. I was so stunned, I turned and ran."

"Where is the stake you used?" Bertoli said.

"I dropped it in the woods behind the house."

"That would be good evidence to find," I said. "Although I'm hardly surprised the angels missed it. They've been too focused on finding evidence to prove Mack's guilt."

Zandra nodded, her attention on the interview. "It's weird. Why didn't they see the wound?"

"Because Mack chewed on it."

She shuddered. "Oh, yeah, possibly. But why didn't Dorian go poof when he got hit with a stake?"

"Nadina missed the kill spot. Still, it would have been a difficult injury for Dorian to heal in his weakened state."

Finn pinched his chin between his finger and thumb. "You've been around vampires for years, so you know when a vampire is staked, death is instant."

I nodded. Finn was thinking the same thing as us.

"I can only think I didn't hit the right target," Nadina said.

"Did you use poison on the stake?"

"Nothing like that. I knew Dorian hadn't been feeding, so he'd be easier to kill. Perhaps my blow was deadly, but I only clipped his heart, so it took him longer to die." She hiccupped and covered her mouth with a hand. "I did it."

"Does that sound right to you?" Zandra said to me.

"It makes no sense. A vampire who gets staked in the heart goes poof. That's how it works. Stake to the heart or take off the head and it's no more vampire."

"I'm no vampire anatomy expert, but Dorian sounded weak because he was refusing to feed. If he was thinking about giving up, he may have used that injury to help him along the way. He knew he wouldn't heal because he wasn't strong enough."

"I'm not convinced. It would have taken him a long time to heal, but he would have done it."

Finn and Bertoli talked quietly for a few seconds.

"We'll be back in a moment." Finn said to Nadina. They both left the room.

Finn came in and joined us. Fortunately, Bertoli wasn't with him. "What do you think?"

"I think we need to see the scene of the crime," I said. "And we take Mack with us. Since the case is as good as closed thanks to Nadina's confession, we won't be disturbing evidence by looking around."

"I guess that'll be okay. Why do you want to visit Dorian's mansion, though?" Finn said.

"Because I'm a cat, and I'm curious."

"What are you really up to, Juno?" Zandra said.

I licked at a patch of dry clay on my paw. "This murder isn't done with us. We're missing something, but I won't know what it is until I find it."

"And you think you'll find the missing piece at the murder scene?" Zandra said.

"Like Finn, I'm always keeping an open mind."

He shrugged. "I've got more questions after that interview. And we need to search the grounds for the stake. Okay, you're on. I'll arrange things with Mack. Tomorrow, we're visiting a murder scene."

Chapter 15

Squeakers and cheesy vampires

The next morning, we were up early and heading to Angel Force to meet Finn before starting work.

He appeared around the side of the building a few minutes after Zandra pulled the van to a stop. He carried a bulky bag as he ran toward us.

The bag moved.

"Get us out of here. I don't want to be seen." Finn hurried to the van.

"What's the problem?" Zandra said through the open window.

"Cythera wouldn't agree to let Mack out, despite my assurances he'd be under my care. She kept reminding me of the last time I looked after Mack and he was animal-napped by a vampire."

"So you snuck him out, anyway." Zandra grinned. "You'll get in so much trouble if you're caught."

"The risk is worth it. Besides, Mack wanted to come along when he learned about the plan. He also said there were things he needed to collect from the house."

"When can I get out of this bag?" a muffled sounding Mack said.

"As soon as we're on the move," Finn said.

Finn sat on my seat, I was on his lap, and the bagged honey badger was in the footwell, grumbling about being dumped on the floor like a pile of unwashed underpants.

Finn unzipped the bag, and Mack's head popped out. He gasped in a breath. "It stinks like used socks in here."

Finn shrugged. "It's my gym bag. It was the only thing you'd fit in."

Zandra sped away from the Angel Force building, and we were soon cruising toward Dorian's mansion on the edge of Crimson Cove.

"I heard about Nadina's confession," Mack said to me.

"What do you think?" I tried to focus on the mystery and not on making perfect biscuits on Finn's flat stomach. This half-angel needed more meat on him.

"Nadina was ditzy but basically a chaos maker. She could never be focused enough or fast enough to stake Dorian. And I was there. I'd have seen her do it."

"You never left his side?"

"Well, sometimes, but never for long. Comfort breaks, food breaks, walking breaks, sleeping breaks."

"So all the time?"

"No! And I wouldn't have missed a staking attempt. Dorian would have complained if he'd been given a new hole."

"What about when you ate him?" Zandra said. "Did you see any holes in his chest?"

Mack wrinkled his snout. "Don't remind me about that. I'm still having nightmares."

"Focus on it for a moment," I said. "You said Dorian had a head wound, so you started eating there, but were there any other injuries? A gaping hole in his chest, for example?"

He shuffled out of the bag. "There was a mark to the right of his heart. A small hole. I didn't think much about it. Could that have been where Nadina staked him?"

"That must be it," Zandra said. "She wounded Dorian, but he healed. Well, almost."

"So she did try to kill him." Mack grunted and shuffled around some more. "I didn't think she had it in her. I figured she'd be too worried about breaking a nail. You really don't know some people."

"Nadina was angry and hurting," I said. "Didn't you notice Dorian was injured when he locked you in his bedroom?"

"No. Although I smelled something strange. It was kind of like old blood, but Dorian was a vampire, so that smell was always around the mansion. But this had an odd tang to it. A bit like a pizza parlor."

"Cheese and dough?" Finn said.

"No, not that. Dorian brought in loads of snacks for me, so I assumed the smell came from them." Mack rested his chin on the edge of the seat, forcing Finn to shuffle over. "Dorian was uncomfortable for the first day, though. He must have been healing from being staked by Nadina. And he wouldn't let me lie on his chest. He always did that so he could easily tickle my belly."

"If Dorian healed from being staked, it wasn't the cause of death," Finn said.

"Does that mean Nadina can go free?" Zandra said.

Finn tilted his head from side to side. "She's confessed to trying to kill Dorian, so there are grounds for charging her with attempted murder. Although the rules on vampires are murky. Some say the undead can't be killed again, so there's no crime to answer for. But if getting staked ensured Dorian didn't survive whatever killed him... I'm going for a maybe there's a charge against Nadina."

"Any sign of the stake?" Zandra said.

"No, but angels have been sent to the woods to find it. We'll need to keep watch for them. They haven't started work yet this morning, but it won't be long before they arrive."

"After their coffee, snacks, meetings, lunch, and filing their paperwork," I said.

Finn gently poked me in the side. "We're not all lazy balls of feathers. Some of us enjoy our job."

"You! Only you enjoy working at Angel Force."

"Bertoli has his moments."

I stared at him until he laughed.

"Okay, he's had maybe five moments of joy at work. But some of the back-room people are fun. The guy who looks after our tech is hilarious and cool if you're into geeky equipment."

"Never met him."

"You should. And the scariest angel werewolf guards the evidence room. Feathers and fangs are a combination you don't want to miss."

"A party at your place so we can meet everyone?" I said.

"Less social diary planning and more murder focus," Zandra muttered.

Finn tickled my head and winked at me. "Done."

Zandra drove for a few minutes, and we arrived outside Dorian's mansion and climbed out.

Mack nudged me once he was out of the smelly sock bag. "While we're here, I'm collecting a few toys. I've been missing my favorite squeaker."

"Fine by me. Who doesn't love a squeaky toy? Especially when it's mouse shaped."

Finn fished a set of keys from his pocket and unlocked the front door. He pushed it open.

Footsteps dashing away made me freeze.

"Should anyone be in here?" Zandra stepped inside and looked around.

Finn joined her. "The place should be empty. All the vamps and drones were told to leave."

I lifted my booping snooter and inhaled. "Someone's been inside recently. Someone with a smell. Not a vampire." I dashed along the hallway with Zandra, Finn and Mack behind us. I turned into a large kitchen and spotted a door swinging shut.

"Hey, stop," Zandra yelled.

We charged through the door and discovered Bryce, Dorian's drone, halfway out a window.

"Bryce! What are you doing here?" Finn marched toward him and caught hold of his arm, preventing him from going anywhere.

He heaved out a sigh and climbed back through the window. "I have a right to be here. This is my home."

"This is also a crime scene," Finn said. "After your interview, I said you'd be informed when you could come back."

"This is my hive. I have to defend it. All the vampires have abandoned the place. They're acting like Dorian didn't exist."

"What they're doing is following Angel Force orders. You should have, too." Finn stepped back. "What if we'd discovered new leads or needed to do another sweep of the place? You could have messed with evidence, and then we'd never figure out who killed Dorian."

He glanced at us and then dropped his gaze. "Sorry. I wasn't thinking straight. I just can't believe Dorian isn't coming back. I know it was wrong to break in, but I wanted to make the place nice and get everything ready in case he showed up."

I walked over and wound around his legs. "Dorian isn't coming back. I'm sorry for your loss, but you need to admit that and move on."

"Move on! And do what? I had my whole life and immortality planned out around that vampire. I knew what I'd do once Dorian turned me. Now, I don't see any future."

Finn clapped him on the shoulder. "You need to figure that out somewhere else. I can't have you staying at a crime scene."

"I thought this was almost over, though. Although I'm surprised to see him here." Bryce glared at Mack, who'd remained back, partially concealed by Zandra's legs.

"Mack's here because he's innocent," I said.

Bryce's eyebrows lifted. "You found out who did it?"

"We have another suspect, but it's possible she didn't do it either. We're still investigating. Which is why you need to leave," Finn said.

"She? Who is it? Do I know her?" Bryce remained firmly in place.

"Don't concern yourself with that information," Finn said. "Now, get out of here before I charge you with breaking and entering and contaminating a crime scene."

"I just wanted to do the right thing by Dorian. I meant no harm."

"Which is why I'm letting you go with a warning," Finn said.

Bryce stuffed his hands into his pants pockets. "Sure. Sorry again. I'll go." He shuffled away and out of the kitchen. A few seconds later, the front door opened and shut.

"I feel sorry for the guy," Finn said. "He pinned everything on becoming immortal. It was his dream, and he's left with nothing."

"I've been meaning to look into Bryce's alibi," Zandra said. "He mentioned he wasn't around when Dorian died."

"He said the same thing during his official interview. When did you quiz him?" Finn arched an eyebrow, but a smile played on his lips.

"Oh, you know, just in passing." Zandra shrugged.

"Uh-huh. Well, Bryce was with a friend. I contacted that friend, and he confirmed it. Bryce is just having trouble letting go and accepting he needs to find a new future."

"Bryce is smarmy and thinks he's more handsome than he is. Smug jerk." Mack nudged me toward the door. "I'm showing Juno my bedroom. You know where the gross murder room is if you need to stare at the crime scene again."

"Sure. We'll be in there," Finn said. "Join us when you're ready."

"And this was your idea, Juno," Zandra said, "so don't be too long. We need your expert nose for sniffing out clues."

"I won't." But I had a feeling Mack was delaying the inevitable, returning to the place where he'd lost his best friend. I didn't blame him. If he needed a few minutes to gather his strength, I wasn't stopping him.

Mack led me to a room and nudged the door open with his nose.

I stepped inside, and my jaw dropped. It was a toy store for familiars. There were shelves full of chew toys, soft toys, balls, tins of treats, soft throws, beds, and so much more, I couldn't take it in.

"You have your own toy room?" I walked around, sniffing everything.

"Sure. Don't you?"

"No! I need to speak to Zandra about an upgrade. This is amazing."

Mack grabbed a grubby pink bone-shaped toy off the floor and chewed on it, making it squeak.

"Take what you like. I haven't used most of this stuff. Dorian used to take me to the store and buy me everything I looked at."

I sniffed some more and discovered a soft gray mouse that I tried for mouth fit and texture. It felt good. I tossed it around between my paws. "Mind if I have this?"

"Be my guest." Mack dragged out a small backpack from a low closet and put a few toys in it then flipped it onto his back. "I suppose we should go to Dorian's room and get this over with."

"Not yet. Since you've been so generous with me, I'll share something with you. Take me to the kitchen."

Mack led the way and stopped outside a shut door.

"This trick will change your life." I hopped onto my back legs, carefully positioned my paws around the handle, and twisted. The door was stiff, and I had to use all my weight to get the handle to move, but it shifted enough, and the door swung open.

"You can open doors! That's incredible. It bugs me I have to wait for people to let me in and out of rooms." Mack looked on in appreciation.

"It'll take practice to get good at it, but it'll be worth it."

"It so will." Mack barged past and headed for the fridge. "Can you open this? It's a different type of handle."

"Of course. It's all about getting the weight distribution right." I flipped around, got my paws under the handle, and then leaned. The door sprung open to reveal a full fridge of untouched food.

"Nice!" Mack hopped his front feet onto a shelf.

"All this food for a house full of vampires?" I said.

"Dorian liked to keep up appearances. And, of course, the drones needed feeding. He always kept my favorite treats in stock. Try this jerky." He tossed me a package.

Neither of us spoke for ten minutes as we gorged on delicious meats and cheeses.

Mack smacked his lips together. "This tastes so much better than Dorian. He was rank."

"He was an old vampire, so I can't imagine him tasting good. Although I can't imagine any vampire tasting delicious."

"It was more than that. He tasted pungent. I mean, the old blood was gross, but there was an intense flavor I hadn't had in ages."

"Intense how?" I finished a chunk of mature cheddar and inspected the fridge to see what else I could have.

"Dorian tasted like pizza."

"Cheesy?"

"No, like that greasy bread they serve in restaurants."

"Garlic bread?"

"Yeah, which is impossible. Dorian hated that stuff. He didn't even like me eating anything with garlic in. He always said he could smell it seeping from my pores."

"No vampire is a fan of garlic, and the old ones become more intolerant. I've heard baby vamps are less affected." I resisted the tray of sausages. "Are you sure Dorian tasted like garlic?"

"I mean, I haven't been exposed to the stuff much. Living with vampires, they don't grow it or cook with it. But Dorian smelled and tasted like a slice of greasy garlic bread. Add in the mix of ancient vampire blood oozing through his veins, and it was an all-round gag-fest."

I'd lost interest in the contents of the fridge and was staring at Mack.

"What? Have I got something on my chin?" Mack wiped his nose on the floor.

"How long was Dorian confused before he died?"

"It's hard to say. It happened slowly. At least a couple of months, maybe longer. Why?"

"And did he lose his appetite around that time, too?"

"That happened more recently. After he fed, he'd feel bad. He even had tests done, but of course, nothing showed up. He was an undead. Tests rarely show them having anything, not even a pulse."

"Where did Dorian get his food?" I paced in front of Mack.

"The same places as always. He had his drones, me, and he'd have the blood bank deliver."

"These food sources were always in the house?"

"Sure. Dorian rarely went out and dined, not in the last few months of his life. Juno, what's going on?"

"I have a theory. Put down that salami." I raced out of the kitchen, and a few seconds later, Mack thundered after me.

"Why? What are you thinking?"

I followed my booping snooter and discovered Zandra and Finn standing just inside a room. "Finn, did you test for evidence of garlic in Dorian's system?"

His forehead wrinkled. "No. Why do you ask?"

"You should. Someone poisoned him with garlic."

Chapter 16

Garlic infused vampire with your fries?

After Mack explained Dorian's uniquely garlicky taste, we were all in agreement more information was needed.

"I'll get the tests on Dorian rushed through," Finn said.

"You could start by giving him a good sniff. That stuff always lingers," I said.

"We can do better than that. I'll make the call. Back in a moment." Finn stepped outside the room.

A heavy sigh from Mack made me hurry to his side. His head was down and his eyes half-closed. "Being here brings back sad memories."

I leaned against him briefly in a show of sympathy. "Use those memories to help us figure this out. Tell me what happened in here."

He huffed out a breath. "Sure, I can do that. I want to help."

"How long had you been in the room before you got worried about Dorian?" I said.

Mack dragged his paws as we made a slow circuit, Zandra following behind. "I was already worried before we came in here. Dorian had been sluggish and sad and kept talking about the past. And he'd been so tired. Vampires need little sleep, but even after he'd had a full twelve hours in fresh grave dirt in his original coffin, he could barely keep his eyes open."

"That could be because of the garlic poisoning," I said.

"I should have realized something was wrong with his odd smell, but I kept dismissing it. Everyone loved Dorian. I never thought someone would poison him."

I made sympathy noises as we trudged along. "So you came in here, settled in for some quiet time, but then it all went wrong."

"I've already told you, I dozed off. Dorian kept saying the same thing over and over and that he was struggling to find a purpose. I told him he had his hive, me, and endless amounts of money. He could do whatever he wanted. But he wasn't listening. In the end, I ate my feelings and fell asleep in a chips and dips food coma. I only woke because there was a thud. That's when I saw Dorian on the floor."

"Where did he fall?"

Mack jerked his chin. "By the plinth behind us. The marble one."

"And he was dead by the time you got to him?"

"Yup."

"That's when you tried to get out?"

"Not at first. I panicked. I yelled and jumped on him, thinking I could get him moving. You see people do that heart pump thing in the movies, but vamps don't need a beating heart to keep going. Nothing made him open his eyes."

"Then you tried to get out?" I said.

"Or get help to come to us. But this place is soundproofed. Nothing I did made any difference."

"Is this where Dorian fell?" Zandra was examining the marble plinth.

"That's right." Mack glanced up then hung his head.

"There's a mark here."

"That's where he went down." Mack stayed away from the small dark mark on the side of the plinth.

"We ran a test on that mark." Finn returned to the room. "It's vampire blood."

"From the head wound," Mack said. "I'm so ashamed. If I hadn't gorged on all the treats because I was frustrated, I'd have held out for longer and not eaten his face."

I patted his paw.

"But why did Dorian fall?" Zandra said. "Could it have been because of the injury Nadina inflicted with her stake?"

"If the small hole in his chest was from that stake, it was almost healed," Mack said.

"I'm certain garlic had something to do with Dorian's death," I said. "Somehow, it got snuck into his food over time, so he didn't know how badly it was affecting him."

"We'll find out soon enough. I got authorization to run more tests on Dorian," Finn said. "We'll do a full tox screen."

"You'll find garlic, but it's a good idea to be thorough. And I'm even more certain Dorian was poisoned after hearing Mack's story again," I said. "Dorian was behaving out of character. He was sleepy, depressed, and off his food."

"If you find garlic poisoning in his system, does that mean I'll go free?" Mack said. "I still feel responsible. After all, I ate the evidence."

"No, you're innocent," I said.

"Hold on, now. You still have questions to answer," Finn said. "It's unlikely you'll be charged with anything relating to Dorian's murder, but you attacked a troop of angels and hospitalized three of them."

"In Mack's defense, he wanted answers about his vampire. I'd do the same for Zandra if she'd been murdered and the angels were being incompetent."

Finn's wings fluttered behind him. "Juno! That's not fair. We're doing our best."

"Is your best the fact you missed the high probability Dorian was poisoned with garlic?"

Finn looked shamefaced. "Maybe we could do better."

"I deserve to be punished," Mack said. "I should have had more willpower."

"You were keeping yourself alive by benefiting from Dorian's leftovers. We'd all do the same," I said.

Zandra and Finn looked disgusted.

"And as unpleasant as it sounds, Dorian would have wanted you to eat him, so you lived." My stomach grumbled. "All this talk of food is making me hungry. We should go to Vorana's and grab breakfast before work."

"You're impossible," Zandra said. "We're at a murder scene, talking about eating a vampire, and you want food?"

"Tell me you're not hungry. I know you've only had coffee."

She shrugged. "I could eat."

"Everyone else in?"

After a few seconds of hesitation, Mack nodded.

Finn shook his head. "Sorry, buddy, we can't. I need to get you back in your cell and hope Cythera hasn't noticed us missing. Then I need to hassle for those test results."

Mack harrumphed his displeasure.

"Next time," I said. "Finn, you focus on that. We'll eat pancakes."

Lady Luck was on our side, and not only did we walk in just as a delicious pancake breakfast was being served, but Sorcha was also a guest at Vorana's table.

"Hey! I wondered where you two were this morning," Vorana said. "I didn't hear you leave."

"We were on an important mission," I said. "Solving crime. We just dropped Finn and Mack back at Angel Force to get things moving."

"Ooh! Tell us everything," Sorcha said. "Wait, let me guess. Does it have to do with a recently deceased vampire and a honey badger with a liking for flesh?"

"Got it in one." Zandra settled at the table in the empty seat next to Sorcha, and I took my usual seat next to Sage.

"The whole town is talking about it," Sorcha said. "What's the latest?"

"It's an ongoing investigation. I really couldn't say." Zandra looked around the group of stunned faces and grinned. "But since it's just us..."

I smiled, making sure not to drool as Vorana placed scrambled eggs and salmon on Sage's plate and then mine.

"People keep saying Mack did it." Sorcha accepted a refill of coffee from Vorana.

"The more we're learning, the less convinced we are Mack had anything to do with Dorian's murder." I gulped down some salmon. "He was in the wrong place at the wrong time, and unfortunately, his hunger meant he had to take a nibble out of Dorian to survive."

Vorana settled in her seat. "That statement almost put me off my breakfast."

It hadn't put me off mine, and I'd already eaten half the salmon.

"Solving murders clearly gives you an appetite," Sage muttered. "Don't dare think about having any of mine."

"Are you still grumpy because you didn't come on the first kitten impossible mission?" I whispered.

"I'm not grumpy. I'm just realistic."

"Keep those realistic thoughts to yourself, because I have a plan, and it involves you."

Her ears pricked, and she looked at me.

I shook my head and glanced at Zandra. My next kitten impossible mission had to be top secret, and I was still ironing out the details of how to get away without making Zandra suspicious.

"If it wasn't Mack, who killed Dorian?" Vorana sprinkled fresh raspberries over her pancakes and drizzled them with maple syrup.

"There have been a few names in the mix," Zandra said. "Initially, I thought it was Remus. He's got a great motive for wanting Dorian dead, since he wanted to expand into his territory. Remus can do that now Dorian is out of the picture."

"Remus is a decent vampire. He's no killer. I'm a great judge of people, and I'm sure he didn't do this," Sorcha said.

"Remus claims to have an alibi, but he's using his drones as that alibi, so..." I said.

"That's not ideal. Drones do anything their vampire tells them. But I still don't think it was him," Sorcha said. "I'd be prepared to stand up and defend him if it goes to court."

"Even though he has a flimsy alibi, I don't dislike Remus. I'm not sure he's our guy," Zandra said.

"I agree. He's almost too obvious a suspect," I said. "And the Oak Park Ridge hive has made overt attacks on Crimson Cove in an attempt to take over. Why change things and suddenly go into stealth kill mode?"

"Let's set Remus to one side for now," Zandra said. "There's also been a connection to the Shadow gang."

Sorcha's fork froze halfway to her mouth. "I thought those guys were finished in Crimson Cove."

Vorana reached over and squeezed her hand. "They are. The gang is behind bars. You've got nothing to worry about."

Sorcha still looked concerned.

"The gang's days are numbered," Zandra said, "but thanks to Remus, we made a connection between Anan Shadow and Dorian. Apparently, Dorian had a miscommunication with the gang, and someone was killed. Dorian refused to pay them the rest of their money because he never agreed to that, and things got nasty. Anan threatened Dorian."

"So it was the Shadow gang. They have contacts everywhere," Sorcha said. "If they wanted someone dead, they could still make it happen."

"You're not still worried they'll come after you, are you?" Vorana said.

Sorcha sighed. "Honestly, sometimes I am. Even though I got a new mattress, new sheets, pillows, and moved my bed to a different position in the bedroom, I still hesitate every time I pull back the covers, because I think there'll be something gross under my pillow."

"I had no idea you were so worried. You should have said something." Vorana hopped up and hugged Sorcha. "No one's leaving any body parts in your bed ever again."

"You should get Tinkerbell to help," I said. "Make sure she's on your bed every evening defending it. That's what a good familiar would do."

Sorcha's gaze lowered as she pulled back from Vorana's hug. "That's another problem I'm dealing with. Tinkerbell is barely speaking to me. She's had such a terrible attitude recently. I even invited her to come to breakfast today, but she refused. I'd love it if she'd protect me, but she has her own issues to deal with."

I grumbled under my breath. I didn't trust that cat. When this was over, I was pulling Tinkerbell to one side and reminding her of her responsibilities. She may not have a full familiar bond with Sorcha, but they should look out for each other.

"You could try a cleansing in your bedroom," Vorana said. "Get out the bad energy."

"I'm willing to try anything," Sorcha said. "Anyway, this isn't about me. At least with the Shadow gang already behind bars, the angels have got their man if Anan killed Dorian."

"This is where it gets complicated, because someone has confessed to killing Dorian," Zandra said.

"Who?" Vorana and Sorcha said at the same time.

"His former girlfriend, Nadina," Zandra said. "She staked him."

Vorana returned to her seat. "I'm confused. If he'd been staked—"

"He'd have gone poof," Sorcha said.

Zandra lifted her hands. "Exactly. Nadina confessed to the murder, but then evidence was found of a healed stake mark on Dorian's chest. She didn't kill him."

"Although the staking most likely weakened him," I said. "And since I believe he was being poisoned with garlic, the combination of being staked whilst also being poisoned could have been too much for him."

"Wow! So many ways to kill a vampire," Sorcha said. "Who poisoned him with garlic?"

No one spoke.

"Maybe we're looking for more than one killer," I said. "What if someone systematically poisoned Dorian to make him weak, so Nadina got a chance to stake him?"

"Hmmm, it's a theory," Zandra said. "Who would Nadina work with?"

"That's a tricky question to answer." Sorcha sipped her coffee. "I know Nadina, and I know the vampires who lived with Dorian. She wasn't popular with them. They saw her as grasping and materialistic. They talked about her not loving Dorian and only loving what he could do for her. None of them would help her kill him."

I lapped up the last of the egg. "What about a disaffected drone? When we talked to Bryce, he admitted to being frustrated because Dorian refused to turn him. Nadina and Bryce have the same motive. Dorian went back on his word to them."

"Bryce is ridiculously handsome," Vorana said. "I can see those two as a couple. The supermodel and the movie star."

"So, Bryce poisoned Dorian slowly to make him weak and confused, then Nadina staked him," I said. "It was a lover's pact. Neither could get what they wanted from Dorian, so they formed an alliance and figured out how to destroy the vampire who lied to them."

Zandra pushed back from her seat. "We need to speak to Nadina and Bryce about this love tryst. This could be what we've been missing."

Sorcha cleared her throat. "I... err... I dated Bryce for a couple of months."

"Go you! He's gorgeous," Vorana said.

"He is, but I ditched him because he was so obsessed with Dorian. All he talked about was wanting to be turned into a vampire. It was unhealthy and boring. He even asked me to bite him, and I'm not a full vamp. It was impossible for me to turn him. I'd have killed him."

"Did he ever talk about being angry with Dorian or wanting revenge because he wouldn't turn him into a vampire?" I said.

"Nothing like that, but he had an unhealthy focus on Dorian. It creeped me out."

"Then we talk to Nadina and Bryce right away," Zandra said. "We found Bryce at the mansion, but Finn made him leave. Has Bryce got somewhere he stays when he's not on drone duty?"

"The drones rent a shared apartment in Crimson Cove. I know the address," Sorcha said.

"Write it down. We'll go see Bryce. Although, should we see Nadina first?" Zandra tapped her fingers on the table. "We have to do this carefully. If one of them tips off the other before we speak to them individually, this could fall apart. And as much as I want to solve this now, if I'm late for work, Barney won't be happy."

The last piece of my second kitten impossible mission fell into place. "You tackle Bryce after work, and I'll speak to Nadina. She's still at Angel

Force, so it'll take me time to get the green light to reach her. You know what the angels are like when processing requests."

"Perfect. We'll get our work done, split up to question suspects, then regroup and swap notes." Zandra stood from her seat. "I hope Barney has easy jobs for us today. I won't be able to concentrate on anything too deadly while I'm thinking about all these suspects."

Zandra thought she'd be having a tough day! Not only would I be by her side making sure the animals behaved, but I had to get the kitten impossible gang together, question a murder suspect, and figure out exactly what was buried beside that spa.

Kitten impossible two was a go.

Chapter 17

Kitten impossible two

"We hadn't considered any of the suspects were working together to kill Dorian, but the theory has potential." Finn's image glowed in the snow globe I sneakily used in Vorana's lounge. "Do you and Zandra want to be here when I speak to her?"

I glanced over my shoulder to ensure Zandra wasn't making her way up from the basement. She'd needed a shower after the day we'd had at work. "That won't be necessary. We trust you to do a good job. Just don't let Nadina off easily."

Finn smirked. "I do know how to interview suspects. I've been around the block a few times."

"I expect you've been on the other side of the table, too."

He was quiet for a heartbeat. "Meaning?"

"I need to know more about your background. Not now, but after this case, we need to talk."

"Why?"

"There are things I must know about you."

"Is this about Zandra's mother? You know we've got to tell Zandra about finding that purse."

"No. Well, it's partly about that. And we will tell her, but not now. I have to know you can be trusted, though."

"Have I let you down so far?"

"There's always a first time. If you're staying in my witch's life, I must be confident about you being in the house, so I don't have to stand outside the bedroom door all night."

"I... Juno." Finn rubbed the back of his neck. "I'll admit, I like Zandra—"

"Not now. Later. Focus on questioning Nadina and get the information we need."

"I am. I will. But... you don't think a happy ending will come out of this, do you?"

"For you and Zandra? It won't if you mess things up, or if I find dirt in your past."

"We all have a little dirt. Even you. But I meant a happy ending for Adrienne. We have to tell Zandra what we know. She needs to be prepared for the worst."

"It's another thing to discuss. Just don't screw up when you question Nadina about her relationship with Bryce."

Finn shook his head. "Anyone would think you're my boss."

"I'd make an excellent boss. I've bossed around thousands of people over the centuries."

"Centuries? Exactly how old—"

"Got to go. I'll catch you later." I cut the connection on the snow globe, hopped off the couch, and was innocently licking my belly when Zandra strode in.

"We're running late to question our suspects. That last job with the swamp monkeys took twice as long as I thought it would. I'm never getting those stains out of my shirt."

"At least you've got the muck out of your hair," I said. "And it doesn't matter about the time, since I need to get into Angel Force to speak to Nadina. Finn's helping me out, so I'm just waiting for news before I leave to question her."

"I'll go to Bryce's apartment and wait outside, see if he's around."

"And I thought I'd visit the spa again, see if I can get anything useful out of the staff. Now they know Nadina is a murder suspect, they could be willing to talk."

"It's worth a try. What time are you questioning Nadina?"

"No time figured out yet."

"Finn can get you in to speak to her, though? His boss isn't being snippy, is she? She doesn't like us."

"It's all arranged. You should go now. The traffic could be bad."

Zandra cocked her head. "In Crimson Cove? It's never bad traffic around here. Anyway, I was thinking about walking."

"Even better." That would give me more time for my kitten impossible mission two.

She looked out the window and jangled her keys. "Nah, I'm exhausted after chasing those swamp monkeys. I could drive to the apartment and then pick up takeout on the way back."

"We've had too much takeout recently. I don't want to get plump."

"We haven't had takeout in ages. Vorana always cooks for us." Zandra narrowed her eyes and studied me. "You're being weird. You're not feeling sick again, are you?"

"I'm fine. In perfect health. You should get going. I have a good feeling about this. We're onto something with Nadina and Bryce working together. We just need to catch them out in their lies, and we'll have two killers off the street."

She shrugged on her jacket. "If you're certain. You sure you're good?"

"Go. I'll meet you back here once I've been to the spa and spoken to Nadina." Or rather, once Finn had spoken to Nadina on my behalf and gotten the answers I needed.

My plan was coming together. All I had to do to make this work was get the timing right. Finn would be speaking to Nadina any time now, while I was on my mission. By the time Zandra got back from speaking to Bryce, we'd have all the information we needed, and I'd have a little something special back in my life.

"Let me know if you run into any problems," Zandra said.

"Will do. See you later." I walked behind her and waited until she closed the front door and walked along the path before chirruping softly.

Sage, Sammy, and Archie appeared from out of the closet under the stairs.

"You're sure you're doing the right thing by hiding this from Zandra?" Sammy said. "She'd want to help."

"She would, but if Zandra got involved, it would mean explaining a few things, and I'm not sure she's ready for them yet."

"I'm not sure any of us are," Sage said. "Only half of what you told me about this mission made sense."

After breakfast this morning, I'd gathered my team and explained the kitten impossible two mission. I couldn't understand why Sage was grumbling. It was simple.

"Any questions before we leave?" I said.

"When are we going to Angel Force?" Archie's fur gleamed, and he smelled of peppermint. The vampires had given him an astonishing makeover.

"Forget Angel Force. We don't need to be there. Finn is helping on that side of things. We're going to the day spa where Nadina spends most of her time and checking the records to see if she's ever late for her appointments. I reckon she's been using that spa as a cover to meet Bryce."

"Her secret lover," Sammy said. "I remember that part."

"That's right. Apparently, she spends all her spare time there, but there are only so many treatments a person can get. If we can find evidence Nadina's been using that spa to go on secret liaisons with Bryce, it'll connect them."

"And make it more likely they killed Dorian?" Sage said.

"That's what I'm thinking. After we're done at the spa, Archie will do a small amount of excavation for me."

Sage wrinkled her nose. "How is this excavation connected to Dorian's murder?"

"Technically, it's not. But while we're at the spa, we should make the most of our visit." And I could do with Archie's enormous paws to plow up that sticky red soil and get to the magic buried beneath it.

I checked out the window and was happy to see Zandra had left her van and was walking to Bryce's apartment. "Gather around, everyone. Join paws, and I'll translocate us to the spa."

Everyone shuffled closer and linked paws.

I dug into my magic, but it was having an off day. Again.

Sage gave me the side eye. "Something wrong?"

"I'm tired. Busy day at animal control. Could someone else translocate us?" I faked a yawn.

"I'll do it," Sammy said. "My magic behaves when I'm around you."

I rubbed my face against his, grateful for his support.

The spell connected, and a few seconds later, we were outside the spa. The front door had been repaired, and visitors would never know two powerful magic users had gone head-to-head in the dirt recently.

The low-level lighting inside showed the building wasn't open for visitors, which was just what I wanted.

"Sage, you're up," I said. "Now's your chance to shine."

Sage trundled over on her wheels and inspected the door then rifled in a small bag on the back of her harness and pulled out a thin metal rod. She inserted it into the lock, held a paw over it, and it flared with blue magic. She pulled the rod out and wheeled back. "That should do it."

I grabbed the handle and leaned back. The door opened.

"Nice job," Archie said. "Where did you learn to do that?"

Sage tucked away her lock picking equipment. "Vorana taught me."

I glanced at her. "Vorana used to break into places?"

"She didn't always own a bookstore."

I'd love to know more of that story, but it would have to be another time. "Sammy, you're our lookout. Stay by the door and alert us if anyone comes toward the building. There could be alarms inside we trigger, and we don't want any angels to discover us."

"I promise I won't let you down." He stationed himself by the door, his ears up and his gaze alert.

"What about me?" Archie said. "I forgot what I'm supposed to do."

I hurried through the door with Sage and Archie. "I need you for the second part of this mission. For now, just make sure you don't drool on anything you shouldn't. This won't take long."

Archie looked disappointed and sloped off to sit with Sammy by the door.

"What are you up to?" Sage walked with me to the reception desk.

"Does no one listen to me when I outline mission plans? I'm solving Dorian's murder." I hopped on the desk and looked around. The receptionist was incredibly neat, and everything looked like it had been lined up with a ruler.

"I get we're here to learn if Nadina lied about being at certain appointments, but what's with the digging afterward?"

"Well, you said Vorana hasn't always been a book store owner. Perhaps I haven't always been a familiar. This is what we're after." I discovered the appointment diary on the top of the in-tray. I tugged it down and flipped it open with my paw.

"If you weren't always a familiar, what were you?" Sage said. "Has it got something to do with your strange power?"

"Shush, I'm concentrating." My gaze scanned down the pages as I looked for Nadina's name.

"Does Zandra know about you?" Sage was persistent.

"Why don't you stand with the others and keep watch?"

"They don't need me. Does she?"

I glanced up from the page. "It's complicated. But I'm with Zandra for the right reasons. Our powers perfectly complement each other."

"Your powers don't even work. And I sense Zandra's got something special going on inside her, but she's holding back. Is that because of you?"

"Of course not. I'll do everything to ensure Zandra becomes the most incredible witch anyone has ever seen."

Sage was quiet for a moment. "But there's more. And it's got to do with what you want Archie to dig up, hasn't it?"

"You're distracting me. Look at this. I've found six days when Nadina was booked in for the whole day, but she missed her first appointments. There's got to be a reason for that."

Sage hopped her front paws onto the desk and examined the appointment diary. "You can ignore my questions all you like, but I'll keep asking."

"Why?"

"You're living under Vorana's roof, and I have to make sure she's safe."

I stifled a sigh and pressed a paw on top of Sage's head. "You have my word. We're no threat to your witch or you. I want only the best for Zandra and any of her friends. Just because I can't tell you everything about my past and what I'm doing in my present doesn't automatically mean it's a bad thing."

She narrowed her eyes at me. "But it's a complicated thing?"

"Yes. And until I've untangled it, gotten everything right, and found a way to make Zandra understand, I must keep some things from her."

"And from your friends. I'm not sure I agree with that."

"Are we friends?"

"Of course. I don't share my breakfast table with just any old cat."

My heart softened. "I consider you a friend too, Sage. And friends trust each other. When the time is right, you'll know everything. And I may just have to call on your help again to make sure I can achieve my goals."

She snuffled around for a second before finally nodding. "Keep looking at the diary entries. What you found seems suspicious."

I flicked my tail at her. Sage understood, and I was grateful she'd stopped questioning me. "It's a pattern. You can understand Nadina being late for one or two appointments, but she missed an entire hour of massage each time. It must have been because she was meeting Bryce."

"Are they a couple, or did they bond over their shared desire to kill Dorian?"

"That's what I'm hoping Finn is finding out." I turned the page with my paw. "Nadina was two hours late after she'd staked Dorian. She said she'd waited in the mansion, and he was about to go into his bedroom when she confronted him with the stake."

"Maybe she was working up the courage to confront him and do the deed."

"Or Nadina needed time to dispose of the stake and calm down before she came here."

"That also makes sense."

"This is the evidence we need to get her to confess." I flipped the diary shut and placed it back on the in-tray. "We've got everything we can. On to part two of our mission." I hopped down from the desk and walked along with Sage. We joined the others.

"There's no one about," Sammy whispered. "It looks like we didn't trigger any alarms when we came in."

"Perfect. Archie, are you ready?" Despite sounding calm, my insides churned like a bubbling witch's cauldron.

"Point me in the right direction, and I'll dig." He wagged his tail.

"You must be careful when you dig. What's underground could have a lot of power in it." And that power hadn't been touched in over three decades. It would want a release. "It could be unstable."

"I'm always careful. I've only broken two vases since moving in with Remus."

We hurried out of the spa, and Sage used her magic to lock the door, so it looked like we'd never been there.

"How do you know about this buried power?" Sammy said.

"It's unique to me."

"I don't feel anything," Sage said as we got closer to the mound.

"What about either of you?" I said to Sammy and Archie. "Do you sense anything?"

They shook their heads.

The power under my paws was like a pounding drum. How could they not feel it?

I paced for a moment until I found the spot with the most concentrated source of energy. "Archie, start digging here."

He sniffed around and scraped out some soil. "It's damp, and it stinks. It'll mess up my fur. I only got back from the groomer a couple of hours ago."

"Pampered pooch," Sage muttered.

"I'm sure Remus will be thrilled to take you again. He's clearly having fun turning you into a civilized hellhound," I said.

"Yeah, he is. And I'm having loads of fun being civilized, too. Stand back everyone, this'll get messy." Archie plunged into the dirt, enthusiastically carving out huge chunks of sticky clay soil.

I scooted back, my heart racing and my toe beans tingling. I was so close to finding something precious that had been taken from me.

"Have you got anything?" Sammy craned his neck as he looked at the increasingly large hole Archie dug.

"Not yet. I still don't feel any magic."

"It's there. Just keep digging." My tail quivered, and my whiskers twitched. "Any second now."

"Hey, I got something."

I dashed over. "Careful. It could be fragile."

Archie backed up a few steps. "It's a lump of metal. Is this what you expected to find?"

I blinked several times. When I'd been transformed into a cat, I'd had no idea where my magic had been concealed. The goblin jerk who'd trapped me in this form and taken most of my power had whipped it away so violently and then vanished, so I'd been unable to track him.

But I'd listened to rumors and whispers over the years, so I knew he'd hidden what he'd stolen in a vessel. Until now, I didn't know what sort of vessel that would be.

"Do you know what it is?" Sammy whispered.

"It's mine. It's me." I pressed a paw on the metal, and the world exploded.

Chapter 18

A power returned

Archie rolled in the dirt, extinguishing flames from his fur and yelping. "What just happened? Why am I on fire? Did I do this to myself?" He rolled and yipped some more.

I was face down in the dirt, my paw stinging as magic I hadn't felt in three decades pulsed through me. "That wasn't supposed to happen."

"Will someone help me?"

I looked over to discover Sage on her back, her wheels in the air. I pulled myself upright and staggered over to her.

Archie rolled out the last of the flames and flopped down beside us. "That wasn't me, right?"

"Of course not! It was Little Miss Innocent here. Stop flapping your slobbering jowls and get me on my paws!"

"I... err... yes. I may have caused that tiny explosion," I said.

With Archie's help, we got Sage the right way up.

There was a groan, and it took me a moment to discover Sammy partially buried under an enormous pile of dirt. "Archie, follow me."

Archie bounded after me, his pristine fur a smoke blackened, charred mess. Not that he seemed to mind. He caught hold of Sammy's tail and pulled him out of the mound of dirt.

Sammy squeaked and wriggled away from the hellhound's sharp teeth.

"Juno, what have you gotten us into?" Sage stomped over, one of her wheels squeaking even more than usual.

I looked at the group, their expressions dazed. Sage was the angriest, while Sammy looked nervous.

I couldn't hide this from them any longer. "What you dug up, Archie, was one of my missing... pieces."

"What piece were you missing?" Sage said.

"Before I go further, I must swear you all to silence. It's important other people don't know about this."

"Why?" If Sage could have crossed her legs over her chest to show her annoyance and still stayed standing, she would. I had a lot of making up to do for tipping her over.

"Because it would make me vulnerable."

"Vulnerable to what?" Sammy said. "You know I'll always protect you."

"And although that's adorable of you, you wouldn't be able to protect me from the monsters who want me dead if they discovered where I was and what I'd become."

"Monsters?" Sammy's tail quivered. "Are we talking werewolves? Golems? Ogres?"

"This is about your weird magic," Sage said. "I knew there was something going on with you. The second we met, I thought to myself, this cat isn't all she seems to be."

"And you were right." I licked a soot blackened paw. "I haven't always been in this form."

"What were you?" Archie said. "A hellhound, like me?"

"No, but I had a different shape and different powers. And although that gave me a lot of opportunities, it also made me enemies. And those enemies are still around and looking for me. Most of them think I'm dead, but I'm certain a few of them keep their ears to the ground in the hope I'll show up somewhere."

"How does this information link to the weird rock that exploded and nearly killed us?" Sage said.

"You're being dramatic. None of you were near death." Although my ears rang, and the stench of charred fur churned my stomach.

"Archie was on fire!"

"And I didn't do it to myself." His tongue lolled out. He looked so pleased with himself.

Sage huffed out a breath. "You said it was a missing piece of you. Explain."

I settled on the dirt and glanced at the pulsing lump of rock. I felt different after touching it, but I hadn't absorbed all its power. And I didn't want it all in one burst. I'd forgotten how strong I used to be, and it would take time to get comfortable with so much magic coursing through me again.

"Focus! You just flipped me on my butt, buried Sammy, and set fire to Archie. We're owed a proper explanation." Sage tapped me on the booping snooter with a claws extended paw.

"Of course. Sorry, I was just thinking." Excitement shivered through me. "I've often wondered what would happen when this day came. I never expected to find it so close to my new home."

"Keep talking," Sage said.

"But only if you want to," Sammy said. "It's okay to have secrets if they keep you safe."

"Not from us. And not when Juno involves us in dangerous things and doesn't give us the full story," Sage said.

"Thank you, Sammy. And sorry, Sage, I can't tell you everything, but you'll know the important stuff." I took a few seconds to gather my thoughts and figure out a start point. "Around thirty years ago, I was changed against my will into a cat. I had a minor disagreement with a powerful goblin. He took offence over a comment I made and punished me using a powerful spell. He caught me when I was sleeping, so I had no opportunity to defend myself. His plan was to turn me into a cat and trap me, keep me as a caged creature to mock. He wanted to parade me through the streets to show everyone I'd fallen from my pedestal."

"Did he do that? Trap you?" Sammy said.

"No. I escaped. I was half-crazed and scared out of my mind. Becoming a successful cat takes work."

"What did you used to be?" Sage said.

"Different. I didn't have four paws." It was too soon to tell them exactly how powerful I'd been. It would only intimidate them.

"Did you have a tail?" Archie said.

"No tail. Just an immense amount of power. The goblin's spell ripped chunks of my power away. He told me he planned to destroy it, but I knew he'd fail. You can't destroy abilities so magnificent." I lifted my chin, remembering the old days. They'd been so good. "That was when I figured it out. Since he couldn't destroy my magic, he'd have to hide it or risk becoming a target for other magic users who wanted a taste of what he'd stolen. I had no idea where or what form my stolen magic would take, but I vowed to get it back."

"And then get your revenge," Sage said. "That's your plan, isn't it? And you want to use Zandra to do it."

"No! I'd never use Zandra for anything. But when we met, I knew how perfect we were for each other. I care deeply for her."

"Because you both have weird magic," Sage said.

"There's nothing weird about Juno or Zandra," Sammy said.

"You're only saying that because you're in love with Juno. You feel it, too," Sage said. "And so does Archie. You can tell by his expression."

Archie simply looked puzzled. "I have gas, if that's what you mean."

"Juno's just extremely powerful, not different." Sammy leaned against me. "She makes me feel safer when I use my magic."

I appreciated him siding with me. "Sage isn't wrong. My power is extremely old. I come from a long line of powerful magic users, so when that power was taken, and I only had my basic abilities left, I struggled." I stared calmly at Sage. "And revenge is on my mind. That goblin took things too far. He took away everything I loved. It took me years to get control over my powers, and then I had to figure out how to use them in this form. And... my power is lessening. Before long, I'll be of no use to Zandra."

"You've told me you had bonds with other magic users before Zandra," Sammy said. "Was that because you were trying to get power from them?"

"Partly. I was willing to try anything to keep what I had. It helped me when I aligned with strong magic users. But as we all know, extreme power creates problems."

"It corrupts," Sage said. "Is that what it did to you?"

I hissed at Sage. She was overstepping the bounds of our friendship. "I was never corrupt. I was fair and benevolent."

She snorted. "You use the word obliterate too casually for my liking. That doesn't sound benevolent to me."

I sighed. How could I get Sage to understand? Only another demi-goddess would know what I'd been through. My gaze drifted around the group again. I could perform a memory wipe and make them forget about helping me locate this power.

I flicked my ears. No, I wouldn't do that. Even though these friendships were new, I valued them. And Sage had hit a nerve when talking about power corrupting. Perhaps there'd been a time or two when I'd misused what I had.

"When my power was taken, I had to change. I could no longer click my fingers—"

"Wow! You had fingers?" Archie said.

I closed my eyes for a second. "Yes, I did. But after I changed form, my power slid away, and I had to become a different kind of magic user. And I'm still learning. I want to be kind and perhaps obliterate a little less often."

"Than you used to?"

"Yes, than I used to." I glared at Sage. "Do you have a problem with that? You kill."

"I do not!"

"You keep a tally of the mice you've killed scratched on Vorana's kitchen door."

"That's different." Sage snorted. "You should have told us. Perhaps we wouldn't have wanted to get involved in this dangerous game you're playing."

"I'd still be here," Sammy said. "I don't mind a little danger."

"Me too," Archie said. "Catching fire was kind of fun. Scary but fun."

"And I appreciate that. But in this instance, Sage is your voice of reason. This was my mission, and I should have done it alone."

"I didn't mean you had to go it alone. Only a fool would do that." Sage sniffed and inspected her bent wheel. "There's no shame in asking for help, especially when it's something this big."

I flicked my tail in her direction. "You're not angry with me for concealing things from you?"

"I also didn't say that. It's not fun being flipped over and not being able to get up. I felt like a stranded turtle."

"I apologise for that happening to you. I didn't know my magic would react so strongly when I made contact with it. We've been separated for too long. It was excited to see me."

"How do you feel now you've found it?" Sammy said. "Will you change form? Get fingers again?"

"Oh, no. This is just the start. My power was so great, the goblin had to split it into many pieces. They could be hidden anywhere. Until I get them all, I won't be all-powerful again."

"All-powerful! Is that a good thing?" Sage said. "You've got a decent life with Zandra. She adores you and is always doing right by you. And you've said loads of times she's perfect for you. Why not be content with what you've got?"

"Because I had so much. And I could do so much more when I wasn't stuck in this annoying fluffy body and controlling my urges to hunt rodents, roll in catnip, and steal off people's plates."

"I think you have a beautiful fluffy body," Sammy said. "I wouldn't like to see you change."

"We all change," I said tartly. "Whether that's form or power. Nothing stays the same."

"It does with me and Vorana," Sage said.

"Really? So you've always had those wheels? You didn't make some great sacrifice to save your witch from something terrible? Perhaps that something involved her lock picking ability."

Sage grumbled to herself. "That's also different."

"Not so much." I nuzzled Sammy, who looked crestfallen. "I won't change that much when the time comes. And I'll still adore you. I don't want my magic back for myself. I have to protect Zandra. She's growing into her powers, and when she finally figures it all out, she'll be incredible. That kind of power and influence will attract danger to her all the time."

"She already seems good at attracting danger," Sage said. "Your witch has gotten herself involved with two murders since she's been here, and her mother's still missing."

"Zandra likes to help people. She always supports the underdog."

"Like me." Archie wagged his tail. "You and Zandra looked out for me and figured out who killed Osorin. You made sure I was safe and wouldn't get in trouble."

"That's right. But I must make sure Zandra achieves her goals, and I need more of my power to do that. More than once, her life has been put at risk because I could not help her."

"So you'll keep searching for your missing pieces until you're strong and powerful?" Sammy said.

"Yes. Discovering this piece was lucky. I only found it because we came to the spa to investigate Nadina's alibi. The rest of my pieces could be anywhere. I'll be searching for a long time."

Sage rubbed a front paw over one ear and then down her face. "I don't think they're scattered all that far. It seems to me you've been drawn to this area for a reason."

"Um... yes. To find Zandra's mother."

"Maybe, but I reckon it's more than that. And if you're as powerful as I think you are, and as old, that kind of magic can only be contained in a few equally powerful places. It's no surprise some of it was hidden in Crimson Cove. For all its sleepy looks, we're a draw to magic users with power. Especially the ones who find themselves in trouble."

I tilted my head from side to side, a tremble of revelation running up and down my spine. "You're right. It would take great power and concealment magic to ensure what was hidden wouldn't be discovered by any magic user who stumbled across it."

"I often am right about these sorts of things. I'm not just a pretty face." Sage bared her yellow tooth nubs. "That's where you should look if you're determined to get it all back. But my advice is to think carefully before you do that. Why mess with such a good situation?"

I bit my tongue. Sage would never get it.

What I had with Zandra was amazing, but what I'd had when I was a demi-goddess was out of this world incredible. And even if I could only get a few pieces back, it would help. I could stand proudly beside my witch and ensure she was never hurt again. And perhaps have some fun demi-goddess style, too.

"What will you do with that magic lump?" Sammy pointed his nose at the uncovered rock. "Do you need to take it with you, or did you absorb all the power?"

"I'm not certain. I don't know what the goblin did to put my power in that rock, but I'll have to reverse engineer it. I got a hit of something, which shows the magic is in there and accessible. I just need to make sure I can get it out safely."

"Without tipping me on my butt again," Sage said.

"Exactly."

"And I suppose you want our help to do that?"

I narrowed my eyes at her. "You can leave any time you like."

"Come on, Sage. This could be fun. I'm helping. And Juno knows how great I am at digging. I bet the rest of it is buried, too. I can be useful."

"Thanks, Archie. I appreciate that. Your digging paws are always welcome," I said.

"And you know I'll always help you," Sammy said quietly. "Just so long as we don't change. I mean, I know we will, but I really like hanging out with you. When you get all powerful and even more amazing than you already are, you'll forget me."

I nuzzled his nose with mine. "That would be impossible. I'll never forget you, Sammy."

"I guess I can lend a paw now and again," Sage said. "But no more secrets."

I placed a paw on the dirt in front of me. "I've trusted you all with this knowledge, but you cannot share it with anyone. Not the vampires, not Vorana, not Zandra. No one must know. Until I'm strong enough to protect me and Zandra, I can't risk this information going any further. Do we have an understanding?"

Archie dropped his huge paw over mine, covering my white fur in mud. "I'm in."

Sammy's paw joined a second later. "Me, too."

Sage huffed out several long breaths before wheeling closer. She stamped a paw on top of the pile. "Well, I haven't got much else to lose. I can barely walk, I'm losing hearing in one ear, and I've got next to no teeth, so I get no pleasure from food."

"But you have spirit and heart, and you love Vorana with a deep and undying loyalty that fills me with happiness," I said. "You're an incredible cat, and I'm honoured you're a part of this adventure."

"A misfits adventure," Archie said.

"There's nothing misfit about me," Sage said.

Sammy glanced at her. "You can be grumpy. And you have a habit of saying what's on your mind, no matter how mean it is. And you have that strange obsession with sitting on brown paper bags."

"What's strange about that?"

"You're missing out on so much. The recyclable white plastic bags are incredible. The feel under my paws when I make biscuits on them is out of this world."

"And I'm the misfit? Weirdo," Sage said.

I grinned at my wonderful motley crew of magical misfits. "With you three by my side and Zandra, we'll find the rest of my power in no time."

"And then what?" Sage said.

"And then... well, that's for me to figure out."

Chapter 19

Unicorn horns don't look good on everyone

Although tempted to use my newly found power to translocate us to Vorana's house, it was too risky to tinker with it until I knew what I was dealing with.

The magic had also felt a little unstable, so I wanted to investigate how much of it was left in the glowing lump of rock before blasting out any more magic.

So, my marvelous Sammy had kindly gotten us back home.

When we arrived, we headed inside. I dashed to the basement with my magical lump of rock and concealed it under a favorite cushion in the corner of the room. I'd find a better place for it when I wasn't distracted by vampire murder suspects.

I hopped up the steps and discovered Zandra, Vorana, and Sorcha in the kitchen.

"Did something go wrong?" Zandra dashed over and inspected me. "You look singed. And what happened to Archie?"

Vorana scooped up Sage while she was still in her harness. "You're not hurt, are you, sweetie? Is that wheel bent?"

Sage grumbled as she accepted multiple kisses on the head and an inspection from Vorana.

I feigned nonchalance. "Archie got carried away with his fire breathing."

Sage shot me a tart look but said nothing.

Archie simply nodded, while Sammy stayed silent.

"That must have been some fire breathing." Zandra kept inspecting me until I batted away her hands. "And your eyes look different."

"They're the same as always. It must be a trick of the light." I blinked and looked away from her. Maybe my magic had given me more of a jolt than I'd realized.

Zandra's forehead crinkled. She went to pet me but then moved her hand away. "If you say so."

I needed to get her mind off my appearance. "I have good news. We got inside the spa and looked through the guest register. Nadina has been late for several morning appointments."

Zandra kneeled and ran her hands over Archie. "I didn't know you were taking anyone else with you."

"Does it matter? Having backup is always a good idea. Isn't it interesting, though? Nadina missed appointments. That's important."

Zandra glanced at me. "It could be. You think she was meeting Bryce and using the spa as a cover?"

"That's what I wondered."

"What did Nadina say when you confronted her with this information?"

"I've got Finn working on that. He said he'd question her."

"Oh! You spent all this time at the spa? What took you so long?"

"It wasn't all that easy to get inside."

"And why are you covered in mud, Archie?" Zandra sat back on her heels. "You, too, Sammy. Have you been rough playing?"

"They had a play fight. Forget about the mud and focus on the clues," I said.

Zandra pursed her lips. She knew something was going on.

"Finn knows not to let Nadina talk to anyone, especially Bryce. How did you get on with him?" I curled around Zandra, hoping to calm her.

She stood and brushed mud off her hands. "There was no sign of him at the apartment."

"We think he's on the run," Vorana said.

"Which suggests he's guilty." Sorcha sat in a chair. "But I've got an idea about where we can find him. Bryce has a favorite hangout. He took me there a few times when we dated. He always goes to the same place when he needs to relax."

"It's worth a try," Zandra said. "We have to confront him with what we know."

"There's a small complication." Sorcha shrugged. "It's also Remus's favorite bar. He owns it."

"Bryce hung out with Dorian's rival?" I tilted my head. "Does anyone else think that's unusual?"

"Bryce said he only went there to get information about what Remus's hive was planning. He was worried they may attempt another takeover bid in Crimson Cove. I was never so sure, though. He always had such a great time when he was there, and he was definitely a regular. The bartender knew his order."

"Bryce was working with Remus?" Zandra said. "They used the bar to connect so he could feed Remus information about Dorian."

"I don't want to believe that, but it's a possibility," Sorcha said. "But Bryce always seemed so loyal to Dorian. He'd defend him against anyone, even when Dorian was in the wrong."

"Dorian lied to him," I said. "He promised Bryce something he deeply desired and didn't deliver. Bryce has been waiting a long time to be turned into a vampire. That's got to make a guy frustrated. Maybe even frustrated enough to turn traitor and kill."

"We should go now," Vorana said. "It's been a while since I've been out, so we can combine business with pleasure."

"We could. It's a fun bar," Sorcha said. "They have karaoke most nights."

Zandra grimaced. She wasn't a karaoke kind of woman.

Sorcha chuckled at Zandra's reaction. "The food is good, too. And they do cocktails. Does any of that tempt you?"

"I'm convinced. Let's go see if Bryce is there," Zandra said. "Then we'll figure out our next move."

We piled into Vorana's small van, which was emblazoned with her bookstore logo. Archie took up most of the back seat, and I squatted next to him, along with Sammy and Sage.

Whilst Zandra, Sorcha, and Vorana chatted in the front, I got everyone's attention. "Are we all still good? We're keeping quiet about what happened at the spa?" I whispered.

"We're good for now," Sage said. "But it's wrong to lie to your witch."

"It's not a lie to deceive. And she'll know the full truth soon."

"Zandra is already figuring it out," Sammy said. "She's so smart."

"I wouldn't be with her if she wasn't clever, but stick to our agreement and nothing will go wrong."

"Where have I heard that before?" Sage said.

"Not from me." I turned away and looked out the window. This situation was getting complicated, but I could handle complicated. I'd managed many thousands of subjects, so a few feisty familiars wouldn't be a problem.

Ten minutes later, we pulled into a crowded parking lot outside the Honeyed Vein bar. The bright fluorescent lights revealed what kind of place it was, as did the throbbing music coming out of the doors.

We headed inside, and the noise and lights grew louder and brighter. There was an iron rich tang in the air as waitresses rushed around with full tray of drinks.

"I see Remus at the back. He always has a private section to himself and his favored vampires of the month," Sorcha said.

"Let's grab that booth over there. We can watch him without drawing too much attention to ourselves," Vorana said.

"Too late for that." Zandra hunched her shoulders as we hurried through the crowd.

We were drawing curious looks. It was no surprise, since the place was mainly full of vampires. But they seemed to know Sorcha and gave her a nod and a smile as we passed.

"You're popular," Zandra muttered as we slid into the booth, Vorana helping Sage onto the red leather seat so her harness didn't get tangled.

"It's not me. It's my café. You won't know this, but I do a late night opening three times a week for night creatures only. Vampires love the café culture, but they don't love the caffeine or sunlight. I serve a special blood brew, along with blood sausage bites, put on some smooth jazz, and create a relaxed scene. It's popular. I'm thinking of opening for a fourth night because of the demand."

I looked around while Sorcha went into detail about her vampire exclusive café nights. Although we were still drawing inquiring looks, the vampires left us alone. They all looked well fed and happy, and I detected no immediate threat.

"Here he is!" Remus's voice boomed across the room. "I knew that outfit would suit you."

We looked over, and my eyes widened as Bryce appeared. He was dressed in a unicorn thong with a multi-colored sparkly horn on the front, his amber pendant, and he was balancing a tray of drinks on his head. His muscular body was bronzed and had a sheen of oil over it. I couldn't stop staring at the unicorn thong. It went right up his butt.

"What is that idiot doing?" Sorcha whispered.

"Looking like he wishes he was somewhere else?" Vorana giggled and clapped a hand over her mouth. "Shall we get cocktails?"

Bryce did a slow turn and attempted a bow without losing the tray of drinks.

Remus clapped raucously, and the vampires sitting with him joined in. "Wonderful. I didn't think you had it in you. Do another spin. You have a wonderful figure. Like a Greek god."

"This is ridiculous. I've had enough." Sorcha pushed past me and stomped over to the private area. She dodged around a vampire bodyguard. "Remus Salamander. You should be ashamed of yourself."

The laughter died as all eyes turned to her. Remus was still smiling, though.

"We should get over there and lend a paw," I said.

Zandra snatched the cocktail menu from Vorana's hand. "Sorcha needs us."

"Oh! Sure." Vorana looked less than thrilled at missing out on her Sex on the Beach.

"Archie, you stay back. Remus won't be happy if he spots you messing with his plans," I said.

"We were friends first. He'll understand why I'm with you."

"Even so, keep a low profile. I don't want you losing your new home."

His tail lowered, but he nodded.

We hurried over, minus Archie, so we could hear what Remus would say about Sorcha's intrusion into the unicorn thong fun and games.

"Sorcha, my angel! It's been too long since I've seen you in here. Join us for a drink?"

"Don't sweet talk me. And stop humiliating Bryce. He doesn't deserve this." She grabbed a jacket off the back of a chair and slung it at Bryce. "Put that on. I'm getting a chill just looking at all that flesh."

Bryce almost lost the tray of drinks as he grabbed the jacket, which landed neatly on the unicorn's horn on the front of the thong.

"I'm having fun," Remus said. "Bryce said he'd do anything to join my hive, so I wanted to see if that was true. I've been meaning to find someone who could fill that thong. Doesn't he do an incredible job?"

"You're playing with him, and that's unkind. You're better than this." Sorcha stood with her hands on her hips and glared at Remus.

He sighed as he lifted his eyes to the sky. "Being alive for such a long time gets boring. I need entertaining. And I am intending to expand my drone numbers. I'm having a turning soon, and not all will survive."

"You're serious about considering Bryce?" The anger in Sorcha's voice remained clear. "Even though he was affiliated with Dorian for so long?"

"Even more so. Bryce has shown himself to be a loyal drone. He was with Dorian for two decades. He waited patiently to get what he desired."

"And you're happy to give it to him, just like that?" Sorcha snapped her fingers.

"Maybe he'll need to undergo a few more trials until I'm convinced of his loyalty." There was a wicked smile on Remus's face. "But as I've just witnessed, he has potential, and he's so willing to please. That's always an excellent drone trait."

"Sorry to interrupt, but you said you'd turn me within the year," Bryce said.

"And I will. Providing you pass the tests."

"You'd better not be messing with him," Sorcha said. "Bryce has been through a lot."

"Ah, yes. You two had a dalliance. Still holding a flame for him, are you?"

"He's a friend, and Dorian misled him for too long. If you're looking after Bryce, do it properly."

Remus's smile faded, and he flashed his fangs. "I always look after my drones. You only have to look around to see that's true. I take offense at your comment."

I hopped onto Zandra's shoulder. "Should we intervene before things get out of hand and everyone's fangs come out?"

Zandra looked over her shoulder and nodded. "Some of the other vampires are moving in." She went to step into the private area.

The vampire bodyguard held up his hand. "Only vampires beyond this point."

"We only want to grab Sorcha and get her out of here. We don't want trouble," Zandra said.

"You're not coming in."

"Allow me to deal with this one." I stared into the vampire's eyes. "You have no reason to stop us from entering. We're friends of the vampires. Step aside. And while you're at it, fetch us a round of drinks. My witch likes something fruity. Vorana wants Sex on the Beach."

The vampire swayed on his feet and then turned and walked away.

Zandra's eyebrows rose, and she stared at me with wide eyes. "Neat trick. It's been a while since I've seen you do that."

I'd impressed myself. I usually had to dig deep into my magic to get it working, but that had happened effortlessly. Perhaps some of my old power was functioning. "Let's help Sorcha before the other vampires realize what I've done."

We headed inside the roped-off zone, closely followed by Vorana, Sammy, and Sage. Archie stayed back, although I could tell he was desperate to be involved.

Sorcha glanced at us, anger making her face tight and her fangs flash. "Let's get Bryce out of here. They've humiliated him enough."

Remus stood slowly and smoothed a hand down his velvet jacket. "No one is going anywhere. I get to choose my drones and my future vampires. Sorcha, while I appreciate your excellent work in Crimson Cove, you have no authority in here. This isn't your territory. And the last time I checked, you had no hive to control. Nor will you ever."

"I never said I had any authority, but humiliating people is wrong. Bryce, take off that ridiculous thong and get your clothes. We're leaving."

Bryce stared at her.

"I have a better idea. Bryce, make your friends leave," Remus said. "I don't like them being here. They're spoiling the atmosphere."

Bryce blinked rapidly. "What... what do you want me to do to them?"

"Anything you like. I just don't want to see them. You have your orders. Obey them."

"He must be having a laugh," I muttered. "Bryce has barely any power. I sense almost nothing from him." Although there was a faint buzz of power I couldn't put my paw on.

Zandra ducked as a chair whizzed over our heads. "Hey! Quit doing that. We're here to help."

"They want to spoil your chances of having a happily ever after as an immortal. Get them," Remus said.

"Is that true?" Bryce held another chair.

"Of course not, you idiot," Sorcha said. "If you want to become a vampire and Remus is willing to help, we won't stop you. But we need your help to figure out what happened to Dorian. Unless you've already forgotten the master you were loyal to for such a long time."

Bryce lowered the chair. "I haven't. I would never forget Dorian."

"Of course, you're still poking around in Dorian's death." Remus shook his head. "Zandra and Juno, I was kind when you came to my home, and I gave you a vital clue in the case, but this is too much. And I see you've even recruited my favorite pet to do your dirty work. Archie, stop skulking and get over here. I've been worried about you. What have you been up to?"

Archie whimpered and looked at me. "Helping a friend."

"Your beautiful coat is ruined. If I didn't adore you so much, you'd be getting a few less treats tomorrow." Although Remus's voice was sharp, he stuck a hand in his pocket and pulled out a chew, which he tossed to Archie.

Archie grabbed it and swallowed it in one bite.

"Sorcha, thanks for sticking up for me, but you need to leave." There was a note of desperation in Bryce's voice. "I don't care why you're here, but this is my only chance. Dorian let me down, so I have to try something else."

"Remus is making fun of you. Don't believe him. He takes months to pick drones, and then years to get them ready to be turned."

"Are you suggesting I'm incapable of creating new vampires?" Remus hissed and bared his fangs again.

Sorcha waved a hand at the watching vampires. "Of course not, but you're building up Bryce's expectations for nothing. He's been through so much with Dorian. He waited a long time to get his chance to be turned, and now that's gone."

"I'm aware of that. I'm also aware Dorian was schooling Bryce, so he'd be prepared for his turning. The fact Dorian failed to follow through with his promise is no concern of mine. Bryce is ready now. If I choose, I could turn him this instant, and he'd survive."

"I'm ready. I need this." Bryce tilted his head, exposing the veins in his neck.

"What you need to do is get rid of these individuals, immediately." Remus turned away. "I'm done with them. My excellent hospitality is over."

Bryce threw the chair, and it whacked Zandra's arm.

"Oh, no! You didn't just hurt my witch." I flew off her shoulder, digging into my magic and flaring it across my paws. I slammed into Bryce's bare chest, sending the tray of drinks crashing to the floor as I knocked him down.

Sammy was right beside me, his fur sparkling with magic. He flopped onto Bryce's face, and the sparkling magic flared out around him, pinning Bryce in place.

Sage wandered over and twanged the unicorn horn with a paw.

Bryce writhed beneath us and yelled muffled curses against Sammy's belly, but our magic held him down.

Remus made a sound of disgust at the back of his throat. "Pathetic. Perhaps he's not the drone I'm looking for after all."

Zandra stepped forward. "Bryce isn't a powerful magic user. Why set him on us when you know he couldn't beat us?"

"I wanted to test his loyalty to me."

"Enough games. Let Bryce go before every shred of his dignity is lost," Sorcha said.

"We're past that point." Remus smirked as Sage kept whacking the unicorn horn. "Why do you want him so badly, anyway?"

"Because we believe he had something to do with Dorian's murder." I settled myself on Bryce's chest.

Remus eyed Bryce for several seconds. "Never let it be said I stand in the way of justice. I'll compel him to tell you the truth. Let him up. He won't run. If he does, my vampires will tear him apart."

We clambered off Bryce, and he staggered to his feet, adjusting his unicorn thong. It looked no less obscene.

"Bryce, look at me," Remus said. "Tell Sorcha and her friends what they need to know."

Bryce's gaze dropped. "Of course. Whatever you say."

I hopped onto Zandra's shoulder as she stepped closer to Bryce. "We found garlic in Dorian's system. Did you feed it to him?"

Bryce kept his gaze lowered but shook his head. "I'd never do that."

"Garlic! How hideous," Remus said.

"I didn't do it," Bryce said. "I loved Dorian. I'd have done anything for him."

"There you have it. He must be telling the truth," Remus said.

"What about Nadina?" I said. "Were you in a relationship with her?"

Bryce's head shot up. "She's not my type. She was also Dorian's girlfriend, so off-limits. I'd never touch her."

"If you weren't in a romantic relationship, did you work together to figure out how to kill Dorian?" Zandra said.

Bryce looked away again. "No. We loved him. We didn't want him dead."

"Nadina wasn't having secret meetings with you when she was supposed to be at the spa?" I said.

"I don't know about any meetings. You'd have to ask her about that."

"Any more questions?" Remus yawned. "We want to enjoy ourselves, and all this talk about murder and garlic is a buzz kill."

Zandra glanced at Sorcha and then at me and shrugged. I was as bemused as her. This wasn't the outcome I'd expected. I'd been certain Bryce and Nadina had worked together. They wanted Dorian dead but couldn't do it on their own. But since Remus had compelled Bryce to tell the truth, he couldn't have lied, so he couldn't be guilty.

"We're done here," Zandra said.

"Excellent. Now, Bryce, you leave, too. You're not suitable for my hive," Remus said.

"But... but you promised. And I did everything you asked."

"You did, and I appreciate that, but after hearing from Sorcha and her companions, you're not to be trusted, and I only allow trustworthy drones into my hive. Leave the unicorn thong and go. Someone else will be worthy of wearing that one day."

Sorcha opened her mouth as if she wanted to argue with Remus, but Zandra caught hold of her arm and shook her head.

I was glad she'd intervened. We were pushing our luck with these vampires if we kept causing trouble.

Sorcha clamped her mouth shut, but her grim expression showed she wasn't happy.

Bryce turned and trudged away, hopefully to find his clothes, and we hurried out of the bar.

"I can't believe Remus! I thought he was a decent vampire. I've stood up for him so many times. He's just a jerk." Sorcha stomped to the van.

"At least we know Bryce is innocent," Vorana said. "You now have one less suspect in Dorian's murder."

"But it takes us back to square one," I said. "Although Nadina must have been doing something she shouldn't when she should have been at the spa."

"The question is, was she plotting Dorian's murder or simply terrible at timekeeping?" Zandra slid into the van, along with the others.

I had no answer to that and no idea who killed Dorian.

What should our next move be?

Chapter 20

Do ghouls look good in yellow?

I was snuggled on top of a pile of unimportant looking paperwork, contemplating taking a few hours to have a serious nap, when fast footsteps approaching Zandra's desk had me looking up.

It was Torrin, and from his frown, he wasn't arriving to ask Zandra on yet another date she could turn down.

"Hey, Juno. I need to speak to Zandra. She about?" He ran a hand through his hair, and his eyes flared yellow for a second. This part dragon was stressed, and his agitation had me interested.

I stood and stretched. "She's with Barney. They've got a difficult case they're figuring out."

Torrin paced the room. "Has Zandra seen Adrienne recently?"

"No. You know she's still looking for her. Why?" He smelled faintly of sweat and saltwater.

He paced some more. "I don't know how to say this, but I think I saw her, and she wasn't looking too good. Less than good. Adrienne was a mess."

My fur bristled around me. "Did she look like she'd been out partying and was coming back from a weekend of fun, or...?"

"I... um... she looked sick. Was she unwell before she went missing?"

Zandra poked her head through the doorway. "Oh, hey, Torrin. I can't stop. Barney's got me on an urgent job with an escaped griffin. It could be messy. Juno, we need to go."

I was going nowhere. I had to find out everything I could about Adrienne. I flopped onto my belly, watching Torrin to see if he'd spill the secret about Adrienne. "I'm not feeling well. I'll sit this one out. You can handle the griffin."

"You never said you were feeling bad this morning. You should have stayed home." Zandra stepped into the room.

I shuffled away. "I could be contagious. Go without me. I'll make my own way home, and Vorana can spoon feed me chicken soup."

"You sure you don't need me? Barney can always find somebody else." Zandra inhaled as if about to yell for Barney. She jumped when he appeared right behind her.

"We need to leave. I just had another message. The griffin is getting too close to Crimson Cove for comfort. And it has a friend. A hungry friend."

"Go. You're needed elsewhere. I'll grab some more sleep, and I'll be fine," I said.

Zandra stepped out of the door then came back in. She pressed a hand against my head and kissed my booping snooter. "Get in touch if you need me. I'll come back. Torrin, keep an eye on Juno for me."

"Sure." He watched Zandra race away with Barney, scrubbing the back of his neck, his brow furrowed as he turned to me. "Don't you think Zandra should know about her mother? You two have been looking for her ever since you got here. This is a lead. I'm certain it was her."

"There's no need to worry Zandra until I know what's going on with Adrienne." I had to think fast. I needed to check if Adrienne had turned ghoul or if she was sick for another reason.

"Are you sure about that? I think she should know."

"I know Zandra better than anyone, and it'll only worry her if you give her half the information. What did Adrienne say when you spoke to her?"

"We didn't speak. I only saw her from a distance."

"So it might not even be her?"

His mouth twisted to the side. "It was."

"Where did you see Adrienne?"

"On the beach, stalking a group of people."

"Stalking!"

"Well, it looked like she was stalking them. She was keeping back but following their movements."

"You said she looked sick. How could you tell if you were so far away?" I hopped off the desk and hurried out of the room. "Follow me."

Torrin did as he was told. Sensible man. "I didn't get too close because she was behaving strangely. I watched from a distance, but I know Adrienne well, since I visit the bakery she used to work in most days. She was following this group as if she wanted to talk to them or give them something but wasn't sure it was safe to approach them."

I stopped at the end of the corridor and looked up at Torrin. "I'll be blunt with you. Could she have been a ghoul?"

His eyebrows flashed up, and he took a step back. "You're serious?"

"As a sabre wielding warlock with a hangover and a death curse hanging over his head. You already know about the Shadow gang's ghoul operation."

"I do. You think... you think they got to Adrienne and turned her?" He blew out a breath. "Would they stoop so low?"

"I can guarantee they would." I wasn't sure how much to tell Torrin, but in my time knowing him, he'd never lied and was an upfront guy. "This stays between us, but Adrienne's purse was found in the pile of belongings the gang planned to sell."

Torrin shook his head. "Why turn her?"

"Adrienne has always had terrible taste in men. She briefly dated Anan."

"Whoa! Why would she do something as crazy as that?"

"That's not the question to ask. Torrin, focus! Could she have been a ghoul? Is that why she looked so unwell?"

He swallowed and let out a slow breath. "Maybe, but I hope she's not. It can't be that. Anan knows loads of unpleasant spells. He could have used one of them on her. Maybe he wanted to mess with her appearance so no one else would date her. He's a possessive jerk. Insane and possessive."

Hope flickered inside me. "If that's true, most spells can be undone."

"But when someone's been turned into a ghoul, that's it for them." Torrin shuddered. "What are you going to do?"

"Go to the beach and find Adrienne. Are you busy today?"

"Always. I was out for a run when I saw Adrienne, but I need to get to the workshop. Why?"

"If Zandra comes by and asks what you were doing here, keep quiet. Distract her. Ask her on another date if you have to. That always makes her anxious."

"Hey! That's not fair. I don't want to make any woman anxious."

"You're missing the point. I don't want Zandra worrying about her mother. Not until I know everything. Do we have an understanding? This'll help Zandra."

Torrin shifted his weight from foot to foot. "If you think it's the right thing to do..."

"I do. Go to work and act like everything is fine. If Zandra shows up, charm her with your dragon breath."

"Watch it, fluff ball, I don't have dragon breath." He glanced over his shoulder. "Do you need backup? Ghouls aren't friendly."

"She hasn't been a ghoul for long, so she'll have memories of her life before she was turned. She'll know me, so she will be unlikely to attack. Even if she gets difficult, I can handle her."

He pursed his lips. "You're feisty for someone so small and fluffy."

"You don't know the half of it. Remember, not a word to Zandra." I raced out of the building and sped toward the beach. I'd been there a few times with Sammy, so I knew the way.

This morning, there was a sharp wind blowing off the sea. It ruffled my fur and forced me to lay my ears flat against my head to avoid the sandy grit stinging my delicate skin.

Despite telling Torrin I could handle things, I felt shaky. Not because I was about to meet a ghoul, but the unexpected blast of my old magic had been a shock. I'd forgotten how strong I'd been, and keeping my magic pent-up had made it feel aggressive and unstable when I'd gotten a taste.

And as much as I wanted to test my new—or should that be old—power again, I wasn't sure how it would react if I unleashed it. And I needed to take care not to harm Adrienne when we met.

The unpleasant smell of rotting fish flooded my booping snooter as I reached the beach, and I hurried to a pile of torn apart raw fish. There wasn't much left, just the tail and a few heads and organs. But there was something else far more disturbing among the fishy remains. A small gray toe.

I should take it with me and get the angels to look at it, but there was no way I'd hold that in my mouth and not gag.

I made a mental note of where it was then scanned the beach, looking for Adrienne. That toe could be hers, and she'd want it back.

There was no sign of her, but there was a small group of people huddled close to the sand dunes.

I hurried over and discovered six miserable individuals in need of a good meal, a wash, and some sleep. "Greetings. Have you been here long?"

A skinny blonde with faded black liner smudged halfway down her cheeks glanced at me. "Where else can we go?"

"We have lots of nice places in Crimson Cove to visit."

"Not without money, you don't."

Were these our local homeless? Some wore designer clothing, but the others looked a little shabby, and all of them appeared lost. I examined their belongings. There were sleeping bags rolled up on the sand and bags containing what looked like cosmetics and clothing.

"I'm looking for someone. I've had a report she's been on the beach. Possibly a female ghoul. Have you seen her?"

Several of them nodded.

"She's around," the blonde said. "She keeps her distance from us, though."

My tail twitched. "Definitely a ghoul?"

"Yes. We were worried she might attack us in our sleep, so one of us stayed awake to keep watch, but she never got close. In the end, we made her a fire, and she sat by it. She seemed confused, not scary like some of them get."

"How old was she?" I said.

The blonde attempted to rearrange her bird nest hair then gave up and let it fall loose. "It's hard to tell with ghouls, but she's a pretty new one. Not much missing. Maybe in her forties. She's wearing a yellow sun dress with pink flowers on it."

My spine shuddered. Adrienne had a dress just like that. "When was the last time you saw her?"

"She was around this morning, wandering behind us. I threw her a sandwich, and she ate it. At least, I think she did. I didn't stick around to watch. Ghouls have lousy table manners."

"She went in the sea a couple of times and caught fish," a guy said. "It was awesome to watch. Not so awesome when she ate it when it was alive. And she left us a fish, too. A trade for the sandwich, I reckon. Smart for a ghoul."

My heart sank. The age and clothing pointed me toward this ghoul being Adrienne. For all her faults, she'd always been generous, sharing money, food, and time with people less fortunate.

I looked back at the group. "What are you all doing here?"

"Our house is a crime scene," the blonde said. "And Dorian paid our rent and bills, but the landlord said we can't stay in the apartment because the money has stopped coming in. He's kicking us out."

"You were Dorian's drones?"

The woman nodded. "We're stuck. The angels wouldn't even let us in to collect our stuff. We used the apartment for a couple of days, but it's not set up for lots of people. It's more of a drop-in place. And now the landlord isn't happy, so we figured we'd get out before we were thrown out."

"Where do you live when you're not at Dorian's mansion?"

"The block on the corner of Sunrise Avenue. The one with the black gates and the sweeping drive. It was a great place, classy, just too small for us, even though Dorian rented us the penthouse."

"And too expensive to keep now Dorian's no longer around," the guy who'd been listening in muttered.

"You're all living on the beach? Don't any of you have jobs to pay the rent?"

The blonde shrugged. "Dorian always took care of things like that. I hate staying here, though. I thought it would be an adventure, but the sand gets in every crack." She tugged at her pants.

I flicked my tail from side to side. "Have you thought about joining another hive? Bryce has been to visit Remus to see if he can get in there. And Remus is recruiting before his next turning."

The group fake vampire hissed.

"Bryce is a traitor," the blonde said. "And a liar. None of us liked him."

"Why? What did he do?"

"He betrayed Dorian. Several of us saw him meeting Remus while Dorian was still alive. He had no loyalty to the hive."

This was a theory I'd also considered. Bryce and Remus had worked together to destroy Dorian. But I had no evidence to prove it. Until now. "What do you think they were doing when they met?"

"Bryce was desperate because he was getting old and flabby." The blonde smirked. "If he didn't get turned into a vampire within a year, his career was over."

"He was feeding Remus all of Dorian's secrets," the guy said. "He hoped his betrayal would get him turned by Remus."

There was more fake vampire hissing.

"Did Bryce try to get any of you involved in this plan? Ask any of you to go with him?" I said.

"He told us nothing," the woman said. "He was so secretive, though. It creeped me out. We're a family, but he never acted like we were."

"And he lied about his alibi," the guy said. "Bryce reckoned he was with some friend, but I saw him at the house the day Dorian was found. If he'd crept back then, he could easily have snuck home and killed Dorian without us catching him. He's a sneaky toad. And I hate all of his movies."

A tingle ran through my whiskers. Bryce had been deceiving all of us.

"He probably locked Dorian in that room and left him for dead," the blonde said.

There were murmurings of agreement from the rest of the drones.

"I don't think that's what happened," I said.

"What do you know about it? You work for the angels?" the guy said.

"They work for me. And I assist them with their more complicated cases. Dorian definitely locked himself in that room."

"Huh! Really?"

I flicked my ears and allowed a glimmer of magic to trickle across my silken fur. "I'm invaluable to the angels. Ask anyone."

"So you know about the crazy honey badger?" the guy said. "Even though Bryce was a creeper, I'm still betting on that badger."

The blonde gave him a gentle shove. "Mack didn't kill Dorian. He was a loyal drone of last resort. I miss that cute little guy."

"I don't. Never trust a honey badger. He bit me once," the guy muttered.

"Getting back to Bryce. He was definitely hanging around the house when he should have been elsewhere?" I said. "You're certain of the time and day you saw him?"

"He was there. Several of us saw him," the guy said.

"Have you told Angel Force he lied about his alibi?"

"We've had other things on our mind," the blonde said. "We're homeless and have no clue what to do next. Although, we're never betraying Dorian and grovelling to Remus. We heard what he made Bryce do with that unicorn thong. It was so embarrassing."

They grumbled their agreement, although not all of them looked happy to pass up the chance to join Remus's hive and get a new vampire sugar daddy.

"You could get jobs," I said. "Save up and rent the penthouse. There's enough of you to cover the costs."

No one looked happy about that idea, either. Drones could be so entitled. Like millennials but with a more gothic dress sense.

"I don't want to go back to that apartment," the guy said. "Bryce's room stinks. It's no wonder the landlord wants us out. He blames us for the rank smell."

"What kind of smell?" I said. "Unwashed socks? Dirty plates?"

"Sort of wet and earthy. And Bryce let no one in his room. He'd lock it every time he left, like he had something precious in there he thought we'd steal."

"He was up to something dodgy," the blonde said. "The landlord will figure it out when he clears the place."

As they discussed what Bryce might have hidden in his room, I took a step back, still looking for Adrienne while my mind churned through this new information. I'd dismissed Bryce as a suspect, but this news put him back in the frame.

But I was here for Adrienne, not Dorian's killer.

I took another look along the beach. There was no sign of my missing ghoul.

I turned back to the group. "If you see the ghoul again, could you let me know? I'm based at animal control."

"Err... sure. What does animal control want with a ghoul?" the blonde said.

"She's important to us."

"Sure, but she's been no trouble. So long as she doesn't try to eat any of us, we're leaving her alone."

"Which is the right thing to do. But she needs help. I'm Juno. Just ask for me. Everyone knows me."

"Hey, you guys. I'm making breakfast," another woman called out. "We've got boxes of cereal to eat up before they get too sandy."

Everyone abandoned me and hurried over to feast on their sandy granola.

I remained on the beach, scouring for any signs of Adrienne. But I couldn't stay much longer, and I needed to get back to Zandra.

I'd found clues about Adrienne but also discovered important new information about a suspect in Dorian's murder.

Which one should I tackle first? The ghoulish mother or the vampire killer?

It was almost noon by the time I got back to the animal control office. I'd asked a few more people at the beach walking with their familiars if they'd seen Adrienne, but they hadn't. She was keeping a low profile and, for a ghoul, behaving herself. And since she was getting her own food, she'd remain stable.

But the sooner I found her and confirmed her identity, the better. Even though Adrienne was feeding herself, she'd be confused and scared. And a scared ghoul was a dangerous one.

I hurried into the office and discovered Zandra glaring at paperwork. She looked up, and her expression softened. "How are you feeling? Did you get a chance to rest? I stopped at the house on the way back from the job, but you'd already left."

"Oh! We must have just missed each other." I hopped onto the desk, and sand scattered across it from in between my toe beans. "I've been busy."

"At the beach?" Zandra shook the sand off her papers. "What are you up to?"

I jumped onto her lap and pulsed out calming magic. It was time for a confession. "Torrin came by this morning with some information."

"I was going to ask what he was doing here. What's this about?" Zandra scratched between my ears.

I looked her dead center in the eyes. "He thinks he saw your mother at the beach."

Zandra's hand stopped moving, and I leaned against it to encourage more scratches. "Was she there? Why didn't you tell me earlier when Torrin was here? I'd have come with you and looked for her."

"I didn't want to worry you if it was a false alarm. And I couldn't find her. I needed to know for certain it was Adrienne."

Zandra sighed. "If she's in Crimson Cove, she must know I'm here."

"I'll keep looking for her. Adrienne will show up when she's ready. And Torrin could have made a mistake. He's not perfect. Remember he thought eating magical hedgehogs was a smart idea?"

Zandra kissed the top of my head. "You're such a good familiar. I'd be lost without you. And I can feel your calming magic, but I'm not freaking out over Adrienne this time. I'm through with her messing with my life. I've been thinking about it a lot since we've been here, and I'm not being her caretaker anymore."

"You're giving up on her?"

"No, there'll always be a place for her in my life, but she's my mother, not my best friend or someone I should emotionally support every day. I've done that most of my life, and it sucks. It doesn't need to be this way, but I've always felt obligated to make sure she's safe and happy. Isn't that the wrong way around? She should do that for me."

"Adrienne can be selfish."

"Sure, and I try not to hold a grudge. I know Adrienne did the best she could with the knowledge she had when raising me," Zandra said. "And the fact things didn't work out with my dad didn't help, so I'm working on not resenting her. I just want her in my life as a parent, not someone I always need to worry about."

I struggled to stay calm and keep quiet. If Zandra knew what Adrienne had become, she'd do nothing but worry. Could I use magic to stop Adrienne from becoming an uncontrollable ghoul? It worked with Elijah, but I'd been able to help him as soon as he'd been bitten. Adrienne could have been a ghoul for weeks, possibly longer.

But before I could work on any sort of magic solution, I had to find her.

"Maybe Adrienne won't change," Zandra said on a sigh. "This is how our relationship will always be."

"She's definitely changed. If it's her, she'll show up soon. Maybe she's keeping a low profile until everything with the Shadow gang blows over. Now they're gone, she has nothing to fear."

"Except she does, since the gang still has influence over this place." Zandra petted me. "Thanks for watching out for her. And me."

A trickle of guilt ran down my spine. I was hiding too much from Zandra, and when it all came out, it could drive a wedge between us. That was the last thing I wanted. But until I'd seen with my own eyes what Adrienne was, I wouldn't worry Zandra about it.

"I spoke to a group of Dorian's drones on the beach," I said. "You're not going to believe this, but they're living there. They're homeless since Dorian died and his money dried up. And they're being kicked out of their apartment, so they have nowhere to go."

"Sucks to be a drone."

"In every sense."

Zandra chuckled. "Yeah."

"That's not the interesting part of the conversation. They told me Bryce was being weird in the apartment they shared. And he lied about his alibi for Dorian's murder."

"Finn checked that out. The friend confirmed they were together."

"Either the friend is lying, or Bryce snuck off when they should have been together. He was seen at Dorian's mansion."

"Doing what?"

"Committing murder? The other drones hate Bryce because he's been sneaking around and talking to Remus."

"Bryce was considering changing sides before Dorian died?" Zandra's eyes widened. "Or did they work together to figure out how to kill Dorian?"

"Why create a false alibi if he wasn't involved?" I said.

"We need to tell the angels this information."

The door opened, and Barney barged in with three large, delicious smelling pizza boxes in his hands. Behind him was a muscular woman with a crewcut and a tattoo of a black wolf on her neck. Behind her was a tall, skinny guy with round glasses and floppy dark hair.

"I'm glad you're here. I've been meaning to introduce you to Lola Martinez and Randal Nix since you started, but you know how things have been. There are always more animals to take care of and never enough hours in the day."

"Or a murder to solve," I muttered. I looked at Zandra, and she half-shrugged. We couldn't run off to find Bryce or speak to the angels without things getting weird.

Barney cleared his throat when no one spoke. "Lola has worked in animal control for ten years. There isn't a creature she hasn't tackled."

"Or been tackled by." Lola pursed her lips. "I've seen them all."

"It's good to meet you both." Zandra's gaze went to the door. "You'll have to give me some tips since I'm new to the job."

Lola nodded. "Barney reckons you're some hotshot with the dangerous animals."

"I wouldn't say I'm a hotshot, but I'm dedicated to doing a good job." Zandra's tone had hardened as they stared at each other.

My hackles rose. This newcomer had a whiff of alpha female werewolf about her, and they never backed down easily.

Randal stuck out his hand and stepped forward. "It took Barney a while to convince me to leave my cave."

Zandra glanced at him. "Your cave?"

"Yep. I'm here to do a system upgrade and check for magical viruses. There's been powerful magic flickering around Crimson Cove that's been distorting the networks for over a month."

Lola crossed her arms over her chest. "It started when you arrived in town."

"That has nothing to do with us." Zandra shook Randal's hand. "You're tech support?"

He grinned. "Something like that."

I held in a sigh. We weren't getting out of this office until we'd played nice with the new people. "Greetings. I'm Juno, Zandra's familiar."

"Hey, cutie." Lola scratched her long, green painted nails through my fur.

I regarded her carefully, trying not to be swayed by her delicious scratching technique. "Werewolf?"

She winked at me. "Got it in one. Did my tail give me away?"

I gave her the cat version of a smile. "No offence, but it's your smell. All wolves have that slightly damp woody smell. It's not unappealing."

She arched a well-plucked eyebrow. "I'll take your word for that."

I looked at Randal, who was rocking back on his sneakered heels and checking his pockets. The man seemed unable to stay still. Maybe it was a nervous tic. "I'm not sure about you."

His cheeks flushed, and he pushed his glasses up his nose. "I'm a tech mage. Well, my mother was a witch and my dad was a high-level tech mage, so I got magic and a love of technology in one hit. I enjoy pulling things apart and making them work better."

"Randal is our genius." Barney flipped open the pizza boxes. "Everyone, grab a slice. Randal helped me design the engines for our vans, so they break down less because of magical interference."

"That was a side project." Randal took a piece of three cheese pizza. "I mainly deal with the communications for animal control and do some freelancing for the Magic Council."

Lola smirked as she chewed on a piece of pizza. "Ignore Randal's crippling modesty. The guy basically runs the communications network for the Magic Council. If he wanted, he could pull the plug, and they'd be in chaos. Nothing would work. They wouldn't get messages, and they wouldn't be able to do that fancy moving of their offices every time a dragon farts and they think they're under threat. It would be chaos. Wars have been started over less."

Randal simply grinned again as he ate his pizza.

"Whatever you're doing, we appreciate it. My mobile snow globe rarely glitches." Zandra remained standing as she ate, hurrying through a slice of pizza. "And I've used the tech on several jobs. It always works well."

"Happy to get positive feedback. If you ever have problems, just get in touch."

"I should warn you, never go to Randal's cave of secrets, or you won't come out the same woman," Lola said. "He fixed me up with so many devices, my head spun for a month while I figured out what they all did."

"They keep you alive," Randal said. "That's all I want to do. Make sure we all have the best operating systems. We've got to keep everyone safe." He tugged at the sleeve of his shirt, but I'd already spotted faded white scars on his wrist. Had he been the victim of something dangerous? It would explain the passion for his work and interest in protecting others.

"Juno, you don't want pizza?" Zandra held out a slice for me.

"We should get going," I said. "We have that... thing. It's been great to meet you both, but we don't want to be late."

"For the thing?" Lola cocked her head.

"I kept your afternoon clear," Barney said, "so you could spend time with Lola. She's got insight into the griffins. And she'll be joining the local team for a few months. She'll appreciate your insights on Crimson Cove."

"Err... I don't have any insights. Couldn't someone else give her a rundown of the town?" Zandra shot me a nervous glance.

Barney set down his pizza. "I can't put her with Oleander for obvious reasons, and Glenda rubs people the wrong way."

"I know them both. Oleander is a giant douchebag, and I refuse to be in the same room with him," Lola said. "Glenda punched me once, so we have a history I'd rather not repeat."

"Do people you work with often punch you?" I narrowed my eyes at this feisty werewolf.

"Only when I call them out on their stupidity and they don't like it." She gave me another wink. "I promise, I'll be on my best behavior, especially since you've got something special about you. If I step out of line, I'm sure you'll use those cute murder mittens on me."

"You'd better believe I would." I didn't want a werewolf causing trouble for my wonderful witch, and this one was wafting trouble around like it was her favorite scent.

"Stay for half an hour. I got this pizza from the new store in town." It was clear Barney wanted everyone to get along. "The guy running it, Voss Black, makes them himself. He even grows most of the herbs he uses, too."

"He was weird when we got the pizza," Lola said. "He insisted on showing us the storage sheds out back, when all I wanted was a free slice."

"I thought his setup was interesting," Randal said. "Voss had these special pots where he grew the herbs. And troughs for the garlic."

"Garlic?" I said. "How was that grown?"

Lola groaned. "Don't tell me you're a gardening geek, too?"

"No, but keeping an active, inquiring mind stimulated is important."

"Don't worry, Juno, I'm not a gardening geek. I'm a tech geek, and I found it interesting. I wasn't just there for the free pizza." Randal shrugged. "You have to use well-rotted manure or garden compost. Never use fresh manure."

"Because the stench puts off customers wanting pizza," Lola said.

"No, although, probably it does, so yes. The garlic doesn't like fresh manure, though. Voss grows the garlic in troughs to keep the bulbs crisp and makes sure the soil doesn't get too dry."

Lola yawned.

Randal ignored her. "Voss breaks up the bulbs into individual cloves and plants them with the flat base plate facing down and spaces them six inches apart and one inch below the soil. And that's just with the regular variety. He grows elephant garlic, too. They like the earth to be damper."

"Damp earth?" I said.

"That's what he said. Why? You thinking of getting into gardening?"

I jumped off the desk. "Barney, my deepest apologies, but we must leave. It's a matter of urgency. We'll be back, then Lola and Zandra can work together. I'm sure they'll get along."

"Good luck with that," Lola said. "I don't get on with most people."

"My witch is wonderful. You'll adore her," I said.

"Do you have to go?" Barney hovered by the door.

"We do." I stared at Zandra. "It's important. A matter of life or death."

Zandra set down her pizza crust. "Sorry, but there's... an appointment I can't miss. We'll be back as soon as we can."

I dashed out the door the second Barney opened it, and Zandra followed.

Once we were out of earshot of the others, I turned and hopped onto her shoulder. "I should have made the connection sooner. But when

Randal mentioned growing garlic and the odd smell, it hit me."

"I'm glad you got hit with something useful, because I have no clue what's going on."

"The drones on the beach said Bryce's room smelled damp and earthy. What if he was growing garlic to use to poison Dorian?"

By this time, we were outside, and Zandra was striding toward the van. "If that's true, I'd say he's looking very much like the prime suspect."

We climbed into the van, and she started the engine.

"If Bryce was growing garlic, it would have been easy for him to slip it into food and feed it to Dorian. Or eat it himself and get Dorian to feed off him," I said.

"And if he was doing a deal with Remus, Bryce had an escape plan set up." Zandra pulled out her mobile snow globe and made a connection. "I need to tell Finn about this."

He answered almost immediately. "Hey, Zandra. How's it going?"

"We think Bryce killed Dorian."

"And we're going to the apartment he shared with the other drones to find the evidence. It's in his bedroom." I leaned over so I could see Finn.

His mouth dropped open. "Okay. What do you need from me?"

"Get Bertoli to gather the suspects at Dorian's mansion then meet us at the apartment," I said. "If there is evidence Bryce poisoned Dorian, you need to see it."

Finn winced. "Bertoli will love being ordered around by you two."

"We wouldn't have to order him around if he did his job properly," Zandra said. "I trust Juno, and she's onto something. Can you help?"

"Always." Finn grinned. "I sure am glad you're on our side."

"What other side would we be on?" I said.

"Err... of course. I just meant... never mind."

Zandra ended the call, and we shot away from the offices.

"I'm glad you're on my side, too, Juno," she said.

"Like Finn said. Always." I hid my guilt again. I was on Zandra's side, but she may think I wasn't when she learned about everything I'd been hiding from her.

Chapter 21

A dirty surprise

The apartment complex Dorian had rented for his drones was exclusive, and it took a few minutes to get someone to open the gates to let us through in our less than exclusive van.

Once we were out of the van and inside the building, we dashed up the stairs to the penthouse. The front door was propped open, and a guy in his early forties was stacking boxes outside.

He looked up as we approached. "I'll be putting this place up for rent in the next couple of weeks, but I'm not doing viewings at the moment. The previous tenants left it in a mess."

"We're not here to view," Zandra said.

He wiped his hands on his dark blue jeans. "Then why are you here? You don't look like a drone. Too much color in your cheeks."

"I'm definitely not a drone." Zandra glanced down at me and raised her eyebrows.

"A friend of theirs? If you're here to plead their case, you're wasting your time. I told them, no rent, no entry."

"Hey, Christian. It's not a problem. They're with me." Finn strode up the stairs, his hand raised.

"Long time no see, Finn." The two guys shook hands. "Missed you at the club the last few weeks."

"Work. What you gonna do?" Finn nodded in our direction. "This is Zandra and Juno. They're helping on a case, and we need to look around the apartment again. Hope that's not too much trouble."

"Sure. But you found nothing the last time you were here."

"We've had some new information, thanks to my trusty assistants." He reached down and scratched my head.

"Partners." I lifted my chin. "We're equal partners."

Finn laughed. "Whatever you say, Juno. We won't be long. We need to look in Bryce's bedroom."

Christian rubbed the back of his neck. "I can't help you there."

"Why not?"

"Weren't you here when they couldn't get the door open?"

"Nope. I sat the first apartment sweep out. I had unloved paperwork needing my attention. What did I miss?" Finn said.

Christian gestured us into the apartment. "Bryce changed the lock on the door or used some funky magic, so it won't budge. I've not been able to get in. I'll have to break it open before I can clear it."

"Didn't anyone come back and try again?"

"The last I heard from Angel Force, they had a suspect in custody. I figured they had all the evidence they needed."

"Does that locked room seem suspicious to you?" I was on Zandra's shoulder, taking in the apartment. The walls were red, the carpet black, and the atmosphere pretentious drone.

"You don't magic lock a room for no reason," she whispered. "Hey, Finn, how do you two know each other?"

"We're in the same amateur alchemists' club. We meet every week on a Thursday evening. At least, we should, but Angel Force has been busy. Too many murders happening since you came to town." He grinned at Zandra.

Christian stopped by a door. "This is Bryce's room. I've tried unlock spells, but the thing won't move. I reckon he made a mess in there, so he didn't want anyone to see."

"I can get it open for you, but I'll damage the door." Finn flexed his muscles.

I wrinkled my booping snooter. Angel show off.

Christian stepped back. "My man. Do what you have to. I can handle getting the door replaced. I'll just take the money out of the deposit I'm holding."

Finn extended his wings, and a faint red glimmer of magic shifted across them. He pulsed out a spell, and the door bent inward, but it didn't break. He rubbed his hands together and tried again. "Huh! This is tougher than it should be. I didn't figure Bryce was powerful."

"He has connections thanks to his acting. You know how groupies love to help. He probably got a spell off some sweetie he'd been smooching," Christian said.

Finn grunted and threw more magic at the door. The wood smoked, but the door stayed in its frame.

I gently cleared my throat. "Would you like us to have a go?"

Zandra chuckled. "Let the girls show you how it's done."

Finn took a step back, happy to admit defeat. "Ladies, be my guests."

I checked our bond. We were firing on all cylinders, and for the first time in ages, my magic was primed and didn't need to be forced into action.

Zandra shot me a quick glance. "You've had a recharge."

"I'm just having a good day." Now wasn't the time to tell Zandra where my power boost came from. It would lead to too many questions.

I curled my tail around her neck, and we blasted out a spell.

The door shattered, and a strong, earthy smell drifted out of the room.

Christian peered inside. "What in the name of all things angel has he been doing? I don't mind houseplants, but this is ridiculous."

There were a dozen deep troughs full of earth placed around the room. Next to them was a pestle and mortar and several glass jars of dried powder.

"No wonder he didn't want anyone to poke around. And he's not allowed a fridge in his room. It's a fire hazard." Christian was wandering around, scowling. He opened the fridge. "It's full of brownies!"

Zandra uncorked one of the glass jars. "Whoa! This is garlic powder."

"And these troughs are full of garlic bulbs," Finn said. "Bryce had a secret growing operation going on."

I hopped off Zandra's shoulder and headed to the fridge, where Christian was inspecting the brownies. He was about to take a bite of one, but I leaped up and knocked it from his hand. "You don't want to eat that."

"It looks good. I love a chocolate brownie."

I sniffed the fallen brownie to confirm my suspicions. "This has two special ingredients you won't enjoy. Drone blood and garlic."

Christian poked out his tongue. "Why make something so gross?"

The three of us shared a look.

I sniffed around some more. "These tainted blood garlic brownies would have made Dorian sick. But he was a strong, old vampire, so they shouldn't have killed him."

"They must have," Finn said.

I had an idea about what really happened to Dorian but needed one more puzzle piece to be certain. "Get what evidence you need, and then we'll visit the waiting suspects. They'll all want to know what happened to Dorian."

Finn raised a hand. "Um... I wouldn't mind knowing, too."

I twitched my whiskers at him. "Soon. It'll all be revealed soon."

"You're the boss. Although... you aren't. Still, I get a feeling I won't go wrong following your orders."

I knew I adored this half-angel, half-demon for a reason.

Finn pulled out evidence bags and collected samples. "Christian, don't touch this room for now."

He backed out of the room. "I won't go near anything. Especially not those gross brownies. Take what you need. I'll be in the lounge when you're done."

Ten minutes later, we were ready to go. Finn had bagged evidence of the blood garlic brownies, photographs of the room, and samples of the garlic powder.

We said goodbye to Christian and headed down the stairs.

"I'll meet you at Dorian's mansion." Finn blasted into the air, and to save time, Zandra cast a translocation spell to get us to Dorian's faster than flight.

"Uh-oh, super grumpy angel alert," I whispered as we arrived.

Bertoli stood at the entrance of the mansion, his arms crossed over his chest and a scowl on his face so intense even I was intimidated.

He tutted when he saw us. "Of course. You two are involved in this charade. Where's Finn?"

"Right here." Finn landed in typical angel style, his wings out and one hand fisted on the ground. "And you need to be nicer to these ladies, since they've figured out who killed Dorian."

"Well, one of us has," Zandra muttered out of the corner of her mouth.

I nuzzled her cheek. I always enjoyed a big reveal.

"This is a big waste of time," Bertoli said.

"We found it!" An angel I didn't recognize hurried toward us from around the side of the mansion. "The stake." She held up a plastic evidence bag.

"Mind if I take a look?" I said.

The angel hesitated. "Who are you?"

"Juno's working with me," Finn said. "We're equal partners. Same goes for Zandra."

The angel crouched and opened the evidence bag. I climbed off Zandra and took a good sniff then gave the stake a thorough investigation. To the average eye, it looked intact, but my amazing cat eyes revealed a tiny sliver of wood was missing.

"Where are the suspects?" I said to Bertoli.

"Waiting in the kitchen," he said through gritted teeth. "What do you intend to do with them?"

"Reveal which one of them killed Dorian. Follow me."

Zandra walked alongside me as we headed into the mansion. "Have you got everything you need to make this happen?"

"The garlic farm, the stake, and everyone's motives and opportunity. It won't take long to get this sorted." I headed into the kitchen to discover Remus, Nadina, Bryce, and Mack waiting for us.

Mack trotted over for a quick nuzzle. He'd had a bath, and the lemony scent was an improvement on his musky, unwashed aroma.

To my delight, Archie was with Remus and his fur restored to its former glory.

He wagged his tail. "Hey! Don't I look like a real hot dog? I got another groom. And they spritzed me with cologne."

"You look amazing. And you smell even better than Mack." I stood with Zandra and Finn. Bertoli remained some distance away, making it clear he wanted nothing to do with this situation. That was his loss. He'd change his mind when the clues were laid out and the killer uncovered.

"You're up, Juno." Finn nodded at me.

"Greetings, everyone. I have brought you here so you can learn who killed Dorian." I walked slowly, eyeing each suspect.

"I heard Nadina confessed," Remus said smoothly, one hand resting on Archie's splendid head.

"I got arrested. I... I thought I'd killed Dorian. I held my hands up to staking him." Nadina licked her lips, her gaze darting around the room. "Charge me. I'm guilty. I feel so bad."

"We'll get to your staking in a moment," I said. "Remus, you had every reason to kill Dorian. You'd get new territory, more power, and take over this mansion."

Remus stopped petting Archie and raised a neat eyebrow. "And yet I didn't do it. You know this."

"True. Despite not having a strong alibi, you didn't kill Dorian. Your methods for expanding your power base are far blunter."

He shrugged. "I never hide my intentions when I want something."

I stopped in front of my favorite honey badger. "Mack was another obvious suspect. He was trapped in a locked room with Dorian. It makes sense he murdered him."

Mack's solid head swung from side to side. "Not me. I didn't do it."

"You didn't. Although the mess you made of the crime scene made it look like you did. You didn't make this easy for us to solve."

"If it wasn't the honey badger, and it wasn't Nadina, even though she just said she did it, who murdered Dorian?" Bertoli said.

I focused on Bryce. "We've just been in your bedroom. You have a green thumb. And you can bake!"

The color drained from his face. "I'm allowed hobbies. There's nothing wrong with that."

Finn placed a bulb of garlic, a vial of dried garlic, and a tray of blood garlic brownies on the kitchen counter, in evidence bags.

Bryce stared at them and gulped.

"You betrayed Dorian. You've been lying to him for months and slowly poisoning him with garlic using his favorite treat," I said.

"No! I mean... yes. Okay, I poisoned him but not with the plan to kill him. And such small amounts of garlic would never have killed a vampire, just made him sick." Bryce hunched his shoulders. "Dorian lied to me. I've wasted my best years on a vampire who never intended to turn me. So, I taught him a lesson. I showed Dorian he wasn't invulnerable and he could be hurt. He needed me by his side to keep him safe."

"We have witnesses who saw you here around the time of Dorian's death," I said.

"That doesn't make me a killer! I heard from the other drones that they hadn't seen Dorian for days, so I wanted to check on him. I could always get him out of a funk."

"Because you stopped poisoning him, so he felt better," I said.

He shrugged. "Maybe. But I couldn't get into the room. I panicked and thought I'd gone too far with the garlic blood brownies."

Nadina sucked in a breath. "You were the one who gave him those? He adored his blood brownies. He'd overindulge and eat a whole tray. Bryce, you killed him! You poisoned Dorian."

Bryce tugged at his bottom lip. "How? You know how much power he had."

Nadina and Bryce glared at each other.

"You want me to arrest anyone yet, Juno?" Finn said.

"In a minute. What Bryce hadn't expected during his poisoning plans was that someone else would try to kill Dorian. Just before Dorian locked himself away with Mack, Nadina struck with her stake."

"Everybody knows that." Nadina still glared at Bryce. "I was shocked when he didn't die in front of me. When they found his body, I figured I'd landed a successful strike, but it took time to take effect."

"You didn't. Dorian would have lived, but only if he hadn't also been poisoned." I let this information sink in for a few seconds. "Both of you wanted Dorian dead, didn't you?"

"Not me," Nadina said. "In a moment of madness, I wanted revenge, but the second I hit Dorian with that stake, I regretted it."

"I didn't want him dead either," Bryce said. "I was punishing him. Proving a point. I didn't know Nadina would go after him too and mess everything up."

"Me! You've been poisoning him for months. You're the killer!" She yanked off one high heel and hurled it at Bryce.

I paced in front of them, keeping an eye on Nadina in case she got the urge to throw anything else. "You're as guilty as each other and as incompetent. Both of you would have failed if you'd made your attempts separately, but because Dorian had been poisoned with garlic for so long and then received a stake injury, it weakened him. And having just examined the stake, a tiny sliver of wood was left in the wound. That made it even more difficult for him to heal."

Nadina covered her mouth with her hand. "I'd have helped him. I didn't know."

"Of course you didn't. You fled the scene and hid the evidence," I said. "Dorian retreated with Mack by his side because he couldn't turn to anyone else when he was suffering. He knew the people he loved were turning against him, so he retreated."

Mack grunted. "It's true. He didn't know who to trust."

"And in his weakened state, confused, in pain, and scared, Dorian fell. He hit his head on a marble plinth in the bedroom. That was a step too far, even for an old vampire. His body wouldn't allow him to heal from all the injuries."

No one spoke. Nadina cried.

"And then I ruined the evidence by eating Dorian," Mack muttered. "I basically framed myself for murder and messed up the clues."

"Unfortunately, you did." I briefly rested a paw on Mack's side. "But you did what you needed to do to survive. Bryce and Nadina jointly killed him, even though they didn't know they were working toward the same end."

Nadina hung her head. "If I could go back in time, I'd change everything. I'd never have attacked him."

"Same here," Bryce said. "I'd planned on stopping. I'd figured out another option to be turned into a vampire."

"Ah, yes. Remus." I looked at him. "You never wanted Bryce, did you? You were using him."

Remus inspected his perfect nails. "I never turn down free information, and I didn't guarantee I would turn Bryce. I'd never trust a drone who betrays his master."

Bryce looked like someone had stolen his favorite felt mouse and washed it in lily scented soap.

Archie lowered his tail and whined. "I thought you were a nice vampire."

Remus petted his head. "I'm an adorable vampire, but I'm also an ambitious one."

He whined again. "I'm... I'm not sure I want to be with you if you mistreat people. If you're not kind to others and you deceive them, look at what happens. Two people Dorian trusted poisoned and staked him. Do you want that to happen to you?"

Remus's mouth opened and closed, and he blinked several times. "My drones obey me. And people fear me. They'd never dare make an attempt on my life."

"I'm sure Dorian felt the same," I said. "Now, he's decaying on a slab after the angels cut him up because the woman who loved him and the drone who adored him broke. It could happen to anyone if they're not treated kindly. Listen to Archie. Your hellhound gives out excellent advice."

Remus's expression turned thoughtful as he petted Archie. "My faithful umbrella of drones and vampires have perhaps cosseted me. This fresh opinion is what I need."

"You'll start being nicer to people?" Archie said. "If you're as nice to everyone as you are to me, you'd never have to worry about anyone staking you or drugging you with garlic."

Remus chuckled and fed Archie a milk bone. "Again, you make an excellent point. I'm glad we found each other."

Archie drooled as he munched on his treat.

I looked at Finn and Bertoli. "You have everything you need to make the arrests."

Bertoli desperately looked like he wanted to protest, but Finn simply nodded. "Bryce and Nadina, you're coming with us."

"Is it okay to come down?" Finn's voice echoed along the staircase and into the basement. "Vorana said you were still here."

I yawned, stretched, and rolled over on Zandra's soft bed. "Of course we're still here. And we're enjoying a lie-in, since we solved an impossible murder yesterday."

"Ignore Juno. She's still revelling in the glory. Come down." Zandra shot me a sassy look as she tugged on her jacket.

A few seconds later, Finn appeared at the bottom of the stairs. "I wanted to drop by before I started work. I thought you'd like an update." He glanced at me, raised his eyebrows, and patted his jacket pocket. There was a hidden message if ever I needed one.

"Are Bryce and Nadina behaving?" Zandra hunted for her boots under the bed.

"Nadina is still tearful and apologizing to everyone, but she's not denying she staked Dorian. And thanks to Juno, and after another look at the stake wound, we found a minute particle of wood inside Dorian."

"I knew it," I said a little more smugly than was acceptable in polite company. "A vampire at full strength would have ejected that wood fragment, but given Dorian's poor physical condition, it must have been a painful injury."

"Combine that with the massive amounts of garlic in his system, and the guy didn't stand a chance." Finn leaned against the wall. "Bryce is also talking."

"He doesn't have much choice, given what we found in his apartment," Zandra said.

"And he knows it. Although he's sticking to the story he never wanted to kill Dorian and just meant to teach him a lesson."

"Which went horribly wrong and ended in murder," I said.

"You got it."

"I'm glad it's over and they've been caught," Zandra said. "Have you got time for a coffee before work?"

"Always, if it comes with Vorana's amazing breakfast muffins," Finn said. "I'll wait here with Juno."

"Err... sure. You two chat. I'll be back in five minutes." Zandra dashed up the stairs.

"I know what you're going to say." I smoothed down some fur and settled on the bed.

"I brought the purse." Finn patted his jacket pocket again. "Zandra needs to know her mother's things were found at the ghoul factory."

"Before we do that, there's something you need to know, too," I said. "There have been sightings of a ghoul in Crimson Cove. And although I haven't seen her, I've heard enough to believe it could be Adrienne."

Finn's eyes widened. "Why didn't you tell me? A lone ghoul wandering about is dangerous. If she's not being looked after—"

"Calm down. She seems to be doing better than most lone ghouls. She's feeding herself and not attacking anyone. Adrienne seems stable. Which is remarkable, given the lifestyle she led when she was, well... not a ghoul."

Finn sighed. "What a mess. How will Zandra take the news? I'm guessing, since she isn't freaking out, you haven't told her?"

"She knows there's been a sighting. She doesn't know about the ghoul part. I'm going for shock, denial, then anger. Zandra rolls through those emotions when she gets information she hates."

Finn glanced at the stairs as Zandra made her way back down. "Let's do this."

I hopped up and stretched, preparing myself for what would be an uncomfortable conversation. "Let me do the talking. She's less likely to snap my head off."

Zandra appeared with a tray in her hands, containing coffee mugs, muffins, and a plate of dried treats for me. Her smile faded as she looked at us. "Have I missed something? There's not a problem with the investigation, is there?"

Finn took the tray and set it down on a small table in the corner. "Juno has something to tell you."

"We both do." I patted the bed with a paw. "Sit next to me."

Zandra settled on the bed, her eyebrows raised as she waited for me to continue.

I drew in a slow breath. "Your mother's purse was found at the ghoul factory. Finn discovered it."

He pulled out the purse. It was inside a plastic evidence bag. "Is this Adrienne's purse?"

Zandra stared at it and then at Finn. "Yes. How long have you had that?"

"I discovered it once we'd moved the ghouls and processed their belongings."

"And you didn't tell me?" She reached for the purse, but Finn shook his head.

"It's still evidence in an ongoing investigation, so I can't let you look at it, but it contains Adrienne's ID."

"You knew about this, too?" Zandra's angry gaze flicked to me.

"Finn told me what he'd found. I suggested we stay quiet until we figured things out."

Zandra stood, her hands in fists. "What's to figure out? Adrienne is missing, she had shady connections to the Shadow gang, and her things were found at the ghoul factory. You don't have to be a genius to work out the ending to that story."

"Adrienne wasn't among the ghouls," Finn said. "That's why we didn't tell you. And I've been tracking any links that could provide new information about her."

"What links?"

"Speaking to Shadow gang contacts, seeing if any ghouls were shipped out early—"

"And were they? How long has Adrienne been a ghoul?"

"If she has been turned, less than a month," I said. "There's something else you need to know. When Torrin came to animal control, he told me he'd seen Adrienne, and she wasn't looking well."

Zandra sank onto the bed. "Is that why she hasn't come here? Is she... is she a ghoul, so she doesn't remember me?"

I pressed a paw on her hand. "I haven't seen her, but a few people have. Their description suggests it could be Adrienne."

Zandra hunched forward. "I'd rather she was dead than that. It's the worst kind of torture. Adrienne was proud of being a free spirit and tied to nothing. Ghouls don't think for themselves. She'll live in a world of don't knows and following orders, never having an independent thought or being able to make a decision. It's wrong."

We gave Zandra a moment to process this sad news.

"There's still a chance it isn't her," Finn said. "Just because the purse was found doesn't mean the gang got her. Adrienne's resourceful. She could have escaped or convinced one of the Shadow gang to let her go."

"Or she didn't make it out? They killed her, and it's someone else?" Zandra's hands were clenched so hard I could see the white knuckles through the skin.

"If she has been changed, being a ghoul isn't so terrible. You saw for yourself that, with the right magic, they're not vicious and can even be controlled," I said.

"Adrienne would never want to be controlled. It goes against everything she is. Or was." Zandra shook her head. "You've made a mistake."

Finn looked at me and gave a small shrug. "You could be right. I'll hold on to the purse and keep making inquiries."

Zandra huffed out a breath. "She's out there somewhere, same as always. Living in the moment and not realizing the world of hurt she left behind. She hasn't been turned."

There was a thud from upstairs and a harsh hiss, followed by a clatter of metal. A scream followed.

"That was Vorana!" Finn was bounding up the stairs, and we were right behind him.

I dashed past him and into the hallway. A row of Vorana's precious books were scattered across the floor, and there was a smear of dirt across one wall.

A series of furious hisses slashed into my ears. I bounded into the living room to discover Sage blazing with magic and attached to the back of a woman who had Vorana pinned in one corner.

Sage had abandoned her harness, and her back legs hung free as magic poured out of her, attempting to destroy the woman trapping Vorana.

Finn and Zandra arrived in the doorway.

"Be careful!" Vorana said. "She tried to bite me."

The woman twisted, and for a second, the world stopped turning. It was Adrienne. Ghoul Adrienne.

Zandra staggered back, Finn catching her by the arm to stop her from falling to her knees.

Adrienne's blank gaze flicked into focus. She stared at me, and her eyes slowly tracked back to Zandra. Horror and shame flooded across her face. Adrienne clamped a black-veined hand over her mouth and backed away, mumbling noises I couldn't understand.

Vorana stood on shaky legs. "Careful, Sage. Don't let her bite you. Please, don't get hurt."

Sage had her claws embedded in Adrienne's back, her magic wrapping around the ghoul and slowing her.

Adrienne backed to the window, still covering her mouth, not seeming to notice the raging cat on her back or the magic pouring over her.

I stepped forward. "Greetings, Adrienne. Do you remember me?"

Her gaze flicked to me, but she was only interested in Zandra.

"We don't want to hurt you," I said. "We'd like to help. Don't be scared. You must be confused about what you're going through. I—"

Adrienne turned and leaped through the window. Glass shattered, wood splintered, and a chilly morning breeze flooded the room.

"Sage!" Vorana dashed out of the room and flung open the front door.

I hurried to the broken window, being careful not to stand on glass, and looked out. Sage was flat on her belly, still hissing and shooting magic at Adrienne's retreating form.

Vorana scooped her up and dashed back into the house, holding her against her chest, one hand running over her to check for injuries.

"I'm fine. Stop fussing," Sage grumbled.

"So brave. My angel. My sweet, perfect, fluffy angel. You scared me so bad." Vorana buried her head in Sage's side and kissed her.

I jumped into Zandra's arms, curling waves of calming magic over her again and again, but her panic grew as her heart raced. I wrapped around her neck and nuzzled her ear with my booping snooter, not sure what to say.

From the stunned expression on Finn's face, neither did he.

Vorana looked at Zandra. "I can't believe what I just saw. Was that..."

Finn pursed his lips. "Adrienne. She must have figured out where you were staying," he said to Zandra.

Zandra nodded, still too stunned to speak.

"I startled her." Vorana's voice shook. "I took some recycling outside, and she was hiding in a bush. I almost tripped over her. I screamed, and she reacted and chased me. Adrienne was only acting on instinct. I don't think she wanted to hurt me."

"It didn't look like that to me," Sage grumbled. "She tried to bite you."

"It's easy to trigger a ghoul," I said. "You acted scared and ran, so you became her prey."

Vorana nodded. "Exactly. Zandra, Adrienne wasn't hunting me. What I'm trying to say is I don't think she's dangerous."

"She's a ghoul," Finn muttered. "They're not known for having great safety records. You don't find many nanny ghouls listed in the wanted ads."

I hissed softly at him. "Not helping."

He lifted his hands. "I'm just saying. A ghoul is a ghoul."

I kept focused on Zandra, who was breathing shallowly and was as pale as a ghost. I didn't know how to fix this. I was failing my witch. "Everything will be fine. Adrienne knew you. She recognized you and stopped hunting Vorana. That's a good sign."

Zandra looked at me, her eyes wide and full of tears. "How will this be fine? My mother is a ghoul."

Despite my newly acquired power, my deep love for my witch, and our friends surrounding us, I had no decent answer.

I booped her cheek. "We'll make this right. Together, we can fix anything."

Whatever it took, whatever I had to do, I'd make sure my witch was happy again.

About Author

K.E. O'Connor (Karen) is a mystery author living in the beautiful British countryside. She loves all things mystery, animals, and cake.

If you want to practice spells, solve a few murders, and spend time with amazing witches and their talking familiars, join her weekly newsletter.

Sign up today.

Newsletter:
https://BookHip.com/GXDVFRA
Website:
www.keoconnor.com/writing
Facebook:
www.facebook.com/keoconnorauthor

Also By

Witch Haven: Welcome to Witch Haven, where nothing is what it seems. Meet four fabulous witches as they struggle with their destinies, deal with misfiring magic, murder, and the irksome Magic Council.

Crypt Witches: Meet Tempest Crypt, a witch who swallows demons, and Wiggles, her talking hellhound, while you enjoy magical murder and intrigue.

Lorna Shadow: A cozy mystery series set in the fun world of a personal assistant who sees ghosts. Meet Lorna, her ditzy sidekick, Helen, and Flipper, the dog who senses ghosts, as they solve crimes and save the day.

Holly Holmes: An adorable cozy culinary mystery series set in the beautiful English village of Audley St. Mary. Each book is full of treats, murder, and twists. Join Holly and Meatball, her clue-hunting dog, as they solve murders and eat cake.

www.ingramcontent.com/pod-product-compliance
Lightning Source LLC
Chambersburg PA
CBHW050755190726
48285CB00005B/1674